JILTED: NICO AND SOPHIE

CLIFFSIDE BAY, BOOK 9

TESS THOMPSON

D1715415

Tess Thompson
HOMETOWNS
and HEARTSTRINGS

JILTED: NICO AND SOPHIE

CLIFFSIDE BAY SERIES

Book 9

Tess Thompson

4kids5cats
EDITIONS

For my aunt and uncle Deb and Les Cross,
who've supported me through lean times and always believed in my
talent.

INTRODUCTION

Dearest Reader,

Thank you for continuing the Cliffside Bay journey with me. If you've gotten to book 9 in the series, I imagine you've followed the Dogs and Wolves all the way from book 1. That you're here means the world to me...truly. I've had so much fun writing this series. I love each of my couples equally, as I do my children. However, I've been pretty excited to write Sophie's love story since she first came on the scene in Deleted: Jackson and Maggie. *Many readers have written asking, when would I write Sophie's story? My answer was always the same. I need her to grow up a little before I find her forever man. Well, that answer led me to her story. She falls for Nico pretty much the first time she ever sets eyes upon him. Sadly, like me, Nico thinks she's way too young to fall in love and get married. In this case, our "old soul" Sophie will have her way with both of us. Read on to find out how.*

For those of you who pay close attention to the timeline of the Cliffside Bay Series, this book actually opens before Scarred: Trey and Autumn *because, well, kissing. I didn't want you to miss out on Sophie and Nico's first kiss, which actually happens before the opening of* Scarred. *Then, we'll delve back into "real" time in*

Chapter Four. Did you follow that? If not, no worries. Just jump right in and enjoy.

Please keep in touch. I love to hear from you. Drop me a note at tess@tthompsonwrites.com. Find me at https://tesswrites.com/ to follow my newsletter or social media.

Much love,

Tess

PROLOGUE

Sophie

Eight-year-old Sophie Woods was sick with a fever. All night she thrashed about, in and out of sleep. She hallucinated. A vision came to her of a man. He stood in a field of sunflowers. His eyes were the color of a blue winter sky and his mouth turned upward, as if prepared to break into a smile at any moment. Next to him, a small black-and-white dog wagged her tail.

A voice spoke to her. "This is the man you will marry. Your one true love. Wait for him."

When the fever broke, she opened her eyes. Her mother sat beside the bed holding her hand.

"The fever's gone," Mom said. "You're going to be fine."

"I had a weird dream," Sophie said. "About the man I'll marry."

Rhona Woods didn't flinch. She believed fully in magic and miracles and that which could be seen by the heart if not the head. She smiled. "Excellent. I can't wait to meet him."

"He'll have a black-and-white dog with bangs that cover her eyes."

"You love dogs," Mom said.

"I think he likes flowers."

"You love flowers."

She closed her eyes, wishing she could see him again.

1

Nico

Nico Bentley had always loved sunshine. Everything vital to his simple life came from the flawless sphere of hot plasma. The fiery star made the oceans blue and the mountains green. Plants and flowers grew under the warmth of its great energy. People grew strong and healthy from its rays.

But then the sun had come to him in human form. A temptress had branded him with her light as bright as a thousand suns.

Her name was Sophie Grace Woods, and she was his sun. His shining star. His greatest temptation.

Like the real sun, he could not turn away from her warmth.

That morning, she'd called and said she wanted a dog for her bar. "A mascot for The Oar. A friend to keep me company at night. Will you come with me to the shelter? They have a batch of puppies."

Who could say no to time in the sunshine? Not him. Even when he knew she would burn him in the end. He said yes, as he always did.

The dog and cat shelter in Cliffside Bay was located behind the post office in a small building that resembled a surf shack. He cringed at the weeds and dead plants in front. "I should offer my services," Nico said as he turned off the car.

"I don't think the shelter can afford a landscape architect."

"Pro bono," he said.

"I'm sure Bernie would love it," Sophie said. "That might get us an in with her. She's very strict about who she lets go home with dogs."

"Bernie?"

"The shelter lady. You know, the Dog Whisperer." Sophie said this in a tone that implied he should know this Bernie. "She comes into the bar every Tuesday night for a light beer and tacos."

"That doesn't really narrow it down." Half the town went to The Oar for Taco Tuesday.

"Anyway, it doesn't matter. Just leave this to me. If I have to throw in extra tacos, I'll do it."

"Are you sure about this? A dog is a big commitment."

"I'm all about commitment." Sophie tossed massive amounts of blond hair behind her shoulders. Her aquamarine eyes snapped in that stubborn, sure way they did when she wanted something, and nobody was going to stop her. Least of all him.

"But it seems like this came from out of the blue," he said. Sophie was impulsive, driven completely by instinct and intuition. She plunged headlong into anything that interested her. He loved her for it, but worried too. Living like that could get her into trouble. And trouble was the last thing he wanted for her.

When he'd first met her, she'd invited him upstairs to her

apartment. While sharing dark chocolate and a Washington cabernet, she'd told him the story of her remarkable life. As an infant, she'd been left on the stairs of a " in San Francisco, then adopted by Micky and Rhona Woods. Her identity had not been known to her or her adoptive parents until her half siblings, Zane Shaw and Maggie Keene, had come looking for her. It was then that she discovered the truth about her birth parents. Hugh Shaw and Mae Keene had had an affair, producing Sophie.

Beautiful, sweet Sophie. Untouchable Sophie.

A connection he didn't at all understand seemed to pull them toward each other. His job was to resist that magnetic propulsion. He was worn out from the energy it took to do so. Stay away from her. That's what he vowed to do, but then, like today, he found himself right by her side.

And then, yesterday, he'd discovered they had even more in common. *Don't think about that now.* He would decide some other day what to do about the latest shocking curve in the screwed-up highway that was his life.

"I've never heard you talk about a dog before," he said.

"I've been thinking about a dog since I was eight years old," she said.

"You didn't have one when you were a kid?" he asked.

"Sure. We had gobs of dogs. My mom never met a breathing creature she didn't love." She unfastened her seat belt. "How come you don't have a dog? You're such a dog person."

"I can barely take care of myself," he said.

"That's not true. You take care of Mrs. Coventry."

"I try to take care of her, but she fights me hard. Yesterday I caught her pouring the granola and yogurt I'd made her for breakfast into the trash." Granola that cost more per pound than even the fancy espresso beans she insisted that they use.

"You hover over her too much. Just because she gave you a

sweet deal on the bungalow doesn't mean you owe her more than taking care of her yard."

"She needs me to hover. Dr. Waller told her she needed to gain some weight. She's almost seventy and has terrible nutrition."

"You should get a dog," Sophie said. "I can picture you with a dog. Someone else to look after."

"Not today." Or any day. He was too busy with work. Plus, looking after Mrs. Coventry was more than enough. "Wolf Enterprises is still getting off the ground. I don't have time."

"People always have time for love."

The world according to Sophie.

"Let's go take a look at the puppies," he said. "A puppy for you and only you."

"Great." She flashed her dazzling smile. God, that smile. His stomach went nuts every single time she smiled.

He ached to kiss her, to take her home and into his bed. But no. He was way too old for her. She was so innocent. So young. Only twenty-two and yet untouched. He was thirty-four. A dirty old man. He hated himself for the lascivious thoughts that tortured him whenever he was with her. He knew, too, that all it would take for her to offer herself to him would be a hint of encouragement. She liked him. Or rather, she *thought* she liked him. She would change her mind at some point, as Addie had. He wouldn't go through that again. Plus, it would be wrong. She deserved someone her own age. A man who was in the same season of life. Not a bitter old man like him.

She opened the door and hopped from the car. He dragged his eyes from her curvaceous rear end to join her.

As they entered, Bernie, a.k.a. the Dog Whisperer, greeted them from behind a desk stacked with papers, a box of dog treats, several leashes, an empty coffee cup etched with the words *Dog Mom*, and an ancient computer. The air smelled of dog food and antiseptic.

"Let me guess. You're here about the puppies." Bernie was in her sixties with springy white curls and pockmarked skin. Small eyes scrutinized them. From the way they narrowed, she seemed to find them lacking. He suspected she liked dogs a lot better than humans.

"Yes, do you still have them?" Sophie bounced on the balls of her feet. "I called earlier."

"We have one left. The runt," Bernie said. "Sweetest one of the litter—but people are put off by her scrawniness. She was sick when they first arrived. Some bastard left them on the side of the road."

How could anyone do that?

"Is she well now?" Sophie asked.

"Yep. She needed some TLC, that's all," Bernie said.

"Is she black and white?" Sophie asked.

Black and white? What did that matter?

"She is. How did you know?" Bernie asked.

"Oh, I didn't. I was curious, that's all." A flash of guilt crossed Sophie's face.

That was weird. But that was Sophie. She was a different kind of girl.

Bernie took them into the back. A series of empty cages lined both walls. "We're plumb out of dogs. I had two older ones early in the week, but they were adopted. Jen is the only one we have left."

She took them to a small cage at the end of the row. A skinny black-and-white puppy sat in the far corner shivering.

"This here is Jen," Bernie said.

Jen was a black-and-white checkerboard. She had black floppy ears and a fluffy white chest and paws. Her face was black on one side and white on the other. Small button eyes were almost hidden behind a wall of bangs.

"She's adorable," he said. *Crushingly* adorable. How could anyone walk away from this puppy?

"Is she cold?" Sophie asked.

"Scared," Bernie said. "She's afraid of people. Another reason she's still here."

Nico's heart hurt. He knew fear. As a kid, he'd been afraid of everything, especially other people. If he could have, he would have hidden in a corner, too. Growing up with his parents, fear was not tolerated. Bentleys attacked life. They took what they wanted with no apologies. The rest of his family did, anyway. He simply suffered in silence and developed an ulcer at age ten.

"She won't do for the bar, then," Sophie said. "I need a dog that loves all people."

"Jen needs her forever person," Bernie said. "Someone who will love her just as she is. She needs a quiet home with a person with a steady temperament. An especially kind and gentle owner who will treat her like a best friend."

He was steady. He was kind and gentle. His best friend was Trey, but he had room in his heart for another. In fact, there was nothing but room in his empty heart. Maybe he would be perfect for her. Could she distract him from his obsession with Sophie?

He took another good look at her. Jen stared back at him, still shaking. His eyes welled. He couldn't stand the thought of her being alone for one more minute. All her siblings had left her. The cage must feel so lonely without them. He was alone, too. "I'd like to pet her, if I may?" Nico asked.

Bernie eyed him for a long moment. Nico put his hands in the pockets of his cargo shorts and crossed his fingers, a habit he'd developed as a kid as a way to cope with intense criticism from his parents. When his fingers were crossed, he was impenetrable. Nothing could hurt him, especially not words.

Could Bernie see all his flaws and imperfections? Would she deem him unfit for dog parenting? His mother had always said he was too irresponsible for a pet. His father had said anyone as meek as Nico could never be alpha dog enough to train a puppy. Maybe Bernie would see the same thing?

He glanced at Sophie. She met his gaze with glassy eyes. She didn't have to say anything for him to know that they shared the same feelings for Jen. One of them had to take her home. Most likely it was going to be him.

"Go ahead," Bernie said finally. "But she might not come to you." She opened the door to the cage. "She's never voluntarily come to anyone."

Nico lowered to the floor and sat cross-legged. "Come here, girl." He patted his leg.

Jen cocked her head to the side but didn't move. She wanted to, though. He felt sure of it.

She was so small. He must seem like a giant. Maybe if he got down on her level, she would be less afraid. He lay on his stomach and placed his head near the door. "Do you want to come say hello?"

Jen inched toward him. Her bushy tail wagged once, then again.

"That's a good girl," Nico said. "I won't hurt you."

Suddenly, she seemed to change her mind and went all in, bounding over to him in two leaps. Then she kissed his cheek.

He laughed and wiped his face with the sleeve of his sweatshirt. "Kind of bold for the first date."

Jen wagged her tail for real this time.

He moved into a seated position and waited. To feel comfortable, she needed to come to him. He couldn't just grab her and pull her into his lap.

With one cute hop, she landed on his lap. He gathered her in his arms. She was about the same size as his two hands put together. He snuggled her against his chest. She shook for another second or two but then seemed to accept that this was the right place to be and went limp. "What do you think, Jen? You want to come home with me?" She looked up at him with her button eyes and sighed. Her stumpy tail wagged harder. His heart turned over. He was in love.

"It's all right now," he whispered to her. "You don't need to be afraid ever again. I'll be with you."

Sophie knelt next to them and scratched under Jen's chin. "Can I be your pal, too?" Sophie asked.

Jen wagged her tail even more furiously.

"I'll take that as a yes," Sophie said. "Now let's get you guys home."

And that was how Nico Bentley walked out of the Cliffside Bay Shelter with a puppy named Jen.

* * *

NICO HELD a letter in his hand. The address was unfamiliar. The sender was not. Addison Schneider. His ex-fiancée. He hadn't heard from her since the day she told him she was in love with her best girlfriend. Although he knew what it said already, he opened it to read one more time.

Dear Nico,

I hope you're doing well. I know I agreed to stay out of your life and not contact you. However, I have something important to tell you. It's about your parents. When I suggested you take a DNA test to learn if my suspicions about them were true, you thought the idea absurd. While I understand that, my cop instincts disagreed. Without your knowledge, I sent in DNA samples from you and both of your parents to be genetically tested. I can never let a mystery go unsolved. The detective in me simply couldn't let it go. I'm sorry.

The results went to our old address and were only recently forwarded to me. I've enclosed them, but the upshot is pretty simple. Your father is not your father. Your mother is only a twenty-five percent match, which means she's either your aunt or your grandmother. In this case, it has to be your aunt. Your mother's sister who committed suicide at fourteen is your biological mother. There is no doubt in my mind.

I'm sorry to interfere in your life. I understand it's no longer my right to do so. That said, I do love you and always will. Getting to the truth of your childhood will explain so much about the dynamics of your family. It might even convince you of your worth, instead of believing the lies your mother has told you about yourself.

I can't tell you how sorry I am about how things turned out between us. I don't know if this is a comfort to you, but I'm happy. For the first time, I'm living my life completely authentically. Having the courage to accept the truth about myself has set me free. I hope these results will do the same for you.

Star wants you to know how sorry she is to have hurt you. Neither of us wanted that. You're the best man we know. I hope someday you'll have what we have together. Maybe then you'll be able to forgive me.

All my love, Addison

With shaking hands, he set aside the letter. His first instinct was to call Sophie. His second was to toss the letter in the trash. He did neither. Instead, he picked up his puppy and sat in the middle of the floor and wept.

Addie had been right. His parents were not his.

Months before their called-off wedding, she'd suggested the idea of DNA testing. It was in the car driving home to their apartment after a particularly horrible family dinner. His mother had been terrible, telling stories about all his failings as a child. How they feared he'd never quit wetting the bed. His obsession with collecting seeds from plants. How he'd let the cat out on accident, resulting in her death by coyote.

Addie had lost it at dinner. She'd actually yelled at the formidable Mrs. Bentley. Despite leaving him for her best girlfriend, Addie had always felt protective of him and had been good to him. She'd loved him very much, just not in the same way she loved Star.

But that night was before all that. They were recently engaged. He'd accepted a dinner invitation from his parents. They'd gone so Addie could get to know them better before the wedding. Unbeknownst to him, Addie had swiped the straws from his parent's empty daiquiri glasses. Then, apparently, she'd sent them in for testing.

On the way home, she'd ranted about his mother. She couldn't understand how a mother could be so cold to one son and so loving to the other. She had good instincts about people. Cop-like instincts, honed from her years in the LAPD. Something wasn't right. She was sure of it. No one favors one sibling over the other so blatantly, she'd said. Unless one of them is not like the other.

It was true that he'd always felt like an outsider in his own family. He'd suspected many times that he wasn't wanted. Their preference for his younger brother had been obvious. Nico had always assumed it was because Zander was inherently more lovable than he was. In addition, Nico was so different from the rest of them. They were all attorneys who hated the outdoors. He was a landscape designer who spent every moment he could outside. They'd cut him off when he'd chosen design school over law school.

With this knowledge, so many events and dynamics made sense.

His mother had had a sister who died at fourteen from suicide. No one talked about her. The only photographs were in his grandparents' bedroom. They had lived north of San Francisco in a house that had seemed perpetually dark. Now he knew. In the shadows were secrets.

When he was ten, during a rare visit to their house, he'd asked his grandmother who the girl was in the pictures. She'd picked up the photograph of the little blond girl with the wide, sad eyes and brushed the top of the frame where dust had settled.

"That's your aunt Tina. She died at fourteen. Hung herself." She'd delivered this news without any emotion. Not unusual. She was a stern, religious woman.

That day, he'd wanted to ask why. Had Tina been sad? Did something bad happen to her?

Now Jen licked his face as he held her against his chest. He had no idea what he was supposed to do with this seismic shift to his life.

He wouldn't do anything. What did it matter? It wasn't as if he had a close relationship with them. They'd barely spoken since he moved to Cliffside Bay. Knowing the truth didn't set him free. He would go on with his life just as he had since he moved here. Only now he'd have a dog to keep him company.

If only she had the power to take away his feelings for Sophie Woods.

"Can you do that, girl?"

Jen wriggled, then whined.

"Yeah, I don't think so either."

2

S ophie

"IT'S NOT like I'm the Virgin Mary," Sophie said to Nico as they reclined on her couch. "But you'd think I was by the way people stare at me in this town."

Nico smiled as he swirled a generous pour of 2013 Walla Walla Syrah around a Riedel glass. "It *is* unusual to have your brother's baby." Long-limbed and muscular with a kind of lazy sexiness that seemed innate rather than honed, the boy rocked a pair of loose-fitting jeans and faded Bruce Springsteen T-shirt that clung to his trim waist and wide chest.

He looked good here in the apartment above her bar and grill. The decor that mirrored the grays, soft blues, and tans of the Northern California coast reminded her of Nico. They were his colors. Most things led back to Nico these days.

She forced herself to look away from him before he caught her gawking at him. Instead, she glanced out the windows that faced the northern slope of town. Tonight, lights from the houses built into the hill sparkled good-naturedly in the comforting blue twilight. Warm summer air drifted in through the open windows, bringing the scents of eucalyptus and the seaside.

"Immaculate conception is one thing, but I was a surrogate. Totally different." Sophie had simply been a surrogate for her half brother and his wife, carrying the baby made from his sperm and a donor egg. Nothing seedy or scandalous, but you'd never know it by the way people in Cliffside Bay chattered about how Sebastian Shaw came to be.

Curled on the rug at Nico's feet, Jen lifted her head to give them an appraising look before dropping her chin into her paws and closing her eyes. A month had passed since the fateful day they brought Jen home from the shelter. She'd filled out several inches in every direction in the past few weeks. The vet had estimated she would reach about twenty-five pounds when fully grown. For now, she was about the size of a medium-sized cat but looked bigger because of her fluffy fur.

"Man, this is a small town though," Nico said. "People love to gossip. There are no secrets, that's for sure. A little old lady at church last week trapped me at the coffee station to tell me how sorry she was my fiancée left me for a woman—and would I be interested in meeting her grandson?"

"Wait, what?"

"You heard me right," he said, talking and laughing at the same time. "She thought that if my fiancée was gay then I must be, too. I'm not sure how she worked that out in her mind."

A giggle escaped. "That's pretty funny."

"Or embarrassing."

"Your particular situation was also unusual," she said.

"True enough." He grinned at her. "Apparently, that's our thing."

She clinked her glass against his. "To us."

"To us." He took a sip of his wine. "How did this come up? Did someone compare you to the Virgin Mary?"

"Not out loud, but guys watch me when I'm behind the bar," she said. "Like I'm some kind of freak of nature. Like I'm scary."

"Wait a minute. You think they're afraid of you?" He turned just his head while remaining in his languid pose. His pale blue eyes were doing that twinkly, laughing thing they did when he thought she was funny. Most of the time, she had no idea why.

Her fingers tightened around the stem of her glass. As always when she was near enough to smell the spicy scent of his cologne, she had to keep herself from touching him. His face seemed molded from the finest clay and smoothed into shape by a sensitive and gifted sculptor. There was no wasted space, no features made without the greatest care to detail.

She tipped her glass to watch the legs on the wine, hoping to distract herself from the ones attached to Nico. "I mean, yes, I did something nice for the family I love, but I'm no one to be intimidated by." She suspected the tanned man taking up more than his share of her couch might be put off by what she'd done. Maybe that's what was mixing up their signals. Why else would they have spent so much time together without him making a move when they were so obviously meant for each other?

"I don't think that's it," Nico said.

"What else could it be?" she asked.

"Sweetheart, are you for real?" Nico asked.

"Of course I'm for real." She studied him while pretending to breathe in the nose of the Syrah. "Why are you laughing at me?

"I'm not," he said, then erupted in laughter.

She flushed with heat and longing. He was so delicious when he laughed. She wanted to crawl onto his lap and kiss the amusement right out of him. "It's not nice to make fun of a friend, you know."

He covered his mouth as if that would hide his amusement. "I'm sorry. It's just you're too cute for words."

"Cute?" She didn't like the sound of that. "Like Jen kind of cute? All fluffy and tail-waggy?"

"That's not the kind of cute I meant."

"What kind of cute am I? Like the ridiculous kind?"

He cocked his head to the side and raised one eyebrow. "Nothing about you is ridiculous. But you're a little naive at times." He smiled, revealing laugh lines around his eyes. She wanted to run her fingers over every one of them. "And somewhat quirky."

"I'm not naive. Not exactly. I'm *definitely* not quirky. I'm boringly normal."

"There's nothing normal about you. That's a compliment, by the way."

A warmth spread over her. No one made her feel the way this man did when he looked at her with those kind eyes. She set aside her wine and reached over the back of the couch for the lighter, then lit the candles on the table. The wicks sputtered and flickered to life. When she turned back to Nico, she caught him watching her. His gaze flickered away.

He's the one. My one true love.

When Nico Bentley showed up at a table in The Oar, Sophie had recognized him immediately. The blue eyes and his mouth so quick to smile were an exact match. It was him. The one. She'd felt it deep inside her soul. When he ordered a glass of a red blend from Washington state, she was pleased to know that not only was he made for her specifically, but that he had good taste in wine. This was a bonus.

She'd thought everything would unravel as it should. However, there was a problem. Nico Bentley didn't recognize *her*. Clearly, he'd never had a dream or a vision. Or he'd come to her crushed by life already, rendering him blind to the one he'd been looking for all along. He no longer believed in magic or miracles.

When she proposed this idea to her mother, Rhona had suggested patience. "Sometimes soul mates take their own sweet time seeing what's right in front of them. Especially male soul mates."

And then there was the problem of the dog. He didn't have one. She'd taken care of that well enough. Now she needed to move this relationship from friendship to the love match they were fated to have. Tonight, she'd vowed to tell him how she felt.

She settled back into her spot and picked up her glass. So far, her confession of her undying love for Nico Bentley wasn't going so well. She shouldn't have brought up her virginity. She could see that now. Just because he was as easy to talk to as it was to breathe didn't mean she should tell him everything. She was doing this all wrong.

"Make the night romantic," her mother had advised over the phone. "And wear something pretty."

She'd dressed in a short jean skirt that showed off her long, tanned legs and a peasant blouse that dipped into her cleavage. She was pretty sure the outfit was a good choice, because Nico's gaze had darted to her chest when she opened the door to let him into the apartment.

Nico sipped his wine. Darn that mouth with those full lips. They taunted her, pulled her toward him as if she had no control of herself. She would give years of her life to feel them pressed to her own.

He shifted, removing his feet from the table as he draped one arm over the back of her couch. "I can guarantee you that's not why guys are staring at you—at the bar or otherwise. They're staring at you because you're smoking hot."

She brought her glass to her mouth, buying time to think through this response. If he thought this, why did he treat her as though she was too holy to touch? "Then why doesn't anyone ever hit on me?" *Why don't* you *hit on me?*

He looked away, the way her little niece Jubie did when she was contemplating telling a fib.

"Nico?"

He let out a long sigh, then turned back to her. "What would be a reason guys would be scared to ask you out?"

"That's what I'm saying, I don't know."

"Think about it this way. Who in your life is intimidating?" He narrowed his eyes and leaned closer as if that would prompt the right answer. "Can you think of anyone who doesn't want guys hitting on you and would make sure everyone knew it?"

She stared at him. Please God, let him be talking about himself. "Is it you?"

His eyebrows came together as he shook his head. "What? No, Soph, I'm talking about your brother."

"No, Zane wouldn't do that."

A muscle twitched on the side of his face. "You might be surprised. That's all I'm saying."

Zane wouldn't interfere in her love life. Anyway, that wasn't where she was going with this. She needed to circle around to them. "What about you? Why don't you ever cross the line?"

He dropped his chin into his neck and pinched the bridge of his nose. "That wouldn't be a good idea."

No going back. She'd made a plan to get her feelings out in the open, and nothing was going to stop her. "Why not?"

Growing up, she'd grown accustomed to being singled out and even talked about. That's what happened when a baby was abandoned on the steps of a firehouse and raised by a high-profile music producer and his wife. She was "that" girl. The one in the newspapers. The one who'd helped launch the safe house initiative. The one who'd won the proverbial lottery when she was adopted by a couple in the top 1 percent. Money aside, her parents were wonderful. She'd had a magical childhood.

Then, at age twenty, there was the discovery of two half siblings. Not totally unheard of but somewhat unusual. What made it special was how immediately bonded they'd felt. Zane had given her 50 percent of their family restaurant, The Oar. Maggie had brought her fully into her life and family.

Everything went her way. That was just the truth. But for the life of her, she couldn't figure out the man in front of her. She knew he was the one. How come he didn't know it?

She tucked her bare legs under her and spoke softly. "Nico, look at me."

He glanced over at her, his eyes reflecting the flicker of the candle's flames. His brows scrunched together before he looked back to his lap.

"Why not us?" When she was a child, there had been music everywhere, drifting up from her father's recording studio or on the old turntable in the family room. Even in the car, her father had played the folk and country music of his artists and others. A constant soundtrack to her life played through her mind, even when everyone else heard only silence. Now an old Judds song played through her mind. "Why Not Me?"

"We're too different," he said.

Her throat hurt as she asked the next question. "Is it because I had a baby?"

He stared at her with widened eyes, clearly stunned. "One hundred percent no. Putting your life on hold like you did was incredible. You gave Zane and Honor the best gift in the world. I admire you more than you can imagine."

"I'm talking about my appearance."

His head jerked backward. "Oh, no. God no. You're perfect. Every inch of you." One side of his mouth rose in a wry smile. "That tiny bit of cloth you call a bikini hides nothing from me or any of the other men drooling over you."

She raised her eyebrows in an attempt to sound flirtatious, even though she wanted to cry with frustration. "You sound jealous."

"I don't appreciate the leers, no," he said, closer to a growl than speech. "You deserve better than that." He threw up his hands. "Anyway, this has nothing to do with how you look. To me, you're perfect. So damn perfect. I've never known a more beautiful woman, both inside and out."

"Then what's stopping you from ravishing me?"

He choked on his wine. "Ravishing you?"

"Yes. Like a throwdown, hotter-than-hot ravish." She set her glass on the table and stretched both legs out on the couch. Her toes brushed his thigh, and a jolt of desire traveled up to her core. "We have a great time together, right?"

"The best." He stared down at her bare toes.

"And we have a ton in common. We're both surfing foodies who love wine, coffee, and thrillers."

Still gazing downward at her toes, he chuckled. "True."

She waited until he looked up at her to continue. "We spend all this time together and I keep thinking you're going to kiss me but then you don't. Do you need permission?"

"Permission?"

"Yes, permission. If so, I'm granting it right now." She gazed into his eyes. Her heart pounded in her chest, but she wore it on her damn sleeve.

"Don't do that." He put aside his wine and covered his face with his hands.

"Don't what?"

"Don't look at me with those eyes," he said through his fingers. "I'm weak, Soph."

"I'm a little in love with you. Not a little. A lot."

His head jerked up as he turned toward her. "You're in love with me?"

"Completely."

"That can't be," he said.

Jen rose from her nap and looked up at them. Did she sense the tension in the room?

The next bit came out in a heated rush. "When I was a little girl, I had a dream. God told me about you. I've been waiting for you. I knew the minute I met you that you were the one. I've been saving myself for you."

"What are you talking about?"

"I saw you in my dream when I was a little girl. You and Jen."

Jen barked.

"That's impossible." He snapped his fingers at Jen. "Lie down."

Jen's ears flattened, but she did as he asked.

"Nico, don't look at me like I'm delusional." Sophie scooted nearer until she was inches from him. "I finally decided I better say something, or this might never happen." She brushed his mouth with the back of her index finger. He closed his eyes when she moved her finger up the side of his smooth cheek. "Do you feel it? Like a spark?"

He nodded. "Yes."

"Do you want this?"

He made a growling sound at the back of his throat. "More than anything I've ever wanted in my life."

Joy flooded her. He wanted her. "What's stopping you?"

Another growl came from deep inside his chest. He pulled her to him, then captured her mouth in a long, hard kiss. He tasted of red wine, and his mouth was so warm. She wrapped her arms around his neck and kissed him back, giving herself to him. Finally. This was it. The moment she'd been waiting for.

"Soph, you feel so good." He pushed her onto her back and covered her body with his and kissed her again, this time almost frantically. She moaned softly when his hands moved to her bare legs.

But as suddenly as it had happened, it ended. With a sudden force, he broke apart from her and leaped to his feet. "I'm sorry. That should not have happened."

Jen scrambled to her feet and scooted backward, away from them.

Sophie touched her fingers to her mouth, too stunned to talk. Why would he say that? The kiss had been so perfect. Just exactly as she thought it would be. "But it was good. Wasn't it? I mean, I'm not the most experienced when it comes to kissing, but I liked it. A lot. Did I do something wrong?"

"No, no, it was spectacular. You're spectacular." He knelt on the floor next to the couch and dropped his head onto the cushion. "Kissing you was just like I knew it would be." His voice sounded muffled against the upholstery, but she heard him just the same. He'd thought about kissing her before. That was a good sign, wasn't it? What could possibly be wrong?

She sat up and pulled her skirt down, aware that her polka-dot bikini bottoms were showing, then splayed her fingers through his light brown hair, the texture so soft against her skin. "What's the matter then?"

He looked up at her, pain in his eyes. "We're not a good match."

"What, no. That's not right. It's the opposite.

"You're way too young for me."

"I don't understand. How does age have anything to do with us? Souls are ageless."

He grimaced and rubbed the back of his neck with the palm of his hand. "I'm thirty-four. You're twenty-two. That's too much of a gap. We're not even in the same generation."

"It doesn't matter. Those are just numbers."

"Soph, I'm ready to get married and have children. You're barely out of college."

"I'm ready for those things too," she said.

"You might think that, but trust me, no one knows anything

when they're in their early twenties. You're going to change a ton in the next twelve years. I'm who I'm going to be."

"I am too." Why were people so hung up on ages? "I've done a lot for someone my age."

He rose to his feet. "I have to get out of here before I do something we'll both regret."

"I wouldn't regret it." Tears sprang to her eyes. She'd never wanted anything more than for him to stay. "Please, don't go."

His face crumpled. "I want to, but I can't do this to you. It's wrong. You deserve someone your own age who doesn't have all this baggage. Someone good and pure, like you."

"I'm not that good. I've just been blessed more than most."

"Sweetheart, you're so innocent and I've been with...a lot of women." He spoke slowly, drawing out each word. "I'm not what you want long term. Trust me."

"It's not like you're the same age as my father," she said.

He cringed. "No, thank God."

"I've seen you leave the bar with tons of women. Some of them had to be as young as me." She'd been seared with jealousy every time she saw him leave with some drunk stranger.

"They were just rebound girls. After Addison jilted me, I needed an ego boost."

Sophie had convinced herself that each time he left with some strange girl it was simply to get it out of his system. Soon, she'd thought, he'd be ready to take their friendship to another level.

"I could be a rebound girl," she said. Once he was with her, she knew he'd understand they were meant to be.

His eyes hardened as he spoke through clenched teeth. "You are not rebound material."

"I don't understand what's happening here," she said. "We're soul mates. Can't you see that?"

"There's no such thing." He closed his eyes as if her words

pained his head. When he opened them, he sighed and rubbed the back of his neck. "There isn't a man on earth who wouldn't want you, but what I want and what's right are two different things."

"That's not how men are. If you truly wanted me, nothing would stop you," she said.

"That's not true. Some of us are more than our base desires." He leaned over and kissed the top of her head. "I'm sorry I got carried away. It's nearly impossible to resist you." He cupped her chin and looked into her eyes. "You're going to make some guy a lucky man someday, but it's not me. We're at different stages of our lives. If we were to act on these feelings— the physical attraction between us—you'd regret it at some point. You'd start resenting me for taking something that didn't belong to me in the first place."

He walked across the room to the door, then called to Jen, who trotted over obediently. With his hand on the knob, he turned back to her. "You'll be fine, Soph. I promise, this is in your best interest."

She clenched her jaw to keep from crying as he and Jen walked through the door. The moment it closed, she burst into tears.

Twelve years between them. What a joke. Math always ruined everything.

* * *

SOPHIE'S MOTHER had often told her there was no shame in succumbing to a good cry. The way to work through sadness and disappointment was to acknowledge your feelings and cry if you needed to. When it came to matters of the heart, no one was more of an expert than Rhona Woods. No one but her mother would do during times like this. Sophie picked up the phone and called her.

The moment she said hello, Mom knew something was wrong.

"It didn't go well with Nico?" Her mother's voice was like honey, sweet and warm.

She told her the details of the humiliating evening. "And then he just walked out the door."

"This poor boy is scared to death of you," Mom said. "If anyone's too young for the relationship, it's him."

"His heart was broken when his fiancée called off the wedding," Sophie said.

"It would make him cautious."

"What do I do?" Sophie asked.

"Leave him be for now. Let him miss you. If you're right about what's between you, he'll come back once he's ready."

"I'm sad, Mom."

"I know you are. It's okay to be sad, because that means you're living in your full truth. You know what you want and you're not afraid to fight for it. When you live so authentically and in touch with your feelings, it opens your heart for injury. But you wouldn't want it any other way, would you?"

"No, I like the way I am."

"That's my girl," Mom said. "Now hang on. Your dad wants to talk to you."

She waited as they exchanged the phone. Her dad's deep, authoritative voice came over the line. "How's my baby girl?"

"Not great." Her voice cracked and the tears came again. "I'm so in love with him, Daddy."

"I know, honey. It's your party and you can cry if you want to." Like most things in life, her father punctuated the situation with song lyrics. "But you remember who you are. Sophie Grace Woods. You're a miracle. It's a privilege for that man to have you in his world. If he's too stifled up to see it, then he's not for you. Never settle for anything less. You hear me?"

"Yes, Daddy." She smiled and dried her eyes.

"We'll call you tomorrow," he said.

After she hung up the phone, she ran a hot bath with a capful of jasmine bubble bath. On summer nights, the noise from the bar often carried upstairs. To escape into her own world, she placed her noise-canceling headphones over her ears, put on her favorite love songs playlist, and sank up to her neck into the water.

The kiss they'd shared seemed to hover on her lips. She'd felt a primal need in the way his mouth had moved against hers. He might think she was too young for him, but his body didn't agree. She suspected his heart didn't, either. If only he could get over this silly idea about age.

When the bath had cooled, she got out and put on her pajamas, then crawled into bed. On her bedside table, the notebook with letters from her biological father beckoned to her. When he died, the attorney had given Zane a letter from Hugh explaining about Sophie. He'd also left a journal for her. In it were letters he'd written to her over the years. Letters he could never send but had saved for her.

She flipped to the entry appropriate for tonight.

Dear Sophie,

Today I went into the city and parked outside your elementary school. I needed to see you come out of your kindergarten class. It's hard to believe you're already five years old. I'm ashamed I've had to follow your mom to figure out where your school is and familiarize myself with your schedule. I vowed when I gave you up for your own safety that I'd never interfere with your life. It's been easier to remain committed to that decision because your adoptive parents are so obviously good to you. My heart hurts to not be able to raise you myself, but I'm happy you're with the Woodses. Still, I'll never be able to ever fully let you go. Which is why I waited outside your school today to catch a glimpse of you.

What a glimpse it was. Your hair was fixed in two ponytails on the sides of your head, and you wore this cute little pink dress that

*matched your cheeks. You look so much like Zane. That fact startles
me every time. When I came home, I dug out some photographs of
my mother when she was a child. You're the spitting image of her. I'll
save them for you.*

*It occurred to me today as I watched a young couple breaking up
in my bar that I should write to you with a little advice about love.
I'm afraid no one gets through life without at least one broken heart.
Rejection hurts. But remember, if a man doesn't want you, it just
means he's not the one God made for you.*

*Here's how to tell if he's the right one. It's very simple, actually.
He'll sacrifice whatever it takes to be with you. Don't be satisfied
until he proves to you that he would give his life for you. For your
mother, I would have given my own life so that she might live. Make
sure he'll do the same for you. Hopefully he won't have to. Or, like
me, be unable to. More about that some other time.*

*My point is to wait for the one who will chase you into the depths
of hell if need be.*

She closed the book and held it to her chest. What about
Nico? Would he risk everything to be with her? From the data
so far, she would have to say no. He wouldn't run into hell or
anywhere else to be with her. In fact, he ran away from her.
She'd believed they were soul mates. For the first time, the
possibility that she was misreading the messages of the
universe presented itself. Was she wrong about their connection? Maybe he wasn't the right one even though she ached for
him. Was it just her mind playing tricks on her? Interpreting a
dream in the wrong way?

She was Sophie Grace Woods of Micky and Rhona Woods
and Hugh Shaw and Mae Keene. Two guardian angels watched
over her from heaven and two were here on earth. Their
messages seemed loud and clear tonight. If she were to go by
his actions, Nico was not the one.

She set aside the journal and pulled the covers up to her
neck to stare at the ceiling. A thump from the bass downstairs

beat as though the building had a heart. Her mother had taught her that not everyone or everything was as it seemed on the surface. Tomorrow was another day. She would simply have faith that whatever was meant to be would happen. Faith and love went together, after all.

3

N ico

THE NEXT MORNING, after a restless night's sleep, Nico woke to find Jen's fluffy black-and-white head on the pillow next to him. She smiled sympathetically.

"Did I wake you?" he asked.

Jen blinked, ruffling her bangs.

Sophie's revelation last night had taken him completely off guard. He thought she liked him, but not that much. For the life of him, he couldn't think why she would. However, all that talk about soul mates had scared him. Was she serious about her dream? Knowing Sophie, she probably was. That didn't make it true.

Over the last few months, she'd kept asking him to do things with her: dinner, movies, wine tasting, surfing. He'd said yes every time but had been sure never to cross the line from friendship to anything physical. He'd never touched her until last night.

He'd known it all along. Once he felt her in his arms, he'd want it over and over again. There was no denying it to himself. He was in love with her.

"She's the strangest woman I've ever met." He rolled over to his back and watched the ceiling fan make a slow circle. "I can't believe I let myself kiss her. You should've stopped me."

Jen whined and inched closer to rest her chin on his shoulder.

"I couldn't help myself. I know, I should be ashamed. I am ashamed. I mean, you probably have more experience in the love department than she does."

Jen sighed in sympathy.

"What am I going to do? How can I stay away from her? I thought getting over Addie was hard, but this is torture. You get that it's wrong for me to love her even though I do, right?"

Another whine, this time with even more empathy.

"After what Addie did, I never thought I'd love someone else. You know, it was just supposed to be me and a bunch of one-night stands from here on out. But then there she was, with that big smile and her kind heart. She's the best person I've ever met. I mean, who has a baby for their brother when they're only twenty years old?"

Jen barked.

"I agree. She's totally special. Remember how she found you for me? Meant to be, right, girl?"

Jen licked his cheek.

Dogs made everything better. Even broken hearts. She always knew when he was suffering. She didn't care that he was always messing everything up and that no woman could ever truly love him. Dogs loved unconditionally.

"That's what I mean, though. She's so sweet, and it's like she

knows exactly what I need before I do. No one in my whole
life's ever been like that. My family dislikes me so much. I know,
I've told you this before."

Jen growled. She understood what jerks his parents were.
Not that she'd met them. They didn't deem him important
enough for a visit. Plus, he was living in a bungalow on
someone else's property, thus proving that they were right. He
was a loser.

He'd been expected to go to law school and join his father's
firm like his brother. They'd made sure he knew there were no
second chances if his "gardening" thing didn't work out.

The conversation had gone as expected. They'd been in the
formal dining room of his childhood home.

"I want to be a landscape architect. I'm switching my major
to botany and then getting a master's in landscape design."

Dad hadn't spoken and walked out of the room, his hand-
made leather shoes squeaking on the over-polished floor. Mom
went all hysterical, calling him selfish and completely without
moral character. By the time he returned to the dorm, they'd
cleaned out his bank account. He'd had to take out loans for
undergraduate and for his master's in landscape design. But it
was all worth it. He loved his profession. Now that Wolf Enterprises was taking off, he'd paid off all his debt and was actually
putting money away. Thanks in part to Mrs. Coventry's
generous offer. Someday, he hoped to have a home of his own,
but for now this was ideal.

"Am I a terrible man?" he asked Jen.

She didn't answer.

"Great. Maybe my mom's been right all along."

From the time he was a little boy prone to physical activity
that included throwing balls and ramming play trucks into
furniture, his mother repeatedly told him, "You are a bad
boy." Or versions thereof: naughty, treacherous, lazy, manip-
ulative.

"I mean, who kisses a girl when he knows it's wrong to lead her on?"

Jen rose to her feet and stood there looking down on him.

"You're right. I'm despicable."

He was a selfish, uncaring, and insensitive lout. Sophie, on the other hand, was as near to perfect as the sun itself, all golden and bright and warming. The most frozen terrain of any man's heart would melt under her smile. She needed better, younger, smarter than him. Once she figured that out, she'd leave him just as Addie had.

Dammit all. He wanted Sophie more than he'd ever wanted a woman. Even Addison. Which was why he was absolutely convinced he must stay away.

Last night, he should never have suggested they open the Syrah. They'd already had a glass of her favorite French Chablis while they prepared dinner together. Well, she prepared dinner while he savored the crisp white wine and watched the stunning woman move around her kitchen as graceful and athletic as a tiger. There was nothing the woman couldn't do. She surfed as well as him or Trey. Melt-in-his-mouth dishes seemed to magically appear from her fingers. Behind the bar, she multitasked while charming each and every customer with her quick wit and pretty smile.

"What am I going to do?"

Jen turned and must have caught a glimpse of her tail because she started chasing it.

"I'm not sure what you're trying to tell me, other than chasing after love seems like a futile endeavor." He pulled back the covers and got out of bed. "Come on, let's go check on Mrs. Coventry."

* * *

MRS. COVENTRY PUSHED the bowl of plain Greek yogurt with

almond slivers and flaxseed toward him. "Dear boy, I'm not sure you've noticed but I'm not a horse." She was from the South and pronounced *dear* as "deah."

They sat at the outside table under the awning. She'd just finished a swim in her lap pool and wore a cover-up over her bathing suit. A wide-brimmed straw hat and giant sunglasses hid most of her small face. The house, perched at the top of the northern slope, looked out to the Pacific. Today, both sky and sea were a vibrant blue.

"It's good for you," he said without looking up from his tablet where he was reading the latest *Architectural Digest*. Jen rested near his feet, having worn herself out chasing the malicious squirrel that teased her mercilessly. She would never catch the creature, but Jen was not one to give up easily. He'd tried to tell her about the futility of the same chase every day, but this was a dog who chased her own tail, so the lesson didn't go far.

"Whatever happened to my poached egg and buttered sourdough toast?" Mrs. Coventry asked in her Southern drawl. "The breakfast I had every day for fifty years. The breakfast my dear, departed husband fixed for me without complaint?"

"Your cholesterol, remember?" He glanced up at her. Seeing himself distorted in the curvature of her sunglasses' lenses, he looked rather like a horse.

"You're the one with the cholesterol." She patted her bony shoulder. "I'm as fit as a twenty-year-old."

"Dr. Waller said you need to put some weight on. Almonds have the good kind of fat."

"Living with you is rather tedious." She picked up her spoon and took a bite, then made a face as though she'd just taken a dose of strychnine. "This is dreadful. Truly."

He ignored her and went back to his article while scooping some yogurt from his bowl and into his mouth.

"I'm not eating this. I'm on strike," she said. "I'll give it to Jen. She'll eat anything."

He waved his now-empty spoon at her. "She's already had her breakfast."

She let out a dramatic sigh and tilted her head toward the sky. "How I loved that toast dripping with butter. The bread just melted in my mouth. My husband knew how to treat a lady."

"He was sleeping with you, so he wasn't thinking straight."

"What's the matter with you this morning?" Mrs. Coventry lowered her sunglasses and peered at him with her sharp eyes. "You're as grumpy as a bear."

"I'm fine."

She narrowed her eyes and slid the sunglasses from her face. "Something's wrong." She tapped the glasses against the palm of one hand. "Let me see if I can figure this mystery out." Her eyes sparkled in a way that perfectly matched her mocking tone. "Oh yes, that's right. You were with Sophie last night. Something happened."

How in the world did she know that? He couldn't even remember mentioning his plans. He must have let it slip. It was never good to tell Mrs. Coventry anything you didn't want her to remember. The woman had a mind like a vault.

"What did you do?" She raised one thin eyebrow. "Did you finally give in and do what you've been wanting to do since the day you met her?"

A string of silent curse words pitched through his mind. This woman was too smart. He ran a hand over the top of his head, still damp from his workout. "I'm not proud of it. At all."

"Glory be, did you finally take her to bed? Shall I pop the champagne?"

He made a sound similar to Jen's bark when confronted with a dog she disliked. "Of course not. I told you she's off-limits. I kissed her and then ran away."

"Why is she off-limits exactly?" Her drawl elongated each

vowel. Usually he found it endearing. Right now, a prickle of annoyance tickled the back of his throat.

"You know why." They'd discussed this at length.

"Her age. How a man could resist that gorgeous young woman is beyond me. Do you suppose there's something wrong with you?"

"Very funny."

"No, I'm quite serious. I've never met a man who could resist a young woman. In fact, many make absolute asses of themselves by marrying a woman half their age after the first poor wife is cast aside."

"That's not me."

"I have more than one friend who supported their idiot husbands during several lean decades only to be left for younger women. But that's not the case here. Sophie's not half your age. Twelve years is nothing." She picked up her glasses and shook them at him. "Which is why I believe this has every-thing to do with your poor self-esteem. I hate to be the one to say it, especially as a feminist, but I blame your mama."

Under the table, Jen laid her chin on his bare foot.

Dogs and plants. So much easier to deal with than women.

"How was it? The kiss," she asked.

He closed his eyes and muttered under his breath. "Like the best thing I've ever felt."

"Oh, for heaven's sake. Why must you torture yourself? It's not only her age, is it?"

"Fine. What do you want me to say? I'm not good enough for her. It's not like that's a secret."

"And you're afraid she'll realize that eventually."

"Something like that," he said.

She reached across the table and patted his arm. "The lies your mother told you about yourself are just that—lies. You're a better man than you believe yourself to be. Perhaps it's time to see yourself as Sophie sees you."

Jen licked his toe. Apparently, she agreed with Mrs. Coventry.

They were wrong. He would stay away from Sophie from here on. Out of sight, out of mind.

Right.

4

Sophie

A MONTH LATER, Sophie dried a glass behind the counter at The Oar. Her brother, Zane, was beside her, filling out a liquor order. She stretched the damp towel into a rope and turned slowly toward him.

"Why are you looking at me like you want to wrap that around my neck?" Zane asked. He wore his usual uniform of board shorts and a Dog's Brewery T-shirt.

"Because I want to." She tightened her grip on the towel.

"What did I do?" His wavy blond hair was slightly unruly, and there were dark shadows under his eyes. Sebastian was teething and had kept him up all night. Her anger almost subsided but not quite. She would get the truth out of him today.

"You're an interfering, bullheaded prig. And don't try to deny it."

"Pardon me?"

She hadn't seen or heard from Nico in a month, other than a glimpse of the back of his head one night while she was tending bar. In the days since their kiss, she'd tried to talk herself into accepting that she'd been wrong about their connection. However, when she learned from Trey that Zane had warned Nico to stay away from her, she had new insight into the situation.

"I'm now privy to your little talk with Nico."

"What talk?" He widened his eyes, all innocent. He couldn't fool her.

"You should be ashamed of yourself. Threatening the man."

"I didn't threaten him exactly." Zane looked up at the ceiling. Sure sign of guilt.

"You did."

Her bartender, Bobby, came in from the back, tying his apron around his waist. An aging surfer with a gray ponytail and a tattoo that read "4:20" on the back of his wrist, he was reliable and easy with the customers. In fact, she'd never seen him flustered once since the beginning of tourist season. He could cut a drunk patron off, escort them into an Uber, and make them think it was all their idea.

She greeted him with a friendly smile. "I'm going to talk with Zane in the back for a few minutes. The sprinkler guy is coming by to check that the new system is working. Will you grab me when he gets here?" They'd had a new system installed at the beginning of the summer, and the company wanted to make sure everything was working as it should.

"You got it, boss." Bobby's mouth curved into a lazy smile.

They walked together to the back office. Zane flopped in the chair behind the desk and crossed his arms over his chest. "What's going on between you and this Nico person anyway?"

Sophie closed the door and leaned against it. His agitation was actually amusing. For a man who'd spent most of his life as an only child, he'd certainly embraced his big brother role. "What's it to you?"

"I told him to stay away from you. I'm wondering if the guy has trouble with directions."

"Why would you do that?" Sophie's fists balled at her sides. "He's the nicest guy in the world."

"I disagree."

"What evidence do you have of that?" She crossed her arms over her chest in a mimic of his own.

Zane grimaced as he unfolded his arms to drape onto the desk. "He's a man. There are no nice men when it comes to their intentions with a beautiful woman. Or in your case, a girl."

"I'm hardly a girl," she said.

"You're my little sister."

"Your sister is a fully legal adult. Did you really threaten him physically?"

"What? No, nothing like that. I merely pointed out that you're twenty-two years old and he's thirty-four. In case he didn't see the problem with the math, I wanted to make it crystal clear."

"You had no right to do that." Her throat started to ache at the injustice of it all. "You've ruined my chances by threatening the man I'm crazy about."

"I didn't threaten him. I *talked* to him."

"Does Honor know you did this?" she asked.

He stared at her with a stony expression. "My wife…does not know. No, she mostly certainly does not."

Sophie laughed despite her irritation. "Right. Because she'd have your hide if she knew you messed with the guy I'm in love with."

"In love with?" He shook his head as though she were some silly little girl who didn't know her own mind. "You're *not* in love with him."

She stuck out her chin and moved closer to the desk in a move that she hoped translated as both aggression and self-confidence. "I am."

"Sophie, he's way too old for you, and he's kind of a loser. The guy doesn't even have his own house. He can't take care of you."

"Oh my God. Can't take care of me? Since when do I need a man to take care of me? If Honor could hear you right now, she'd banish you to the couch for a month."

He rolled his eyes. "My wife doesn't tell me what's what."

Sophie laughed again. Harder this time. "Good one."

"Anyway, that's beside the point. He's too old for you. You're barely out of high school."

"I'm a college graduate who runs a business and gave birth to your son."

He sighed and closed his eyes as if she were really trying his patience. "Sophie, you don't have any experience with men. And you're way too immature to be thinking about marriage."

"I'm not." She tapped her temple. "In here, I'm a hundred years old."

"That's part of the problem. You feel old because you're wearing grown-up shoes when you should be like those kids out there." He pointed toward the bar. "I should never have let you take on so much responsibility."

"I wanted this. I love this," she said.

"I feel guilty."

"Why are you changing the subject? Don't try to distract me with this other stuff. You're going to fix this with Nico. He needs the green light from you."

"I'm not fixing anything, Sophie Grace Woods."

"You're not my father."

"Our father would never approve of you dating a man twelve years your senior. Especially when you're, you know, a..." He trailed off.

"A virgin?"

Her brother had the decency to blush a deep pink. "Right. I can't help but think we've robbed you of your young adulthood."

The stricken look on his face softened her, rubbed away a few of the angry edges. "I'm exactly where I want to be. I love the bar and the brewery. I love my nephew, and I'm proud I was able to help you and Honor have Sebastian. You know that."

"And we're grateful beyond measure."

"I know. And, like the idea of Nico and me as a couple, we had to convince you that having me be your surrogate was a good idea." Honor had had a hysterectomy for health reasons when she was a teenager. Even though she didn't have any eggs because of an early hysterectomy, Honor had wanted part of their baby to come from Zane.

Sophie was not one to give up on an idea just because it was hard. She'd known almost instantly the solution to their infertility issues. Her womb. Boom. Done.

Although it had taken Sophie, Honor, and Zane's best friends, the Dogs, to convince him, he'd finally come around. Sophie had been impregnated with an embryo made from Zane's sperm and a donor egg. Nine months later, the perfect Sebastian Hugh was born.

Oh, that baby. Honor said Sebastian reminded her of Zane and Sophie's father, Hugh, both in personality and appearance. Sophie hadn't had the privilege of being raised by Hugh Shaw. He was already lost to dementia by the time she and Zane had found each other. Hugh had passed away shortly after Sophie met him. All she had of him were the journal he'd left her and the stories from family and friends. The longer she lived in Cliffside Bay, the more convinced she became that Hugh Shaw had changed every resident's life in one way or another.

Zane glared at her. "Yes, I was reluctant. But now I can't imagine life without Sebastian."

"None of us can. And you have me to thank for it." She grinned, enjoying a little too much how her good humor agitated him further.

"It's made you want a baby of your own, and for that I'm sorry."

"You shouldn't be. Having Sebastian made me aware of how much I want a husband and baby of my own. That's nothing to be sorry about."

"You're way too young for all that." Zane was now shaking his head as if she were certifiable. He picked up one of those stress-reliever balls from the desk and squeezed it so hard she thought it might pop. "Did you sleep with Bentley?"

"None of your business." *I want to be sleeping with him.*

She wondered if Sebastian would inherit his father's bull-headed stubbornness along with his blue eyes.

"What do you like about him so much anyway?" Zane asked.

"He loves food, dogs, the beach, and wine." The sap had rescued a little mutt named Jen when Sophie had asked him to come with her to find a dog. She'd come home dog-less and he'd ended up with Jen, who made him sneeze unless he took an allergy pill every morning. "To sum it up, he's perfect for me. I just wish he agreed."

"You sound like a stalker," Zane said.

She waved her hands in the air as if she were smacking someone. "Do I need to remind you of the telescope you had pointed at Honor's house?"

Zane's entire face and neck were now red instead of pink. "That wasn't the same."

"It was totally the same. You two were friends. You were madly in love with her but couldn't get the courage up to ask her out."

"We'd known each other for years. We know nothing about

this Bentley guy other than he can plant a mean hanging flowerpot."

"Zane, I'm not Jubie. You don't get to dictate what I do. I'm a grown woman, and if I want Nico, I'll have him and you won't say one word about it except, 'I'm happy for you, Sophie.'"

Zane threw up his hands. "If the guy really liked you, he would not have backed off just because I threatened to run him out of town."

"So you *did* threaten him?"

"Semantics."

Her eyes stung as she stared at her brother. The brother she'd never even known she had until two years ago. The brother she adored. The brother she'd love to throttle right at this moment.

"You should let this go. Find a guy your own age. One who you can have fun with, like you're supposed to when you're in your early twenties." His voice softened, obviously spotting the tears that welled in her eyes. "Okay now, don't cry."

Too late. The tears spilled down her cheeks. She brushed them away, embarrassed. "We kissed. I know he feels the same tug I do. He just won't admit it."

"Are you kidding me? Why'd he kiss you when he thinks you're too young for him?" Zane's eyes returned to snapping with fury.

"He went all remorseful and self-hating the minute after he kissed me."

"Well, he should have."

They were interrupted when Bobby knocked on the door and poked his head through. "The sprinkler guy just called. He has to reschedule. His wife's in labor."

"How exciting," Sophie said. "I love babies."

Bobby winked and headed back down the hallway toward the bar.

She stood in the now-open doorway and looked over at her

brother's stubborn face. "Anyway, it doesn't matter. If you or Nico think either of your reservations about my age or innocence or whatever else you two misguided fools have in your heads is going to stop an epic love story from unfolding, you're both high. No one can outrun destiny." She glanced at the clock above his obstinate head. "I have to go. Dinner rush is about to happen."

"Wait," Zane said as he jerked up from his chair and came around to the front of the desk. He put his hands on her shoulders. "I'm sorry I interfered. I simply can't stand the idea of you being hurt."

"I know," she said softly.

"Maybe you should go back the therapist you went to after Sebastian was born."

She rolled her eyes and stepped away from him. "That was postpartum and all kinds of weird hormonal stuff. I'm fine now."

"Are you sure you're not delusional about him?" Zane said.

"Once again. One word. Telescope."

Zane laughed. "All right, fine. But I swear to God, if he hurts you, I'll run him out of town."

Too late. He already had hurt her. There was no way she was telling her pontificating brother that truth. A brave face was what was needed with a bit of bravado on the side. "Don't worry about me. You take care of your sweet family, and I'll look after myself, okay?"

"Fine."

She gave him a quick hug and made for the door before he started talking about sending her to a place where she could "rest" her nerves.

* * *

LATER THAT EVENING, there was standing room only in the bar

area as Sophie lifted a pint glass from the stack under the counter. She tipped it just so and watched as a creamy dark ale crept to the top. A briny breeze drifted in through the French doors that opened to the front patio, mitigating the hoppy scent of spilled beer, sweat, and sunscreen. Two drunk strident-voiced bachelorette parties raised the noise meter to unparalleled levels. The gaggle of women in the first group were now going through a list of tasks for the bride-to-be. Apparently, number five consisted of asking a man to carry her from one end of the bar to the other.

Sophie exchanged an amused glance with Bobby before he poured tequila into a line of shot glasses for a buff guy wearing a backward baseball cap and his two equally muscular friends, who were in the throes of flirting with two of the bachelorettes. One of the girls laughed and pushed into the baseball guy's chest before accepting the shot. Cliffside Bay would be crawling with hungover people in the morning.

What would it be like to be that free? To smell of seawater and sunscreen instead of spilled beer and kitchen grease? She had responsibilities. A staff who relied on her. Profits, quotas, and inventory to worry over.

She loved it all. As her dad always quoted from his favorite song, "Me and Bobby McGee," freedom was just another word for nothing left to lose. She didn't need freedom. She needed this place. Especially with her broken heart. Work was the one thing she could always count on to cheer her and strengthen her.

As the night continued, the bachelorette parties grew drunker as the men hovered near, ready if one of them gave a nod of interest. Every table was filled in the restaurant area. The bar area was crammed with so many bodies that people could barely move. The waitstaff hustled about delivering drinks and dinners, while Sophie and Bobby did their best to keep up with the demand.

After the dinner rush, the pace slowed. Both bachelorette parties left, as did most of the men who'd been hovering around waiting to escort them back to the lodge. Around ten, the place had emptied by half.

She glanced at a blue-eyed boy at the end of the counter. Slumped shoulders and a morose gaze into the bottom of his nearly empty pint glass told her his story. This was a man with a recent broken heart. He looked up, perhaps feeling her eyes on him, and peered at her through black-framed glasses.

"You need another?" she asked as she slung a dish towel over her shoulder.

"I shouldn't but I will." He was nice-looking, with brown curls, full, sensual lips, and a nerdy, intellectual vibe. The guys he'd come in with were gone, but he'd obviously stayed behind. He wore a white T-shirt that was tight against his broad chest. She didn't know what he looked like below the waist, as he sat on a stool at the end of the bar, but she had a feeling it was as good as the upper potion. "I'm not driving."

"Are you staying at the lodge?"

"How'd you know I'm on vacation?" he asked, pushing his glasses farther up his nose.

"This is a small town, and most everyone comes in here at one time or another." She drew him another IPA from the tap.

"I'm moving to a small town in a few weeks," he said. "Emerson Pass. Have you heard of it?"

She smiled. "Strangely enough, I have. Some friends of mine were married there last Christmas. It's like a postcard."

He sighed, then thanked her for the new beer. "Yeah, it's a romantic place. If you're one of the lucky ones."

"Lucky?"

"In love. Which I'm not." He took a long drag from his beer. "I was supposed to be here for a romantic getaway with my girlfriend. I was going to propose, but she broke up with me."

"I'm sorry." She pushed a dish with nuts and pretzels closer to him. Her instinct to soothe was always associated with food.

"She said she couldn't see a future with a guy who wants to be a high school teacher."

"Well, that's kind of shallow, isn't it?" She clucked sympathetically. This guy was lucky to have escaped. "Teaching is one of the world's most important professions."

He nodded. "My family doesn't think so. They couldn't understand why I'd want a PhD in English. *Dickens is for sissies.* That's what my father said after I'd spent three years working on my thesis." He took another drag from his beer. "Sometimes it seems like there's never been one person in my life who's ever understood me."

"Maybe that means you haven't been hanging out with the right people," she said.

For the first time, the corners of his mouth lifted in a slight smile. "Maybe." He held out his hand. "My name's Darby."

She shook his hand, warm and large with just the right amount of dark hair on his knuckles. Clean, trimmed fingernails. The curls at the base of his neck were an added bonus. "I'm Sophie. My brother and I own this place."

"You own it?" he asked as his eyebrows lifted.

"Yes, family business."

"I figured you were a college student working here for the summer," he said.

"No, I graduated a few years ago. Fast track. Graduated at twenty." As they chatted, she pulled clean glasses from the dishwasher and stored them under the counter.

"Good for you," he said. "Seems like it would be fun but a lot of work."

"That about sums it up." She filled another dish with the nut and pretzel mix. Out of the corner of her eye, she saw Jamie Wattson come in the front door and head for the bar. Sophie waved, pleased to see her new friend.

"Hey," Jamie said as she slipped onto the stool next to Darby. She wore her dark blond hair up in a messy bun that highlighted her tanned, toned shoulders. Jamie never seemed to pay any attention to her appearance. She didn't need to. The girl was a natural beauty. In loose jeans and a tank top, she was certainly a contrast to the overdone bachelorettes with their high heels and heavily made-up faces.

Sadly, Darby didn't look up from his glass to notice.

"What's up?" Sophie asked. "Night off?" Jamie worked as a waitress at Dog's Brewery most nights.

"Zane kicked me out. He said I've been working too many shifts without a break, and he's worried I'm going to turn into a workaholic like you."

"Zane needs to mind his own business," Sophie said, resisting the urge to roll her eyes. "You look pretty tonight." She said this a little too loudly, but Darby didn't seem to have a clue that a gorgeous woman had just about fallen into his lap.

"Mom fell asleep watching reruns of *Downton Abbey*. I took that as a sign to come out for a drink." She and her mother lived in the Victorian just a block south of The Oar. When Trey, her brother, had moved into the cottage of his fiancée, Autumn, Mrs. Wattson and Jamie had moved into his vacated apartment. "I shouldn't spend money on drinks, but sometimes a girl needs out of her cage."

"You want a glass of wine?" Sophie asked.

"Nope. It's a martini type of night." Jamie reached into the snack bowl and fished out a broken pretzel. "I got bad news today."

Sophie filled a metal shaker with ice, vodka, and a smidge of vermouth. "About the inn?"

"Yeah. I was outbid." She popped the pretzel in her mouth and chewed as Sophie shook the contents of the drink. "Again. At this rate I'm going to be saving and making offers on run-down inns until I die."

"I'm sorry. Did you have your heart set on this one?" Sophie poured the contents of the martini into a triangular glass, pleased to see slivers of ice floating on top. She speared a few green olives with a toothpick to finish it off.

"I tried not to, but I did." Jamie sipped delicately from the martini. "It was so perfect. I mean, it needed some work, but only cosmetic. Trey said he'd help me. We'd even been looking at swatches. Which was the kiss of death. Never look at swatches." Seemingly, for the first time, Jamie's gaze slid sideways to take in her neighbor. Her eyes widened.

"This is Darby," Sophie said. "He loves Dickens."

Jamie turned to face him. "Sure, I know Darby."

Darby seemed to wake from his stupor. He adjusted his glasses. "Hey, it's you. The waitress who witnessed my most humiliating moment."

"I served him...and his date at the brewery last night," Jamie said to Sophie before turning back to Darby. "How's your hangover?"

He lifted his pint glass. "A little hair of the dog."

"Good call," Jamie said. "You've got a good excuse."

"Because I was dumped on the night I was going to propose?" he asked.

"Yeah." Jamie grimaced. "Doesn't get much worse than that. And trust me, I've been there. The whole staff felt so bad for you." She turned back to Sophie. "We had the engagement ring in one of those little chocolate cakes and champagne on ice."

Darby groaned. "So embarrassing."

"No way," Jamie said. "We're used to stuff happening like that. On any given night, someone's getting dumped."

"That's super depressing," Darby said.

"Which is why yours truly stays far away from any romantic entanglements," Jamie said.

"Did I do anything embarrassing last night?" Darby asked. "I can't remember much after the fourth tequila shot."

"No, you were fine. Other than buying a round of drinks for the entire bar," Jamie said.

He went white as he tore his glasses from his face and dropped his head into his hands. "Oh God. I can't afford that."

"Don't worry about it. Zane didn't charge you," Jamie said.

"He was dumped at the altar once," Sophie said.

"So he understands my pain," Darby said.

Jamie smiled kindly and patted his shoulder. "He does. I can't lie, dude. Last night was a sad scene. She was kind of brutal." She turned to Sophie. "It was like two minutes after I delivered their steaks, and she pulled the trigger. Then she had the nerve to take her dinner home in a doggie bag."

"Brutal." Sophie excused herself to pour a pitcher of blonde ale and set it and two glasses on the counter for one of the servers. She listened to the conversation between Jamie and Darby while she opened two bottles of Mexican beer.

"You smell really good," Darby said to Jamie.

"Thanks." She caught Sophie's gaze and widened her eyes for a split second.

Sophie turned away so Darby wouldn't notice her smile and continued to listen as she poured a few glasses of wine.

"Anyway, it wasn't your destiny to be with what's-her-name," Jamie said.

"There's no such thing as destiny," Darby said.

"I guess that's why you study Dickens and not Hardy."

"How did you know about Dickens and Hardy?" Darby asked.

"English major," Jamie said.

A customer at the other end of the bar gestured to Sophie down for another round. "You guys enjoy yourselves. Everything's on the house tonight."

"Thanks, Sophie. I accept," Jamie said.

"That's so nice of you," Darby said.

"The brokenhearted have to stick together," Sophie said.

As she walked away, she heard Jamie say to Darby, "How about if I keep you company tonight? I'll tell you my life story to distract you from your woes."

A few minutes later, Sophie's heart sank when she saw the next drink order pop up on her screen. The request was for a pitcher of Dog's Brewery IPA and a glass of the featured red blend from Washington state. She could count on one hand the number of patrons who ordered her monthly rotation of either Walla Walla or Paso Robles reds. One of whom was Nico Bentley.

Sophie scanned the restaurant. Sure enough, there was Nico with the rest of the Wolves at their regular table in the far corner near the window. They must have sneaked in while she was talking to Darby.

She filled a pitcher with the IPA. Should she go over and say hello? The largest of the men, Rafael and Stone, always sat in the chairs that faced the bar section; Trey and Nico sat with their backs to her; David took the end.

"Bobby, I'm going to take this order out myself," she said as she poured a glass of a Walla Walla blend.

"I thought you were going home early tonight?" Bobby asked.

"I am. After this. I just want to deliver this order myself." She stacked the glasses, wine, and pitcher on a tray.

He winked at her. "No kidding? Can't imagine why."

"Be quiet or I'll fire you," she whispered, and kicked him lightly in the shin with the tip of her Birkenstock as she passed behind him with the tray balanced on one hand.

"Be cool," Bobby said. "Act like you don't care."

If only she could. When it came to Nico she was anything but cool.

She wove through the crowded restaurant until she reached them. All five men looked up at her.

Stone greeted her with a wide grin and a soft look in his

dark blue eyes. He knew all about her feelings for Nico and had great empathy for her situation. He'd loved Pepper for a year before she'd give him the time of day. Actually, she'd hated him. Now they were getting married. Proof that miracles happened every day. One just had to be patient.

"Hey, Sophie," Stone said.

She set the tray on the table and unstacked the pint glasses, then set them in front of the four beer drinkers. "You boys eating?"

"We already put our order in." Rafael grabbed the pitcher and started to pour beer into each of the glasses.

Nico fiddled with a coaster, breaking it in half, then quarters. Sophie set the glass of wine in front of him. He smiled up at her, but his faded blue eyes were flat. The eyes of a stranger. "Thanks, Soph."

She swallowed the ache in her throat. *Be cool. Pretend that I don't care.* "This is a red blend from Washington. The grapes are from Red Mountain. Mostly cabernet with some Malbec and Syrah."

"Nice nose," Nico said as he swirled and sniffed and completely avoided further eye contact with her.

"Busy night?" Trey sent her a sympathetic smile.

"We've had a great summer," Sophie said. "By this time of night things are usually settling down. You should have seen it a few hours ago. What brings you guys in so late?"

"We've been in the city," Trey said. "Picking up our custom-made tuxedoes for the big lug's wedding." He gestured toward Stone.

Stone grimaced as he ran a hand through his hair. "Pepper knew exactly what she wanted."

"Down to the fabric," Rafael said.

"Drinks are on the house tonight," she said. "To congratulate Trey on his engagement."

Trey smiled. "Thanks, Sophie. That's nice of you. Is the word out already?"

"This is Cliffside Bay," Sophie said. "News travels fast. I stopped into the bookstore this afternoon and Mary told me. She'd heard it from Autumn herself, who'd come in earlier with a sparkly ring on her finger."

"It took some doing, but I finally got the girl," Trey said.

"Have you set a date yet?" Sophie asked.

Trey shook his head. "Autumn's deciding if she wants to be a winter or spring bride. I told her whatever she wants is fine with me. All I care about is making her my wife."

"The fewer days you're shacking up with my sister the better," Stone said.

Trey arched one eyebrow. "You've been living with Pepper for half a year already."

"Pepper Shaker wanted her castle wedding in France," Stone said, with a fatalistic acceptance in his voice. "Planning this kind of wedding takes time. *A lot* of time and money."

"And custom tuxes," Trey said.

Stone and Pepper didn't have to worry about money, given her inheritance from her late father. Sophie kept that observation to herself.

"I thought my wedding with Lisa was complicated," Rafael said. "Given Pepper's plans, I can see I was wrong."

"Lisa and Pepper had their weddings planned out before they found their grooms," Stone said, chuckling. "We're just along for the ride. Lucky bastards."

"Truth." Rafael tapped his glass against Stone's.

"Personally, I'm psyched Pepper chose France for your wedding," Sophie said. "I'm going early to meet with some wineries over there." She'd arranged for Bobby to run things while she was away.

David gestured at her with his pint glass. "Rough gig you've got here, Woods."

She laughed. "Someone has to do it. All right, I should scoot. I've been here since before the lunch rush and have a hot bath waiting for me upstairs."

Finally, Nico looked up at her. "You work too hard, Soph."

Their eyes locked, and the rest of the world ceased to exist for a moment. "No, I like it this way." She blinked, and he looked away. "Have a great night, guys. I'll see you later." After sharing one of her best fake smiles, she headed toward the bar area. She passed by several couples on the small dance floor, swaying to a ballad coming out of the jukebox. When she arrived back behind the counter, Bobby gave her a concerned look as he put away a stack of glasses.

"You all right, kiddo?" Bobby asked as he stepped over to her.

"Yes, fine." She smoothed a strand of hair from her face. "Just tired."

"He's a fool. You know that, right?" Bobby asked.

"I guess. Sometimes I wonder if it's the other way around." Her attention was drawn to the end of the counter where Jamie and Darby were still talking, both animated. "How are the love-birds doing?"

Bobby chuckled and mumbled something about busy-bodies under his breath.

She made Jamie another martini and took it to her. "I'm going home, so I thought I'd say good night."

Jamie's eyes flashed with mischief. "Thanks for the drinks. Darby and I might head out soon too. We thought we'd share an Uber."

Darby was looking down at his beer, looking suspiciously nonchalant. Nothing like a hookup to help a person get over a broken heart. Or so she'd heard.

"You two have a great night," Sophie said.

"You too," Jamie said as a flush rose to her cheeks.

Sophie left them and turned her attention back to Bobby, who was putting a maraschino cherry into a piña colada.

She untied the back of her apron and folded it over her arm. "It's been a long day. You okay to close up?"

"You got it," Bobby said.

She poured herself a glass of wine. "One for the road."

"Remember what a catch you are," Bobby said. "Don't give that guy another thought."

She gave his shoulder a quick squeeze and waved goodbye to Jamie and Darby, who didn't notice her. They were too busy kissing.

Good for them.

The easiest way to her apartment entrance was to exit onto the back patio, which meant she had to walk through the restaurant section. She lowered her gaze as she made her way around the tables toward the patio entrance. Seeing Nico again before she could make her escape would make a disheartening exit worse. But no, her traitorous eyes just had to look over at their table to find Nico watching her. Her cheeks flooded with heat. She averted her eyes and nearly stumbled. Her full wine-glass tipped and splashed drops onto her hand. When she finally reached the back door, she stepped out onto the patio.

The night air cooled her overheated skin. She breathed in the scent of the ocean as she meandered over to an empty table. Her feet ached after such a long day, and she should really just go upstairs and go to bed. However, the idea of being alone in an empty apartment was like going to a party where you were the only guest. She would drink her glass of wine out here in the cool air and then go up and take a long bath. Maybe have another glass of wine and let herself have another nice cry over stupid Nico. He was right to stay away. Seeing him only made her heartache worsen.

Sophie released a tired breath as she lowered onto the bench. From somewhere in the grass, a cricket chirped. The leaves of the old oak tree that grew next to the building fluttered in the breeze. Behind her, couples nuzzled or talked softly. She pulled a paper napkin from the dispenser on her table and wiped her hand of the spilled wine, then took a long drink from her glass.

String lights glowed from the overhang. She ran a finger along the weathered wood of the original picnic tables from the early days of The Oar. For fifty years, lovers had been etching their initials into the pine. One night, she and Maggie had found the initials of Hugh and Mae—clandestine lovers who had made Sophie on a night much like this one.

From behind her, the sound of the screen door opening and closing broke into her thoughts. She turned to see Nico standing there, the lights from the rafters shining in his eyes. He held a glass of wine in his hands. Without saying anything, he crossed over to her. He didn't meet her eyes as he shoved one hand in the pocket of his jeans and shuffled his feet. "Can we talk for a minute?"

Hope flooded through her. And damn, hope was a dangerous drug. "Sure."

First he set his wine on the table, then sat across from her. Shadows under his eyes were more obvious under the white lights. Stubble on his face told her he hadn't shaved for several days.

He moved his glass of wine in a circle but didn't say anything.

"What's going on?" she asked.

He raised his chin. "Nothing, really. I just thought we should talk. I miss...seeing you."

Her fingers tingled with excitement. *Stay calm*, she told herself. *There's no reason to jump to any conclusions that he'd suddenly come to his senses.* "You know where I am most days, right?" she asked gently. "You can come by and see me anytime."

"Yeah, I know. It's just I feel bad about how things went... you know, because of the...thing."

"You mean when you kissed me?"

He cleared his throat as he picked up his glass of wine and bent his head. His hair was cut into short spikes with the front slightly longer, like an attractive awning over his forehead. She knew how those silky strands felt in her hands now. What she would give to feel them again was embarrassingly high. The entirety of her bank account; her first child. But her first child would be his if she had her way.

"Soph, are you listening?"

She blinked and focused on his face. "What? No, sorry. I was thinking about something else. What did you say?"

"I said I wanted to clear the air," he said. "Make sure we could still be friends. I mean, it's kind of awkward the way it is now."

"You've been avoiding me, so when you come into the bar it's bound to be weird." Sophie studied him as she tilted her glass to her mouth and took a sip of her wine.

"I haven't been avoiding you."

"Seems like it." A spot in the middle of her chest stung. He'd most definitely been avoiding her.

"I thought we could both use a little space." He picked up his glass but didn't drink. Instead, he swirled and sniffed. "I get a little funk on the nose."

"A bit, yes. Just the nose though." Nico didn't like the funk of some Washington reds. He often said it smelled of blue cheese.

He sipped from his glass, holding it in his mouth for a moment before swallowing. She clasped her hands together under the table to keep from touching him.

"Nice finish," he said.

She looked out to the grassy area and then to the gravel

parking lot behind as a couple got into a car. "What do you want? Because this isn't helping."

"I'm weak when it comes to you, and I'm sorry for letting things get out of hand."

"*I'm* sorry you consider kissing me a sign of weakness." Her eyelids burned with the effort not to cry.

He groaned softly as his eyes darted around the patio. "Lower your voice, please. I don't want people gossiping about you."

"No one's paying any attention." Several of the couples were making out. Another pair had their heads together, talking low as he ran his hand up and down her back. One couple was obviously fighting, given how the girl had her arms crossed tightly over her chest and the violent way the man shook his leg under the table.

She thought of Hugh's passage in the letter to her. A bar witnessed so much life on any given day: heartbreaks, first meetings, couples celebrating anniversaries. Was there any better explanation for why she loved her job? She was a witness to life.

"What I mean is it's not fair to lead you on like I did." His voice dropped in volume and timbre. "Not when it can't go anywhere."

She winced inwardly as the hammer pounded hard in her chest. *Hold your breath. Do not cry. Keep it light.* "I wasn't sorry we spent so much time together. The more we were together, the surer I was that you're the one. I didn't regret finally getting to kiss you." She rested her elbows on the rough tabletop and leaned closer to look directly in his eyes. "But I regret this. I regret that you're running away from something beautiful because of some stupid social convention."

"I'm not the man you've saved yourself for," he said.

"Why do you say that?"

"Because I'm not in love with you. I'll never be in love with you."

She recoiled as if he'd physically hit her. A smack would have hurt less than hearing those words come out of his mouth. Defeated finally, she hung her head, ashamed as tears gushed from her eyes.

"Please don't cry. I mean, I can't be in love with you. I can't let myself go there. You and I are all wrong."

"I don't agree." She lifted her head, aware that her mascara was probably running down her stupid face, but she didn't care any longer. Her belief that they belonged together had been all wrong. Nico didn't love her. She'd practically forced him to say it—bullied him into being cruel to her when he was trying to let her down easy. "But I can't make you love me."

Despite his admonition to lower her voice, his raised in obvious frustration. "I can't love the wrong person again. I just can't. I don't have it in me to recover and rebuild—start over again like I did. Not after what happened with Addison. I'm not strong enough to watch you walk away when you figure out that you need a few more years to grow up—to do the stuff that women in their early twenties should do. And eventually you will want that. I can't let myself fall for you." The last sentence was a series of hard staccato notes.

"You don't know I'll walk away. Not for certain."

"I can't take that chance." He looked her straight in the eyes. "The woman I loved with all my heart and soul—the one I wanted to grow old with—completely blindsided me even though I should've seen the signs. They were so close. Addie's eyes lit up when Star came in the room. She seemed more alive when they were together. I'd hear them talking and laughing on the patio or on the phone, and I'd feel jealous. Like, why doesn't she laugh that way with me? When something good happened, she called Star first, then me. I was such an idiot."

His voice cracked. He looked away before taking a sip from his wineglass.

He'd never talked about his ex before, other than a flippant comment here or there. Naively, she'd imagined he was over the whole thing. How stupid she'd been to think so.

Nico continued in a flatter tone. "It was the thought of the honeymoon that finally made her face the truth about how she felt about Star. She said, and I quote, 'I can't bear to be away from her for that long. It hurts physically to think of being apart from her.' Turns out, Star felt the same way." He paused to rub his eyes with the heels of his hands. "Do you have any idea what it's like to love someone who quite simply cannot love you the same way?"

"Yes, I do." She wiped under her eyes and glanced down at her fingers, now blackened from the runaway mascara. "I really do."

"Do you understand why I can't go there with you? I see all the signs this time and I'm not going to make the same mistake twice. You know that guy with the glasses you were talking to at the bar earlier?"

"What about him?"

"He's the type you should spend time with. And later, like ten years from now when you're finally ready to get married, you'll find a guy like that to grow old with. But Sophie, that guy is not me."

"You're wrong. You're wrong about me, about us, and about all these signs you think you see. You're blind to the possibility of us because you can't let go of the past. This has nothing to do with my age." As she spoke, she understood how right she was. He was too afraid to love again. "You've put me in a box that has no relevance to reality. So, yes, you're right. *That guy* isn't you, even though it should be." She stood, wiping her face with her hands. "If you care about me at all, don't come in here again.

Seeing you take home one sorority girl after another is too painful."

"I'm sorry. For everything." He reached for her but pulled back at the last second.

"Me too, Nico. For me and for you." She strode across the patio and down the stairs to the grass, then around the building to the door of the stairway that led up to her apartment. She punched in the code and entered. With vision blurred by tears, she held on to the railing up the skinny flight of stairs until she reached the door to her living room. Once inside, she closed and locked the door behind her. A bubble bath, more wine, and a good cry were coming her way. Again.

This would be the last time she would cry over Nico Bentley.

5

Nico

AFTER SOPHIE LEFT, Nico remained at the table, unable to move other than to bring the glass to his idiot mouth. The lights from her apartment came on, creating a pattern in the patch of grass between the patio and the parking lot. He'd hurt her, made her cry. His beautiful Sophie. No, he reminded himself. She was not his to have. His heart seemed incapable of remembering what his brain knew with unequivocal certainty. Becoming romantically involved with Sophie would destroy him. He'd already been ripped into a million shreds once. As he'd said quite truthfully to Sophie, he wasn't sure he could recover a second time.

Still, he longed to be with her upstairs in her cozy living room. Her place was all blond floors and light-filled rooms decorated in tones of pale blues, greens, and tans that mirrored the terrain outside the windows. Like her, every inch of the space reminded him of his two favorite things in life: sunshine and sea. The evenings he'd spent with her were some of his happiest since he'd moved to Cliffside Bay. *Come on, now. Tell the truth.* Spending time with Sophie were some of the best times of his life. He adored the woman. Everything about her was perfect for him. Except her age and her innocence. Which were two huge things. Too much to overlook, even though he wanted to.

He tried not to think of her upstairs, probably undressing to take a bubble bath. She loved baths. They soothed her tired feet and shoulders. He could imagine only too well the way the suds would slide down her long legs and curvy hips as she got up and out of the bath and into his arms.

Out of the corner of his eye, he noticed Trey and David come out to the patio. When Trey had called with the suggestion that he move to Cliffside Bay and take a job as the landscape architect for Wolf Enterprises, Nico hadn't hesitated. He'd come to lick his wounds and find some kind of way forward from the awful blow of his canceled wedding. Jilted. Thrown over for a woman. He'd known that the only way through was to focus on his work. Trees and flowers never let him down.

"Thought you might need another," Trey said as he placed a second glass of wine in front of Nico.

"Thanks, man," Nico said.

David and Trey, both with fresh beers, sat across from him.

"Stone and Rafael had to go," Trey said. "They are going up to look at the property up north in the morning and want to get an early start."

Nico nodded, trying to care about the possible renovation, but couldn't muster it.

"You all right?" David asked. "We noticed Sophie didn't come back inside."

"We came out to investigate," Trey said. "We were hoping you two were still out here."

"Together," David said.

"She went upstairs." Nico gestured upward as if they didn't know where she lived.

"Man, we need to talk about this," Trey said.

"We think you're insane not to jump on this thing with Sophie." The corners of David's mouth twitched. He rarely smiled, and when he did it was like the muscles of his mouth had atrophied.

"Me? Crazy? Haven't we already established that?" Nico asked in an attempt at a joke.

"I've known you a long time," Trey said. "You're in love with her."

He thought about lying for the second time that night but didn't have the energy to hold all his feelings inside. "I'm madly in love with her. It's true. Which is why I'm keeping my distance. Because pursuing this now will bring the worst fall of my life when she leaves me."

"Okay, then," David said. "Mind if I give it a try instead?"

Nico examined his friend. Was he joking? David's crystal-clear blue eyes stared back at him without a smidge of humor. In fact, he'd never seen David look quite so serious.

"You want to ask her out?" Nico asked. The nerve of this guy. He had no business dating Sophie.

Why does he have no business dating Sophie? Some voice out of nowhere was now talking to him. Great.

Because I don't want him to.

Very selfish of you.

Whoever you are, please shut it.

Now he was fighting with someone in his head. This was crazy even for him. Usually he just talked to a dog.

"So, you're okay with David taking her out on a date?" Trey asked.

"Sure. It's a free country." Nico managed to pinch out the appropriate answer even though he thought his throat might be closing up like the time he ate a mango and had to be rushed to the emergency room.

"Dude, you're so full of it." David actually broke out into a legitimate grin. "You'd rather eat that glass than see me taking her out."

Nico glared at him before downing the rest of his wine and picking up the other glass.

Trey regarded him from across the table with narrowed eyes. "What's the matter with you? This amazing woman wants you, and you're pushing her away."

"I already told you," Nico said.

"You don't really think she's too young, do you?" David asked. "I mean, she runs two businesses and is more mature than most forty-year-old women out there."

"I *do* think she's too young." Nico sighed. He didn't want to go into all this again tonight. The talk with Sophie had exhausted him.

David tapped the table with his fingers stained from drafting ink. "Not that I'm the one who should be giving you advice in anything related to women, but I'm going to anyway. One day very soon she's going to meet someone else and you're going to kick yourself for being so stupid."

Nico watched as David's cheeks colored. Had he loved someone once and let her get away?

"That happen to you?" Trey asked.

David nodded. "There was a girl I loved in college. I let her slip away because I'd already promised Marigold I'd come back for her. It was my code of ethics or whatever. Or maybe I was just really afraid to step out of my comfort zone and risk getting hurt. Marigold and I'd been together since high school. She was my sure bet. Solid as a rock. We all know how my marriage turned out." His gaze drifted up and to the left. "I wonder what my life would be like now if I'd been braver then?"

A high-pitched screech penetrated the relatively quiet patio. For a moment, Nico couldn't place the sound. Then it came to him. A fire alarm.

"Fire alarm," Trey shouted over the unmitigated shriek.

They all jerked to their feet. The back door burst open and patrons streamed onto the patio. For an instant, Nico thought it might be a false alarm. Everything seemed exactly as before the alarm sounded. However, a second later, he smelled smoke. His gaze darted to the two small square kitchen windows to the right of the patio. Black smoked streamed out, clear in the light thrown from the stringed bulbs. "Smoke there," he shouted as he gestured toward the windows.

The glass shattered as angry orange plumes of fire erupted from both windows.

"Fire's in the kitchen," David shouted as he grabbed his phone from the pocket of his jeans.

Trey was already by the door yelling to people to run around the building to the front. The patch of grass between the patio and fence wasn't safe.

Flames spread from the window frame up the side of the building toward the residence above.

Panic surged through him as ferocious as the flames. Sophie was upstairs. The kitchen butted up to the stairwell to Sophie's apartment. Those stairs were the only entrance or exit from her place. All around him, people spilled into the night. Sirens shrieked their approach.

From the window next to the kitchen, he heard banging. A woman's face appeared. "Oh my God, there are women in there," Trey said.

"We'll get them," David said. "You go get Sophie."

Nico ran down the steps around the side of the building to the door of Sophie's apartment. First, he tried turning the knob.

Locked. He pounded on the door, screaming Sophie's name. Terror turned into adrenaline. He kicked down the door and entered the skinny stairway. Heat hit him in the face as if he'd jumped in an oven. Oh God, the fire was right behind the wall and spreading fast.

6

S ophie

WITH HUGH'S journal in her hands, Sophie slipped into the bathtub. She'd run the water extra hot but not too deep so she could keep her precious gift dry. With her noise-canceling headphones playing her sister Maggie's latest album, she turned to the first page. Like a novel from childhood, his words always soothed her when she was upset. They also reminded her that true love was often fraught with more than a few bumps along the way.

DEAR SOPHIE,

You're two years old today. This is also the day of your mother's murder. Her name was Mae O'Malley and she was slight with big green eyes and hair the color of a new penny. She had a lot of freckles, which she hated. When we were seven, she tried to scrub them off with a metal brush. You can imagine how well that went. She loved dancing and theater and had a lovely voice that elevated the church choir every Sunday. She starred in all the school plays. She was as close to perfect as a person could be.

From the time we were small, I worshipped her.

Mae and I were born in 1960 and grew up together in Cliffside Bay. Her parents owned the local inn. My mother owned the only bar in town, which had been passed onto her by her father. Our families were intertwined by business and church. There was not a space of time in my memory that didn't include Mae. That is, until her death two years ago. Now I have only memories.

Missing people is an awful thing. There's such an emptiness and hunger that cannot be filled by anything the world offers. My people are the only thing I want. Nothing else will do. And yet, even as I know this, there's nothing to be done. You're both gone.

There's rage, too. Anger is a beast that continues to grow inside me. I can't shrink it down to a manageable size. Even if I could, I wouldn't want to. The beast fuels me, keeps me going, counteracting the grief by keeping me alive.

As I sit here tonight in the fading light with the sunset painting the sky pink and orange, it occurred to me that all this pent-up grief and anger might be lessened if I wrote to you every so often. Someday, if God allows, you might read these letters and know the story of your birth and those who both made you and mourn you.

Back in the day I used to dream of being a writer. I was always fond of detective novels and hoped one day I might try to write one. But I took over the bar and grill instead and the years kind of rolled along. Zane came, and I had to be his only parent. Between him and running the bar, there wasn't much left of me at the end of the day. I thought, at least, I could write to you. There would be something left behind when I'm gone. Words are life, after all. Nothing can erase them. Not even time.

I should tell you a little about the man who murdered your mother. I'll say up front that as much as they tried, the police could *never pin anything on him. Just like he'd done all his life, Roger Keene escaped unscathed. I know the truth. Lily and Doc Waller know it too. And God help her, so does little Maggie Keene. Keene pushed Mae down those stairs. She didn't fall. Someday, he'll pay. It may not be until he reaches the gates of Hell, but it will happen.*

I'm getting ahead of myself in the story.

Keene and I have a history that dates back to our high school days. When we were teenagers, this town was even smaller than it is now. Our class only had twenty-one kids. Keene and I had a few things in common. We were both good athletes being raised by single mothers. My father died in a motorcycle accident when I was a baby. Keene's father was never known. He and his mother lived in a run-down house outside of town. He was the high school quarterback and I was the guy who could catch his throws and run like heck to the end zone. We were sort of small-town heroes, I suppose. Despite these commonalities, Keene and I were mortal enemies. From the time we were in grade school, I knew that under those good looks and the smooth talk was a bully. On the football field he'd shown me more than a few times his temper and his tendencies toward violence. I'd seen the glint of rage in his eyes when one of the boys on the team made a mistake. More than once I stopped him from hurting one of our teammates with his fists. I knew his heart, and it was black as the darkest night.

All through high school, Mae and Keene were an item. They were "the" couple of our class. Prom king and queen—that kind of thing. I can still see her sitting on the bleachers during our football practices wearing his letterman jacket. She was so pretty with the sun glinting off her hair and those big eyes in that heart-shaped face.

One night at the end of our senior year Keene, Mae, I, and a few others were down on the beach. Someone had built a bonfire and we were all sitting around drinking covert beers. Keene had wandered off to smoke dope with a few of the other guys, but I stayed behind with Mae. Waves crashed into shore, and the chilly night air smelled of sea and woodsmoke. We sat on a blanket with our backs leaning against a large piece of driftwood I'd dragged over to the fire. Across from us were two of our other friends, chatting about going away in the fall for college.

I was only half listening because Mae was beside me, and when that happened everything else faded into the background.

I loved Mae Keene with all my heart.

Yes, even way back then, I loved her.

And she loved Roger Keene.

"Did you tell your mom about the scholarship?" Mae's gaze was directed toward the fire. She wore bell-bottom jeans and a bulky white fisherman's sweater. She sat cross-legged and held a long stick in her hands, which she occasionally used to poke the logs.

It was a simple answer. I hadn't told my mother that I'd been admitted to Berkeley or that I'd won a scholarship. You might be wondering why. The answer was pretty simple. Both my mother and I had secrets. Hers was that she was sick. Mine was that I wanted more than anything to go to college, and I'd found a way to do so. I knew her secret. She didn't know mine.

"Ma needs me to take over at The Oar. She's sick." My father's family had owned the bar and apartment above it for twenty years before I was born. When he died, it was the only thing he left us. Before my mother took it over, the place was more of a saloon. No one but a man would've dared step inside. She saw an opportunity to turn it into a bar and grill and attract tourists and families. She got a loan from the bank and put in a kitchen and changed the decor. All those years later, she was still making payments to the bank. Business was good enough to cover our expenses and the loan, but not enough to put any money away.

"What do you mean, sick?" Mae asked.

"Cancer." Quiet enough so the other kids couldn't hear me, I leaned close and told her about how I'd seen the diagnosis on her desk in her office. "She doesn't know I know. I can't leave her. She needs me."

Mae didn't say anything for a long while. She poked the fire. Sparks rose into the air as the logs shifted. "How bad is it?"

I heaved a pebble out toward the shore. "The cancer's everywhere. All over her body."

We both knew what this meant. Neither of us could say the words out loud, but the truth lived heavy in my chest, burdening me with the inevitable knowledge that my hardworking, uncomplaining mother would soon be gone from this world without ever having lived.

"I wanted you to get out, have more," Mae said.

"People like me don't get out." My voice cracked as I admitted this truth to myself. I was stuck.

"People like us don't get out," she said.

Like I said earlier, Mae's family owned an inn. The only one in Cliffside Bay. Like us, they lived in a few rooms upstairs. And like us, they were always on the brink of not being able to pay the bills. Her parents were older than most, having had her when they were already forty. I knew she felt obligated to stay and help them, just as I did. However, the thought of her growing old before her time like my mother made me sick. She was special.

"You should go, Mae. Go to New York. Get out and don't come back."

She continued to poke the fire. "Roger told me I don't have a chance to make it in show business. He's right. I'm too shy and scared to go away from here."

My blood boiled. I wanted to toss my beer bottle against a rock, but I loved our beach too much to soil it with broken glass. Roger had no right to tell her any such thing. What did he know about show business? He just wanted her to stay because there was no way he was getting out of this town, either. Roger wasn't exactly college material. The only reason he was about to graduate from high school was because of sports. The coach made sure he passed classes by leaning on the other teachers.

I didn't say any of this, of course. We were good friends but not good enough for me to say all those hateful things about the boy she loved.

"We're leaving to get married right after graduation," Mae said. "Eloping."

My heart about stopped. Eloping. That meant I'd never have a chance. See there, that's the sad truth. I'd been holding on to this hope that she would see him for what he was and be done with him. I'd swoop in like a seagull on a tourist's discarded sandwich. If they were married, that would be it. I'd never have a chance.

"Why aren't you saying anything?" she asked.

As luck would have it, the girls on the other side of the fire decided it was time to get up for another beer. We had our stash hidden behind a log a little farther inland.

"Aren't you happy for me?" she asked. "I'm going to marry Roger. I've loved him forever. You know that. There's no one else for me."

I turned to her. The firelight reflected in her eyes. In that oversize, bulky sweater she looked small and incredibly vulnerable. I thought about Keene's violent streak. I remembered a time when he'd tugged on Mae's arm so hard that she cried out in pain and another when he'd shoved her against the wall at a party simply because she asked to go home.

And my heart broke. Because I saw her future in the flames of that fire as clearly as if I'd been watching it play out on the drive-in movie screen.

For the first time in the history of our relationship, I didn't hold back even though I knew it would alienate her from my life. I had to. I wouldn't have been able to sleep at night had I not said the truth.

"Please look at me when I say this," I said.

She tilted her face my direction. Her eyes widened but her mouth clamped shut in a stubborn line.

"If you marry Keene, it will ruin your life."

She blinked. Tears gathered in her eyes. "Don't say that. How can you say that?"

"I've seen how he treats you. Do you think I don't see what he's like?"

"I don't know what you mean."

"I know you do. In your heart of hearts, you do."

She turned her face back to the fire, then tossed her stick into the flames. Several tears traveled down the side of her face. It took every ounce of control I had not to wipe them away.

"Roger says you're in love with me."

I swallowed as my stomach turned over.

"Is that why you're saying this?" she asked. "Because you want me for yourself?"

I drank the dregs of my beer before answering, knowing this might be the last honest exchange we ever had. "It is true that I love you. It is also true that marrying Keene will ruin your life. It may even end your life."

"You're wrong. You're just jealous and spiteful." Her voice broke.

"I've been jealous for a long time now. That's true. But as far as spite goes, you couldn't be further from the truth. I'm the only one in your life who wants what's best for you."

"You don't know anything about anything, Hugh Shaw. You just think you do—going around acting like a preacher and all high and mighty like you're better than the rest of us."

I could barely speak from the ache in my chest. She'd never said one cross word to me in all the years of our friendship, and it hurt bad. "I'm not better than you or anyone else in this town except for Roger Keene."

"You have no right to say such a thing to me."

"Maybe I don't, but I sure couldn't live with myself if I didn't try." I untangled my legs and rose to my feet. "I know you hate me right now, but if you ever get in trouble or it gets too bad, come to me. I'll always be here."

And I left her there. She married him the day after graduation. Her parents had no choice but to let him move into the residence section of their inn. When my mother died a few months later, Mae *came to the funeral and said how sorry she was and gave me a hug. When I looked carefully at her face, I saw a bruise on her cheek under heavy makeup. For nineteen years we were friendly when we saw each other in town or when she came into the restaurant with Keene, but not close like we'd once been. Strangely enough, she didn't have Maggie until almost ten years into their marriage. As you most likely know by now, Maggie and Zane were born the same year. She told me later that she stayed on birth control because she didn't want to risk having him hurt a child like he did her. Maggie was an accident. A happy one, of course.*

Well, that's all I have time to write tonight. I'll tell you more of our story in another passage. For now, happy birthday to my beautiful girl.

Love,

Hugh

Sophie set the journal on the table next to her tub and sank into the water up to her neck. With her eyes closed, she listened to her sister's crystalline voice singing about love. She wondered how it was possible to love someone so much who didn't return those feelings, or even worse, loved someone else.

Her thoughts drifted to Mae. She wished she could know exactly what it was like to be her, to love a man like Roger instead of a man like Hugh.

If only Hugh knew how much The Oar meant to her. She'd come running as fast as she could to this town and the business he'd built for her and Zane. She was proud to run it and proud to live in this community. Her birth parents may have thought it best to "get out," but she knew in her heart this was where she belonged. The last few years had been joyous for her. How she wished she could tell him how grateful she was to have this anchor in her life. And how she wished he were here so she could ask him for advice about her disastrous love life.

She turned up the music and let the tears spill from her eyes and into the bathwater.

7

N ico

NICO PUNCHED in the code to the apartment. Thank God Sophie had given it to him months ago. He ran up the stairs two at a time. By the time he reached Sophie's doorway, the fire burst through the wooden steps below. They were trapped upstairs. He twisted the doorknob, and the door opened. He almost tripped as he ran inside and shouted for Sophie. Smoke was seeping up through the floorboards.

"Sophie? Where are you?" He ran across the living room to the kitchen. The light was off in the tidy kitchen. An open bottle of red was on the table. She'd opened wine, but no Sophie. *Bath. She's in the bath. She can't hear anything because she listens to music through her noise-canceling headphones to drown out the pulsing beat of the jukebox in the bar below.*

Utter fright choked him as he ran across the living room to

her bedroom. The door, slightly ajar, revealed a dark room. He didn't bother to knock. The bed, neatly made, did not have his girl. The door to the master bathroom was closed, but a strip of light under the door told him she must be in there.

He burst through the door and there she was, naked in the tub under a pile of suds. Her eyes were closed. Thick headphones covered her ears. A half-full wineglass sat in the corner of the tub.

"Sophie." He shouted at her as he lunged forward.

Her eyes flew open. She tore off her headphones.

"Sophie, the restaurant's on fire. We have to get out of here." His terror morphed to anger. "Can't you hear it?"

"What?" She blinked at him as she sat up straight. Suds cascaded down her chest. Her hair was up in a damp bun.

"I have to get you out of here." The roar of fear in his mind had masked the sound of the sirens, but now they sounded loud and clear. The bathroom had only a skinny window near the ceiling. Through it, he spotted stars, as if everything were normal.

She continued to stare at him, obviously too shocked to comprehend what he was saying.

"Get out of the tub. We have to get out of here. I think the stairs are on fire."

Sophie blinked and then stood. "My robe." She pointed to a terry cloth robe that hung on the back of the door.

He pulled it from the hook just as she stepped out of the water. "Put it in the water. Get it fully soaked," he said. Frantic, he grabbed a stack of towels neatly folded on a shelf and plunged them into the water. "Please hurry, baby. We're on borrowed time." He wrung out the towels and shouted at her. "Put on the robe. Now."

She stood holding the wet robe against her torso, her eyes wide with terror.

"Please, Soph, listen to me."

She nodded and wrestled her arms into the heavy material.

"Put on those, too." He pointed at a pair of pajama bottoms folded on the back of the toilet. "We're going to have to climb out of here."

Nico pressed the wet towels against his chest. "Stay behind me."

They ran out of the bedroom and into living room. Flames had engulfed the front door. Sophie screamed. A sound filled with such terror that it might have stopped his heart for an instant. He cursed as he looked toward the bank of windows that faced the street. They'd have to go out the windows. Two stories. They would have to jump. He ran to the windows with Sophie right on his heels. Below them, a crowd gathered. Still no fire trucks, only their lonely squawk in the distance. He spotted Trey and David, motioning frantically toward the apartment. They knew he and Sophie were up here. Of course they did. The green leaves of a tall oak fluttered at him, as if trying to communicate. *Come to me. Use me.* Her thick branches were perfect for climbing from the bottom up, but what about the other direction?

The flames were spreading farther across the opposite wall. Black smoke stung his eyes and chest. "Hold your sleeve over your mouth," he said to Sophie. "And get close to the window."

He glanced at the shelf next to them for something to break the windows with and spotted a large dictionary. No, that wouldn't do. He needed something heavier.

As if she read his mind, she reached behind the shelves and came back with a steel baseball bat. "Intruders," she said, hoarsely.

He smashed the large window, once, then again, then again until it shattered. A curved branch close to the window would serve as a good first step. "You're going to scoot out to that big branch, okay?" Thank God she was tall and blessed with long limbs.

She nodded. "But how?"

"I'm going to hold on to you while you reach for that skinny branch. Do you see there?"

"Yes, okay."

"Straddle the window frame first." He held her by the waist as she lifted one leg over the ledge. When she had it straddled, she looked back at him. "I'm scared."

"I'll keep hold of you as you swing your other leg over."

"Yeah, okay. I can do this." She muttered this under her breath, but she was shaking violently.

"I'm right here. I won't let go." He wrapped his arms tighter around her waist as she lifted her other leg over the ledge.

"What if I can't reach it?" she asked. "It seems really far away."

"I know it does, but that's just your eyes playing tricks on you. I'll give you a little push as you do a pull-up on that branch, then swing your legs out to straddle the wide one."

"A lot of straddling going on here," she said with a nervous laugh that turned into a sob.

"You can do it, baby." He spoke into the wet shoulder of her bathrobe. "I've got you from behind."

He felt her take in a sharp breath. "I'm ready."

"Here we go." *Please God, stay close to her.*

She lurched forward at the same time he nudged her. Easily she reached the skinny branch with both hands, then swung her legs up and over the larger one, straddling it like a gymnast on a bar.

"You're awesome," he said, meeting her scared eyes with his.

"Nico, I forgot my dad's journal." Tears streamed down her face.

He knew instantly what she meant. The journal her father had left her. "Where is it?"

"The bathroom. On the little table by the tub."

Without hesitating, he ran back into the bathroom. There it was—just a black notebook, but her life was in there. Her father's life.

By the time he was back in the room, the fire had spread across the floor and engulfed the couch in a blaze so hot he had to wrap a wet towel around his head. Coughing, he stumbled to the window. He looked down below to see Sophie standing between Trey and David. *That's my strong, brave girl.* She'd managed to find her way all the way down the tree. He almost wept with relief. All three of them squinted up at the window, obviously looking for his return. He tossed the journal out to them. David caught it, then yelled something up to him he couldn't hear. The roaring of the blaze behind him was as loud as a freight train.

Without calculating too much, he shrugged off the wet towel and scooted onto the window's ledge. He took a deep breath, then jumped to the branch, swinging like a wild animal, just as he had in childhood. When he was wrapped around the large branch, he whispered a silent thank-you to the tree.

His feet landed on grass just as the fire truck arrived. He ran across the street to where Sophie and his friends waited in front of the grocery store. Sophie threw herself into his arms. He held her tightly, feeling the rapid pace of her heartbeat against his own chest.

"I was so afraid," she said. "So afraid you wouldn't come out."

"It's all right. I'm here. We're both safe."

She became almost deadweight in his arms. He gently helped her to sit under the oak in front of the grocery store. The sister oak to the one that had saved them. Probably planted at the same time by a man or woman with the intention of making their town beautiful with no idea that someday one of them would save two people from an awful fire.

As she slumped against the trunk of the oak, Sophie's wet bathrobe, stained with dirt and speckled with bark and leaves, gapped at the chest. He pulled it closed and sat next to her with his arm around her shoulder. Around them, patrons and curious onlookers huddled together in front of the grocery store entrance, watching as part of the history of their town was decimated in front of them. The heat of the fire was like standing too close to an open oven, but no one seemed to notice. Including Sophie, who had not stopped shaking. From fright or the wet robe or both?

"It's all going to go, isn't it?" she asked.

Stunned into silence by the sight in front of him, he merely nodded. What could he say? She was right. The building could not be saved. Everything was happening too fast. He wasn't an expert, but he knew the bottles of liquor had boiled in the thousand-degree heat and popped their tops, thus feeding the flames. If the initial fire had indeed started from the kitchen, the vats of oil would have also exploded.

The building crackled and hissed like an enraged monster. Great clouds of orange flames billowed out the picture window and engulfed the outside tables and umbrellas. In his imagination, he saw the old wood of the beautifully crafted counter destroyed, as well as the tables and booths where so many had spent enjoyable afternoons and evenings.

Like wicked tongues of that monster, flames suddenly burst from the upstairs windows. He shuddered. Minutes ago, they'd stood in that exact spot.

His attention turned to the firefighters as they wrestled huge hoses from the sides of their truck. A ladder sprang up from the top of the truck, and one of them climbed it while carrying a hose with him.

The firefighters turned the mouths of the hoses toward the fire. Great torrents of water gushed from the hoses but seemed to have little effect on the blaze.

The flames licked their tree. Leaves melted. The branch they'd reached for caught on fire. Not the tree, too?

Sophie sobbed into his shoulder. "Hugh, I'm so sorry," she whispered.

Awful billows of black smoke rose in the air as the firefighters continued to spray the fire.

Bobby appeared by their side, seemingly out of nowhere. He dropped to the ground and took Sophie in his arms. "I was scared to death you didn't make it out."

"It was Nico," she whispered. "Or I wouldn't have."

Bobby closed his eyes for a second before turning to Nico. "You're one brave son of a bitch."

Out of the corner of his eye, he caught sight of Zane Shaw pushing through the crowds. Dressed in sweats and a rumpled T-shirt, with his thick blond hair sticking up in all directions, he looked as if he'd been asleep when he got the call.

Zane was at the front of the crowd now, standing with one hand covering his mouth. The orange glow of the inferno illuminated his face as tears streamed from his eyes. Then he jerked violently and shouted Sophie's name. He moved in a circle, obviously scanning the flock of onlookers for his sister. "Sophie? Where's Sophie?"

Nico hadn't realized David and Trey were standing so close until he saw them rush over to Zane. They each took an arm and led him over to where he and Sophie still huddled under the tree. "See, Sophie's here," David said.

"Safe." Trey helped Sophie up as Nico used the tree to support his weight until he was also on his feet. Shaky as his legs were, he kept one hand on the bark.

Sophie flung herself into her brother's arms. They stood holding on to each other as their family's business continued to burn. "I was upstairs when it started," Sophie said, then explained about her headphones and that she'd been completely unaware of the fire. She spoke in short, staccato sentences, as if she might cry at any moment. "Nico rescued me. I might've died otherwise." She shivered and lifted a hand toward the upstairs of the building. Her voice rose to a higher pitch. "Do you see there? We escaped out of the windows right before the fire took over the entire upstairs."

"Thank God you're all right." Zane wiped his eyes. "I always liked that tree." He turned to Nico and held out his hand. "Thanks, man. That took a lot of guts. I'm thankful."

Zane kept hold of his sister's arm but directed his question to David and Trey. "Everyone got out?"

"Yes, everyone's okay," Trey said. "The staff in the kitchen were able to escape through their door. The customers all ran out the back or front."

"A lady shouted to us from the bathroom window," David said. "There were four women trapped in there. The fire was in the hallway, so they couldn't get out that way. We dragged a table over to the window and broke the glass." He explained how they'd used a rock they'd found in the parking lot to break the window. He pointed to four women Nico didn't recognize who were now being looked at by paramedics.

Sophie had gone perfectly still. "Bobby, where's Jamie?"

"She went home with the young man before the fire started," Bobby said. "She's fine."

"Thank God." Sophie buried her face in Nico's shoulder. Nico instinctively tightened his hold on her.

"Sophie," Zane said softly. "Do we know what happened? How did the fire start?"

Sophie lifted her head. "I don't know."

"We think it started in the kitchen," David said.

"I thought I heard an explosion," Bobby said. "Like a bomb went off. Then everything went up in flames."

Zane's eyes were fixed once again on Nico. "How'd you know Sophie was upstairs?"

"We'd talked before she went up there," Nico said. "I watched her walk around the building."

"When I think what might've happened if you hadn't known—" Zane's voice broke.

"It's okay, Zane. I'm fine." Sophie smiled at him through her tears. "Everyone's fine."

Zane reached out to Trey, who steadied him. "Jesus, I can't believe this," Zane said. "Dad's whole life is right there." He watched the burning building with unblinking eyes. Nico could only imagine his thoughts. This was his father's business. Zane had worked there all his life. He'd grown up in the apartment overhead until only a few years ago when he'd married Honor.

The firefighters still had their hoses pointed into the flames. Several areas were now obscured by thick black smoke.

They all watched in silence as the building collapsed board by board.

"I'm sorry, Zane," Sophie said, sobbing.

"It's not your fault. Probably a grease fire." Zane rubbed his hands over his face. "It happens in kitchens all the time, but why didn't the new sprinklers go off?" he asked under his breath, as if talking to himself.

"I don't know," Sophie said. "The guy was supposed to come earlier today, remember? But he's having a baby."

Sophie, usually so confident and well-spoken, seemed completely undone and terribly young. A tremendous tenderness stirred in Nico. He should protect her at all costs. From guilt and lame maintenance workers. From every little and big thing that came her way.

A terrible crash penetrated the night as one side of the building fell.

"I can't believe what I'm seeing," Sophie whispered, clutching her father's journal in her hands.

"It's all right," Nico said. "No one was hurt. That's all that matters. We can rebuild."

"It's gone. All gone," Sophie whispered. "Everything Hugh built is gone."

They all watched in horror as the rest of the building collapsed in a smoky black mass.

8

S ophie

JUST BEFORE DAWN, after statements and eyewitness accounts from the staff, Sophie stood on Main Street with Zane and Nico. Trey and David had finally gone home. Nico had followed Trey back to Autumn's to get clothes for Sophie to change into but had returned a half hour later. She'd gratefully accepted the leggings and T-shirt until she realized she had nowhere to change. Zane had directed her to his car, where she took off the disgusting damp bathrobe and dressed.

They had a few answers about how the fire had started, but those facts only led to more questions. The cooking staff had told the police they'd been in the process of closing up when a loud explosion sounded in the corridor between the kitchen and bathroom. The fry cook, who'd been closest to the explosion, believed it to have been a common homemade pipe bomb. No one had seen who'd thrown the bomb. Whoever had done it, they guessed, might have knowledge of the kitchen layout, because it exploded very near the deep fryer. Whatever it was burst into flames, which, according to the dishwasher, took off like a bat out of hell. The fire alarm went off seconds later. They'd escaped out the kitchen door that opened into the alleyway and had run around to the front to help get customers out as quickly as possible while warning everyone not to go toward the back. With the large picture windows all open, people had been able to spill out to the street quickly and without trampling one another.

Meanwhile, Trey and David had rescued the ladies in the bathroom and Nico had gone upstairs for Sophie. The fire captain said between the deep fryers and booze, the fire had quickly spread to the second floor.

Now, finally, bleary from smoke and lack of sleep and the horrible knowledge that the place she and Zane had loved so much was gone, she worried her legs might collapse beneath her. There was the staff to think of, too. Even if they rebuilt quickly, there would be months and months without work. Would insurance cover the costs to rebuild? And what about the lost revenue?

The ground under her feet seemed to quiver as the thoughts piled up one after the other.

The reality that her apartment and her things were gone hit her like a fist to the gut. She clung to her father's journal and took in deep breaths. Passing out at this point would be ridiculous. The worst was over. And she was alive. Thanks to Nico.

He'd charged through the gates of hell to save her.

They stood there now, looking at the charred embers. The fire had burned so hot that almost nothing was left. They could make out metal parts, remnants of the walk-in cooler and freezer, but mostly it was lumps of nothing recognizable.

She realized she was clutching something in her hand and looked down to see a small bottle of pills. Doc Waller had given it to her with the instruction to take two before she went to bed. Something to take the edge off, he'd said. She handed them to Nico. "Put these in your pocket."

He did so without comment, but his forehead was all wrinkled up as though he was worried about her.

"Sophie, you'll stay with us until we can figure out a place for you to live," Zane said, sounding as exhausted as she felt. "You'll have to sleep on the couch or in Honor's office."

Next to her, Nico steadied her with a hand on her shoulder. "You should stay with me, or rather with Mrs. Coventry. She has an enormous house with several guest rooms."

Zane was eyeing him suspiciously, so Nico quickly pointed out that his apartment was separate from the main house.

"Mrs. Coventry won't mind if Sophie spends a few nights there. It'll be more comfortable for her."

Zane ran his hands through his hair. "It would probably be better. The kids get up so early, and there's really no space for you. Tomorrow, we can ask Brody and Kara if you can stay in their pool house." Brody and Kara had a huge home about five miles out of town. She didn't really want to stay with them, but she might not have a choice.

"It's the best option for now," Nico said, sounding surprisingly authoritative. "Mrs. Coventry will be happy to help in whatever way she can."

Sophie had met Mrs. Coventry a few times when she'd been over to visit Nico. She was seventy years old and skinny as a pubescent boy, but as sharp as a Wall Street wizard.

"Sure, if you're sure," Sophie said.

"I'm sure." Nico stuffed his hands in the pockets of his jeans.

"Go on then," Zane said. "I better get home. Honor's waiting anxiously for a full report."

She and Zane hugged. "Don't worry, kid," Zane said. "We'll get everything figured out. Just not today."

They said goodbye and walked down the now-empty street

to Nico's car. Mrs. Coventry lived on the top of the northern hill, just two doors down from Lisa and Rafael's new house. She was a wealthy woman. Something about textiles, Nico had told Sophie once.

Nico held the passenger door open and she fell into his SUV. The sun wouldn't come over the eastern sky for at least two hours, but there were no more visible stars or moon. They drove up the hill toward his place in silence. When they arrived, Nico parked in front of his bungalow and turned off the engine. His place was detached from the main house. Small but charming, it was painted light gray with white trim. He looked over at her. "It's still the middle of the night. We can't wake her. You're going to have to stay with me. We need to get some sleep."

She nodded, too tired to argue. Not that she wanted to. There was no place she'd rather be than with Nico.

She jolted forward in the seat as she realized she had no purse. "I don't even have my purse. No ID. Credit cards. Nothing."

"We'll get all that sorted out tomorrow."

"If not for you, I would have burned up." She felt the tears coming again.

"Come on, let's get you in a warm shower." He reached out to tuck a strand of her dirty hair behind one ear. "It's all going to be all right."

"Promise?"

"I promise."

When they entered through the front door, Nico's dog, Jen, rushed toward them. Nico dropped to his knees to load the ball of black-and-white fur into his arms. Her stubby tail wagged as she licked Nico on the cheek.

"All right, girl," he said as he set her down. "I'm sorry it took me so long to get home."

Next, Jen went to Sophie, who knelt to give her some pets.

Jen licked her hand in greeting.

"Hello, sweet girl," Sophie said, giving her a good scratch behind her ears.

When Sophie rose to full height, Jen ran back to her doggy bed by the bookshelf and curled up in a perfect circle and placed her chin on her paws. She watched them with curious eyes as they danced around each other. "What now?" Sophie asked, looking around the apartment.

Decorated in light colors and sparse furnishings, the thousand-square-foot space was cozy and seemed especially welcoming at the moment. Other than the bedroom and small bathroom, the kitchen, dining room, and living room were a shared space. She liked small homes. They were easier to be close to the people you loved.

"Are you hungry?" he asked.

"Not really. What I really want is to take a shower and change into my favorite pajamas."

He gave a weary nod. "You take the first shower. I'll find something for you to sleep in. There are towels and everything else you need in the shower." He reached into his pants pocket. "You should probably take a few of these."

"Don't tell my mom. She would be upset to know I didn't just have some of her granola tea concoction." She held out her hand, and he plopped two pills into her palm. A second later, he gave her a glass of water, and she obediently swallowed whatever drug they'd given her.

She thanked him and went into the bedroom. His bed was made, and other than a sweatshirt and a small pile of laundry on an armchair, the room was tidy. There was no artwork on the walls or much personal stuff. This was the home of a man in transition. All his things were in storage, he'd told her, until he could either buy or build a home of his own.

She peeled off her borrowed clothes. The T-shirt had been too small for her, stretching across her full breasts. Not that she'd noticed until then. Escaping with one's life gave every-thing a new perspective. In the shower, she soaped her entire body and scrubbed away the scent of smoke. Numb, she found her thoughts sluggish, as if her brain had been affected by the smoke. Nico. Why had she come here to his small apartment? Why had he wanted her here? It was a strange move on his part, after what he'd said to her earlier in the evening. Their conversation now seemed like a different lifetime.

She used his shampoo to wash her hair. As she rubbed her scalp, she almost broke down, remembering her own bath-room. Nothing would be left. No towels, soaps, makeup. Her razor. She couldn't even shave her legs. Her favorite shoes and the dress she'd planned to wear to the wedding next month were nothing but ashes now. She had to face facts. The entire apartment was gone. The restaurant was gone. Would Zane even want to rebuild? Was The Oar something of the past? Now that Dog's Brewery was so popular, maybe he would want to take the insurance money and do something entirely different. Maybe he wouldn't even want her to run it.

What would she do then?

Go home to her parents? Try to find a job there? *Don't be ridiculous.* Her home was here in Cliffside Bay now. She had the wine bar, even if Zane didn't want to rebuild. But surely he would? The place was Hugh's legacy. Her thoughts were tumbling all over now, zigzagging around her mind like an out-of-control child.

Her parents. She needed to call her parents and tell them what happened. Not now. Tomorrow morning. Right now, they would be asleep in their home in San Francisco. Her father probably had important work to do tomorrow with one of his new recording artists. Waking them would do no one any good. They were unlikely to hear it in the news. No one in San Fran-cisco cared about what went on in Cliffside Bay.

She turned off the water and stood there in the doorway of the standup shower, shivering. A towel. She needed a towel.

She grabbed one from the stack on the shelf over the toilet and wrapped it around her shoulders.

Dots swam before her eyes. And then, nothing.

9

Nico

NICO HEARD the crash from where he'd been sitting on the floor outside the bathroom. Sophie had looked pale and glazed when she'd headed off to the shower. So much so that he'd worried if she would be all right alone.

At the sound of a thud and then breaking glass, he jumped to his feet. Jen leaped from her bed and ran to him, nails clicking on the hardwood floor. He charged into the bathroom with Jen at his heels. Fortunately, the door didn't have a lock. Not that he was thinking about propriety at the moment. The small shelf with his glass containers of toiletries was turned over and shards of broken glass were scattered on the floor. Sophie was passed out on her stomach. Her legs were bent, but not unnaturally. They didn't appear to be broken as far as he could see. A towel was underneath her, spread out like a super-hero's cape. Nothing else covered her. Not one thing between his eyes and her long-limbed, tanned, smooth body. Nice tan lines. He swallowed and averted his eyes. What kind of pervert noticed such things when the girl he loved was lying on the ground with a probable concussion?

Silently, he talked to God. *Why are you doing this to me? I've tried to be such a good person.*

He'd been resisting yanking off her clothes for months and months and yet he'd seen her naked twice in one night. While in terrible peril, he reminded himself. Off-limits because of, you know, a fire almost killing her, and now here she was passed out and lying in broken glass. God must have one heck of a sense of humor.

He pushed all thoughts aside as he dropped to his knees at her side. Jen sat on her haunches, her dark eyes worried under her fringe of white bangs. *Forgive me, God, for what I'm about to do.* He scoured every inch of Sophie with his eyes, looking for cuts. She seemed unharmed. At least the back part of her. Who knew about her front?

He knelt and scooped her into his arms and rose to his feet. She was not a light girl. Dense was more like it, especially unconscious. And her limbs were all long and dangly and flopping this way and that. He was strong from surfing and working outside carrying heavy equipment and plants, but this challenged him. Then there were her luscious, round, full breasts pressing against him. He'd been with some pretty women, but not one like this. Sophie was a warrior princess, strong and tall, and so damn gorgeous.

He wanted her under him. On top of him. Beside him. *God, why are you doing this to me? I've tried so hard to resist her.* Sophie had been in his heart and mind since the first time she let loose that sunshine-personified smile. His heart had started beating again. Now she was in his arms. Naked.

Her eyes fluttered open. "What happened?" she asked in a half croak, half whisper.

"You fainted."

Jen barked for emphasis.

Sophie shook her head in that stubborn way that drove him absolutely intoxicated with lust. "Impossible. Girls like me don't faint."

"Uncommon circumstances," he said. "Or, otherwise, no."

Jen ran ahead to the bed and stood there waiting with her tail wagging at warp speed, as if she knew that's where Sophie belonged just then.

She wrapped her arms around his neck. "I don't feel so good."

"I know." He grunted softly as he turned sideways to get them out of the bathroom through the skinny door.

"I'm heavy."

"Not for me," he said, panting slightly as he crossed the room to the bed.

"I have a lot of muscles," she said, sounding half-asleep.

Yes, you do. Miles of them in your legs alone.

"Which makes me heavy." Her head plopped onto his shoulder.

"Again, not for me."

"Liar," she said. "I feel a little loopy."

"It's the pills."

"Maybe I should've just had some of my mom's hippie tea," she said.

"You're talking a lot for a girl who just fainted in my bathroom."

Jen whined. "Get in your bed, Jen," he said to her in his best alpha male voice. All he needed was to trip over his small dog with Sophie in his arms.

Jen gave him a dirty look as she trotted out of the room to her bed in the living room.

Nico folded over from his waist to place her on the bed. Her arms remained around his neck as he tried to set her down gently. She was still damp from the shower, too, which made her stick to him. How did men do this in the movies?

The weight of her pulled him down with her, and they landed together with a thud on top of the comforter. She made a little oomph sound as though he'd hurt her. Then her legs spread slightly to accommodate him. He raised his head. "I'm sorry." His damn body was betraying him. He was hard under his jeans, and the damn nuisance was pressing into her belly. That belly. Curved just right. And those generous hips. Great, now his hands were stuck under her. The two of them were practically glued together. All he had to do was lean a little closer and he could kiss her. A hard kiss that could go on and on.

She looked up at him. "Nico?"

"Yeah?" They were so close he could count the freckles on her perky nose.

"Is that what I think it is?"

He nodded, then hung his head. "I'm sorry. For guys, sometimes things happen even when you really don't want them to."

"I've never felt one before."

"What?" *That* brought him back to reality. She'd never felt an erection before? "You've never messed around with a guy to the point where things happened?"

She looked up at him with her enormous eyes. "I've only kissed a few guys. And never horizontal."

"How is that possible?"

"I've been waiting for the right one."

Holy Batman. What was he doing? This was even worse than he thought. He was the biggest jerk in the entire world. He'd known she was a virgin, but figured she had some experience with men. But she'd never... It was too much. He'd been right all along. Sophie was innocent and way, way too young for him. Did she have any idea how many women he'd been with? Not a ton compared to some, but enough to make him a definite man-whore compared to her experience. She deserved so much better than some old, slutty guy on top of her.

He would not, could not, be that guy.

Still, moral conviction aside, it took every ounce of control he possessed to roll off her and practically fall onto the floor.

She curled up on her side, watching him with a concerned furrow of her brow. "Did I say something wrong?"

Her breasts were just right there, all pink and plump and pressed together between her arms. He took in a deep breath. "No, you're...you're fine." Better than fine. He swallowed hard for the fiftieth time in the last thirty minutes. "I'm kind of mortified."

"Why?"

"You're naked in my bed." So very naked. *And I was on top of you with a very inappropriate body part pressed against you.*

She giggled and rolled her eyes. "My mother's a hippie chick. She taught me that a body's just a body. Nothing to be ashamed of."

Sophie's mother. Her sweet, carob-cookie-making mother who probably didn't have this exact scenario in mind when encouraging Sophie to be unashamed of her body. Okay, that was better than thinking about baseball to get rid of his exuberant, salacious, hard-as-a-rock friend. *Erection has left the building.*

Blanket. He needed a blanket. Anything to cover her up from his treacherous eyes. He jumped to his feet and snatched a knit throw from the end of the bed and practically threw it on top of her.

"Are you cold?" He paced back and forth from one end of the bed to the other.

"A little."

"Get under the covers," he said. *Please, just get under them and cover up your luscious body.*

She scrambled upright, all legs and bouncing breasts, and

pulled back the covers. Her long legs slid under them, then the rest of her. "But this is your bed."

Relief flooded him. Now that she was no longer exposed, he could relax a little. "I'll sleep on the couch tonight."

"That doesn't seem right."

"I'm a camping type of guy. I've slept on much worse." He sat on the edge of the bed and tucked the covers around her. "Should you go to bed with a wet head?"

"I'll be fine." She stared at him so intently he had to look away.

"Nico."

Her husky voice drew him back to her. "What is it?"

"I don't even have a pair of shoes." Her voice suddenly sounded hollow and scared.

He couldn't stop his hands as he brushed away the wet hair from her cheeks. "Pepper or one of the girls will take you shopping. You can get new shoes."

"I liked my old shoes. All of them. And all my baking equipment."

"This is all fixable, Soph. A few shopping trips. An insurance payout. The Wolves can rebuild The Oar. You guys can even make changes you wouldn't have been able to before. David's a brilliant architect."

"We could make the place greener, I suppose," she said, brightening.

"Solar panels, for example."

"Maybe an herb garden," she said. "In planters in the back."

He could have made planters for her before the fire. Why hadn't he ever thought of that? "I can make boxes that hang over the back railings."

"That sounds nice." She moved her gaze away from him and stared up at the ceiling. "I *am* worried about being closed for so long."

"We'll get you up and running before you know it," he said.

"We're going to miss the rest of August revenue."

He understood her concern. Before Wolf Enterprises had taken off, his personal finances wouldn't hold up to two or three months without business. He didn't know if Sophie was the same way. "Will you be okay?"

"Money-wise?" she asked.

"Yes. I mean, do you have enough in the bank to get you through some lean months?"

She nodded. "I've got tons in the bank. I hardly have any expenses. Zane and I own the building, so it's not like I had rent."

Must be nice to own your own home. He looked around the tiny apartment where he'd spent the last year. Mrs. Coventry was generous to give him the space in exchange for his help. However, having his own house was the dream. Affording a place in this town seemed like a pipe dream at this point.

"Maybe I'll do something different upstairs," she said. "Higher ceilings. Bigger windows."

He shook his head, marveling at the way she could so quickly find the positive in every situation.

"What?" she asked.

"Nothing, really. I was just thinking you're very adaptable. Most people would need at least a few weeks to wallow."

"Life is all in the way you look at it," she said.

"You're right, of course. But not everyone can live that way."

She shot him a look that told him she was quite aware of how he limited himself.

Nico ignored her commentary on his life. Safer to stay with practical discussions. "You and Zane can meet with David as early as tomorrow," he said. "He'll start working on plans for you guys whenever you're ready."

"Why didn't you kiss me just now?"

He hadn't seen that segue coming. The pills seemed to have

stripped all inhibitions from her. He hadn't thought there was any wriggle room there.

"I could tell you wanted to," she said. "I mean, I'm not the most experienced person in the world, but even I know what an erection means."

He hung his head and wished he could sink right through the floor. "Sophie, what kind of man would I be if I did all the things I want to do to you? Especially right now?"

"Because you don't love me?"

"Right." God might strike him down right then and there for being such a complete and utter liar. The thought of how close he'd come to losing her made him sick to his stomach. If he'd had any doubts about his feelings, he certainly didn't now.

"I want you to love me so badly." Her eyes filled with tears.

"Oh, Soph." *I do love you.*

She gave him a sad little smile. "I really thought you did. All this time I thought you felt what I did. And then you risked your life to save me. Hugh told me that's when I would know if a man was right for me. You did that. So now I'm confused again."

He almost spilled it then. All of it. Throw caution to the wind. Love her for as long as she'd allow him to. Before he could, she continued.

"I lied a bit before—about why I'm so untouched, so to speak." She brought a hand up from under the covers to brush a piece of lint from the blanket from her face. "I've been kind of freaked out by guys. Before you, that is."

"Did something happen to you?" He'd kill whoever hurt her.

"No, nothing like that. It's just that I was kind of a late bloomer and super shy around boys. Plus, I went to an all-girls school, so there wasn't really that much opportunity to meet anyone. In college, I was so busy studying and everything so I could finish early that I didn't really have time. The longer it was, the more stigma I felt around the whole sex thing. You know, like I was weird. Which I am, obviously."

"You're not weird." Special. Flawless. Untouchable.

"Then I moved here and started working like crazy at the restaurant, and after that I was pregnant, you know, so no one wanted to date me even if I'd been interested. I definitely didn't want to lose my virginity like that. I mean, there was a baby inside me. What if a guy's thing hit Sebastian in the head, for example?"

"Um, no." He felt his skin flushing hotter and hotter the more she went on. "I don't think that's how it works."

"How do you know?"

He wet his dry lips with the tip of his tongue. "I just do."

"Well, that's good to know. I was too shy to ask Dr. Waller that question. Another awkward thing about being a pregnant virgin. Anyway, all that to say, there's a reason I'm the way I am. Finally, I met you, and I decided I wanted it to be you."

"Soph."

"I know. You don't want me even though you do."

He nodded. What else could he say? That sentence pretty much summed it all up.

"But what if you did this as a favor to me?"

"Did *this*?"

"Have sex with me. You could teach me things. Then, when I met the right guy...the one that isn't you, I'd be ready."

He simply stared at her. Not only was she too young and naive for him, she might also be suffering from smoke inhalation and a drug-induced state that had affected her cognitive thought processes.

"No strings attached," she said.

Famous last words.

"You've gone through a tremendous ordeal tonight," he said. "You're not thinking clearly."

"Actually, it's the opposite. I might've died in that fire never having had sex. That's even more of a tragedy than merely dying young."

A dry laugh escaped from his belly. Sophie Woods was one of a kind, that was for sure. He glanced down at his sports watch. It was almost four in the morning.

"Regardless of your logic or lack thereof, it's time for us to get some sleep, and I need a shower."

She yawned, as if his words reminded her of how tired she was. "At least think about it, okay?"

"No promises," he said as he rose to his feet.

In the bathroom, he righted the shelf and cleaned up the glass before getting into the shower and washing away the horrendous night from his skin.

When he returned to the bedroom with a towel wrapped around his waist, Sophie was asleep on her back. For a moment, he watched her sleep. How many times had he imagined her like this? Peacefully asleep in his bed. Only in those dreams, she was wrapped in his arms.

He pulled on a pair of sweats, feeling a hundred years old, and dragged himself into the other room. Jen lifted her head and wagged her tail, obviously hopeful that he'd ask her to join him.

"This couch isn't big enough for the both of us." He opened the storage chest that also served as a coffee table and brought out a blanket. Using a throw pillow for his head, he settled onto his side. Jen cocked her head and made a sad whine. "Come on, then."

Jen smiled and leaped from her bed and curled up next to his feet. He closed his eyes, comforted by the small dog, even as the scenes from earlier flashed through his mind—flames and black smoke and the way the building had collapsed in on itself. And the noise. He hadn't known fire would be so loud.

He shivered, thinking of Sophie. How close she'd been to death. Him too, for that matter.

They were safe, he reminded himself. No reason to go down the bad path, imagining things that didn't happen.

Sophie was in his bed, he realized with a lurch. *God, give me strength.*

What about her offer? He knew in his mind, even though every other part of him screamed otherwise, that Sophie's proposition had little to do with her desire to have her first experience over with and everything to do with her desire to have him change his mind about her. For that reason, he could not succumb. They'd both get hurt if they got involved. Neither of them needed that. He had to remain strong.

Finally, he fell into a deep and dreamless sleep.

10

S ophie

SOPHIE WOKE to the sensation of something wet and cold on her forearm. She peeled her tired eyes open. Jen stared back at her from those shiny black buttons under her white fringe. "You need a bang trim. Did you know that?"

Jen's tail wagged hopefully as she let out a friendly whine that communicated both hunger and a need to use the outside facilities.

The clock on the bedside table told her it was after nine. She knew most days Nico was up before six to take Jen out and make sure Mrs. Coventry had her coffee and breakfast. Nico was a man of routine, which she always found counterintuitive to his laid-back vibe, but he was nothing if not a study in contrasts.

She groaned as she remembered parts of her conversation

with Nico. Had she really offered herself up as a sex toy? What had those drugs done to her?

Jen whined again, this time with more urgency. "All right, girl. Hang on. I'll take you out." Sophie threw back the covers and swung her legs to the floor. She wore no pajamas and had nothing to put on, other than the clothes from last night that smelled of smoke. She looked over at the dresser. Would Nico mind if she borrowed a few things to wear? Given how rushed he was to get her under the covers, she figured he'd rather have her clothed than naked. With this in mind, she opened a few of the drawers and found a pair of boxer shorts and a thick sweatshirt she would wear without a bra.

Dressed, she turned back to Jen. "All right, let's get you outside and fed." She grabbed her only worldly possession from the bedside table. While Jen did her business, she would gather strength from one of Hugh's passages.

Jen wagged her tail in response. Sophie padded across the hardwood floor of the bedroom and opened the door. She winced as it creaked, then tiptoed into the living room. Nico was curled on his side on the couch, fast asleep. A pang of guilt tugged at her for taking his bed. The sofa looked more like a love seat under his long, trim frame. She stared at him for a moment, taken in by the sheer beauty of the man.

Asleep, he looked peaceful but also older, which was strange, as usually it was the opposite. In the bright light of the morning, the shallow lines that were etched into the corners of his eyes were more evident. Whereas when he was awake, his face was so animated, and his eyes twinkled and danced. He'd always appeared ageless to her.

People said she was an old soul, more mature than her age, but she disagreed. She felt wise but not old. The secrets of the universe had been taught to her by her mother. Be curious. Be amazed. Be kind. These were age-old adages that kept a person youthful. These were the qualities she saw in Nico. Ones that were innate to him, not taught as they'd been to her. He didn't talk often of his parents, but she knew enough to know their philosophies of life were more along the lines of: be aggressive, make money, take what you want. She often wondered how he'd become the man he was, sensitive and kind and so content to be outside with his plants and flowers. She'd never once heard him talk about anything materially important to him. He was of the land and the sea.

Jen licked her bare leg, bringing Sophie back from her Nico musings to the task at hand. A pair of Nico's flip-flops were near the door. She slipped her feet into them. They were only slightly too large. She had enormous feet for a woman. Her petite mother had always told her they went perfectly with her long legs and to love them for their ability to take her wherever she wanted to go. Sophie agreed and thanked them by having regular pedicures and painting her toenails bright colors. Today, they were crimson pink. She wore a toe ring for extra sparkle.

She grabbed a plastic bag from the roll on the table near the door for Jen's morning gift, then opened the front door as quietly as she could. Jen slipped out and ran toward a patch of grass under a eucalyptus tree, ears flapping like happy flags.

While Jen did her morning work, Sophie took in her surroundings. Like many of the homes built into northern slope, the front of the house faced westward toward the sea with the driveway in the back. Painted white with dark brown trim and a flat three-tiered roof, Mrs. Coventry's home had both Spanish and French architectural influences. She knew this not because she had much knowledge of architecture but because Nico had told her. Formal landscaping included tall, skinny shrubs and precisely trimmed hedges. Double-sided dark-trimmed doors were made more formal by an intricate design in the window above. A wide cement driveway separated the detached garage and Nico's bungalow from the house.

This was a beautiful home. She hung her head, reeling for a moment. She no longer had a house. A lone ant went one way, then the other, on the cement driveway. Poor guy looked as lost as she felt.

No matter, she told herself. The building was just a thing. A building could be rebuilt. She would start again. Zane would have a plan by now. He and Honor would have talked it over in their modern farmhouse kitchen with strong cups of coffee.

She opened the book Hugh had left her and skimmed to the one that continued the story about what had happened to bring him and Mae together at last.

Dear Sophie,

For years Mae and I were friendly but not friends. She'd come in for dinner sometimes with the Wallers or I'd see her down on the beach or at school functions. I hadn't wanted to be right, but I was. Bruises can't lie. She tried to hide them under long-sleeved shirts and makeup, but I knew they were there. By this time Lily and Doc Waller had moved to town. The three kids, Jackson, Maggie, and Zane, were thick as thieves. Doc and Lily were my best friends. The Wallers knew the truth too, but Mae never admitted it to us. She always had an excuse. She fell or ran into a door or some such thing. Like women do who are in that situation. They're scared. The Wallers tried to get her to leave many times, but again, she was too scared.

As far as us, she and I never talked about anything deeper than the weather or sports. When she came in for dinner with Keene, I always had one of my staff take care of them. I couldn't stand seeing her with him.

Then, when the kids were about eight, Keene took a job down in Texas. Mae started coming by The Oar more often. On slow nights, she'd bring Maggie in with her and I'd give them a meal on the house. Maggie and Zane would do their homework in the office, and she and I would talk while I closed up the place. At first, we talked about superficial subjects or about the kids. One night, she came in with

Maggie, and I could tell she'd been crying. I sent Maggie back to the office to hang out with Zane. Rain was coming down in sheets outside the windows. The bar was empty other than us. I poured her a glass of Riesling. That's what she liked. I didn't ask her what was wrong. I'd figured out by then that Mae didn't tell you what was what until she was good and ready. I went about my business, drying glasses from the rack and storing them under the bar, then going through receipts from the dinner rush, which weren't much. All the while I could feel all the words she hadn't said to me for eighteen years just hovering in the air between us like a thundercloud before it bursts.

It took half a glass of wine before she started talking.

"Roger left before Christmas for Texas," she said. "I don't think he's coming back."

I froze with a towel in one hand and a glass in the other.

"He went for a job down there."

"I thought he was working at the feed store," I said.

"He was fired six months ago. Since then, things have been lean. Not many guests at the inn this time of year, either."

"Why don't you think he's coming back?" I asked.

She shrugged and lifted her gaze to the ceiling. "Just my gut. I think he met someone down there."

I didn't say anything to that. It had been my experience tending bar all those years that women almost always knew when their man was cheating. I'd consoled a lot of women over the span of my career.

She looked me square in the face. "I can't say I'm not relieved."

"Then what's made you cry?"

"I don't know how I'm going to support us on my own. He's never allowed me to work. I don't know how to do anything but run the inn, such as it is, and take care of Maggie."

"Come work for me. I can always use someone reliable."

She narrowed her eyes and gave me a pinched smile. "I can't take pity work. Especially not from you."

She was a different person without her husband in town. It was like she blossomed. Started smiling and laughing more. Lost that pinched look around her mouth.

On summer nights after I closed the bar and Maggie was sleeping over at the Wallers', your mother and I would come out to the patio to talk. She loved sweet white wine, and I'd have my Bud Light. Glad for the privacy, we'd talk in low voices. I shared things with her I'd never told anyone. I told her about Zane's mother and how she'd left the baby with me and gone back to her rich family. She understood the utter terror it was to raise a child alone.

After a time, she got up the courage to ask for a divorce, but it was like he'd disappeared off the face of the earth. Letters went unanswered or were sent back with "no known address" stamped on them. Then we found out she was pregnant with you. We made a plan to marry and got an attorney involved to get the divorce proceedings going. That got his attention. The thought of her with someone else threw him into some kind of jealous rage, even though he had another woman. He came back here to punish Mae. Well, you know how all that turned out by now.

I wish to God he'd never returned. Things would have been so different for all of us. My only consolation is that you are with such a good family. They've been able to give you so much that I'd never have been able to. By the time you read this, maybe you'll know all of us. Other than your mother, that is.

If you know Maggie, you'll have a lot of insight into what Mae was like. They were similar, what with their red hair and freckles and delicate dancer-type frames. Mae was soft-spoken and sweet but timid. She never did have much confidence in herself, which is how she ended up married to a monster in the first place. I know just by looking at you from afar that you're nothing like that. You're more like Zane, full of spirit.

I know it's easier to choose anger and bitterness over forgiveness. I'm not saying I haven't struggled over the years. But one thing that's always helped me—when I feel sad or angry, I look around to find someone who has had it worse off than me or is struggling in some *way, and I put my focus on them. Doing something kind for others always makes me feel better. It's selfish, really, if you think about it, but baby girl, getting along in this world is hard. If you can find a way to ease the pain for yourself and others, it's best to do so.*

JEN, having finished, sidled up next to her, ears down as if apologetic about the gift she'd left. Sophie used the plastic bag to scoop up the evidence. She wasn't sure where Nico took such a deposit. A simple shed at the other end of the driveway caught her eye. Perhaps they kept the trash cans in there? Trying the door, she found it open. Inside were trash cans, recycle bins, and garden tools. She dropped the doggy poo into the appropriate container. As her eyes adjusted better to the dim light, she noticed a bag of dog food and a bowl with Jen's name etched into the side.

She used the cup next to the bag to scoop some food into the bowl and took it out to the yard. Jen let out an excited bark when she saw her breakfast. Sophie set it down on the concrete. Jen sat back on her haunches and looked up at Sophie. "You're a good dog. Go ahead. Eat."

After permission, Jen wasted no more time on niceties. She scarfed her breakfast with great enthusiasm. Sophie laughed. She appreciated any creature who enjoyed a good meal.

When Jen was finished, she smiled up Sophie and wagged her tail.

"Are you allowed to run around without a leash?" she asked Jen.

Jen tilted her head to the side, as if trying to understand the simple human's question, but failing. Obviously giving up on attempting to communicate, Jen lowered her nose to the ground and sniffed. She must have caught a whiff of something interesting, because she bounded across the driveway and around the back of the bungalow. Sophie sat on the bottom step in front of the main house's doors and hugged her knees to her chest. She should call Zane and check in, but she had no phone. Why hadn't she thought to grab it? She couldn't even remember what she did with the headphones she'd been wearing when Nico burst into the bathroom. The entire time it took them to get out of the apartment was blurred, like a memory from long ago. This was probably her brain protecting her. She supposed she should be grateful.

Jen returned with a dirty tennis ball in her mouth and dropped it at Sophie's feet. Sophie, never one to deny anyone a romp, tossed it across the driveway. Jen barked and leaped after the wildly bouncing ball.

"Once you start, she'll never stop," said a voice behind her.

Sophie, startled, turned around. Mrs. Coventry, wearing a swim cover-up over a one-piece suit, stood framed in the doorway. She had tan, muscular legs, especially for a seventy-year-old. Sophie jumped to her feet, embarrassed. Who was she to just hang out in front of the woman's front door?

"Mrs. Coventry, I'm sorry. Did we wake you?"

The older woman wore a large straw hat and enormous black sunglasses that covered most of her pixie-like face. She shook her head. "No, no. I've been up for hours. I swim first thing in the morning." Her round vowels and slow pace were soft as a feather.

"Good for you." As she often did around petite women, Sophie felt suddenly like an Amazon.

Mrs. Coventry's mouth lifted into a smile that wasn't exactly warm, but not unfriendly either. "You run The Oar. Hugh's old place."

"That's correct. Zane's my half brother."

"I knew Hugh, of course. Everyone did."

"Seems like it," Sophie said.

"My husband knew him better than I. We moved here after Paul retired, and he and Hugh became good friends. They fished together or watched football." Her gaze drifted toward town. "Paul died five years ago. Before Hugh's memory failed." Nico had shared his concern for Mrs. Coventry with Sophie. He thought she should go out more. Do things. Get involved with the community or make friends. Go to church. But after her husband died, she'd holed up in her house.

"He got bad in the end," Sophie said. "Before I could get to know him, actually. He was already lost by the time Zane and Maggie found me."

"That's a shame. He was a fine man. A good person, genuine and without airs. Paul found him refreshing after spending most of his working life with men who thought they were much more important than they really were."

"I hope it's all right that I'm here?" Sophie asked as she shifted from one foot to the other.

"Yes, yes. Nico can have visitors anytime he wants." She must have raised her eyebrows because her glasses moved up and down. "I realize he's not a monk."

"Oh." Did he have visitors a lot? Her stomach turned at the thought of how many women he would have brought up here over the past year. "It's not like that. My restaurant and apartment burned down last night, and I needed a place to crash."

Mrs. Coventry ripped off her sunglasses. "The Oar had a fire?"

"Yes. It's gone. Burned to the ground." Sophie tried not to tear up, but it was impossible.

"How awful. You poor dear." Mrs. Coventry's eyes were a light green and intense, sharp. Eyes that saw through facades.

"Thanks. I think I'm still in shock. Nothing's really sunk in, other than the fact that I have no cell phone or purse or credit cards. Or clothes or shoes." She held up one foot to show her Nico's flip-flops.

"Terrible thing to have happen." Mrs. Coventry clucked her tongue. "I'm so sorry, dear." She squinted into the sun. "I'm afraid you're much taller than I am or I'd be happy to lend you something to wear."

"I'll go into town and buy a few things later."

"Thank goodness you weren't harmed."

"Nico rescued me." She told the older woman the entire story of her rescue.

With her hands over her mouth, Mrs. Coventry exclaimed, "What a brave, wonderful man."

"I think so too."

"Is he sleeping?" Mrs. Coventry asked.

"Yes, we were up until four in the morning."

"I wondered why Nico wasn't up and fussing over me to eat my granola." Her green eyes flashed. "The boy's obsessed with my nutrition."

"He's very fond of you."

She placed her hand over heart. "Yes. And he's a gentle soul —can't stand the thought of anyone suffering."

"True."

Behind them, Jen let out a happy bark as she ran toward the house with the ball in her mouth.

Mrs. Coventry's gaze swept the length of Sophie, then returned to her face. "You're Hugh's daughter. No doubt about that."

"Do I look like him?" Sophie was always eager to hear anything about her father.

"Your eyes and coloring, obviously. But there's something in your spirit that makes you especially like him. He was always full of life. So curious and eager to help anyone who needed it."

"I'd like to think I'm like him," Sophie said.

Mrs. Coventry didn't reassure her further. She wasn't one to coddle, Sophie suspected.

"Are you hungry?" Mrs. Coventry asked.

"Starving."

"Well, you better come inside and fix us both some

granola," said Mrs. Coventry. "Nico doesn't allow me to have eggs anymore. He's like an old lady."

Jen dropped the ball and barked. Mrs. Coventry gestured toward the dog. "Yes, you can come too. Isn't she the most adorable dog that ever lived?"

"For sure."

Jen waited for them at the door, panting.

Sophie and Jen followed Mrs. Coventry into the house. The insides were as dramatic as the exterior, with vaulted ceilings and shiny cherry floors and stark white walls with brown trim around the windows. They passed by a sitting room with a pale Oriental rug and formal furniture that looked uncomfortably stiff. In fact, the house didn't appear to have inhabitants. Everything was in perfect order. Not a pillow or vase out of place. Like a museum, only with less art on the walls. In the kitchen, the pale gray granite countertops and dark-stained tables and trim were the only hints of color. Everything else was in white. An ornate chandelier hung over the island. Another hung over the table by the picture windows that faced west.

Outside the windows, separated from the house by a smooth sand-colored patio, was the bluest pool she'd ever seen. She gasped at the sight. "Your pool's so pretty."

"Thank you. Swimming has been a part of my life since I was a young child." Mrs. Coventry took a bowl from one of the drawers and filled it with water from the spotless white sink, then set it on the floor for Jen. "Do you swim?"

"Yes, I love the water. I surf, too."

"Surfing is in your blood, I suppose?"

"I think so, yes." Sophie watched as Jen slurped up the water from the bowl, splashing it all over the shiny floor. "Is this all right?" She pointed at the dog.

"We'll wipe it up when she's finished," Mrs. Coventry said. "Jen knows the routine." She gestured toward a closed door. "The pantry's there. I'm going to shower and clean up. Make yourself at home. Nico buys a silly amount of groceries for me, so help yourself to whatever you please. There's an espresso machine if you'd like coffee."

"I'd love nothing more." Sophie followed her gaze to the metal espresso maker. It was an industrial model, probably better than the one she had at the bar. The one she *used* to have at the bar, she reminded herself. Would insurance cover all the equipment they had to replace?

She really needed to call her parents and Zane. "May I use your landline? I need to call my family. I didn't make it out with my cell phone."

"Whatever you need." Mrs. Coventry gestured toward the phone on the other side of the kitchen as she passed by. "I'll be back shortly."

Sophie thanked her. After she let Jen outside and cleaned up the water, she made herself a double espresso and added a dollop of half-and-half she found in the refrigerator. Enjoying the scent that wafted through the kitchen, she inhaled and centered herself before making the call to her mother.

"Hello?" Mom sounded wary, probably because this was an unfamiliar number.

"It's Sophie."

"Where are you? I don't know this number. Are you at Nico's?"

Nico's? How did she know that?

"Did you stay the night with him?" The excitement in Mom's voice caused her to sound slightly out of breath, as if she'd run up a hill. Which would never happen. Rhona Woods was more the tai chi and yoga type of woman. Mom thought running was the perfect metaphor for all that was wrong with their society. Too much running like hamsters on a treadmill instead of being in the moment.

"Mom, no. I mean yes, but not the way you mean."

Mom seemed not to have heard the end of Sophie's

sentence, given the next thing out of her mouth. "Has he finally come to his senses and realized only a complete fool would pass you up?"

"No, not yet anyway." She flushed as she recalled how they'd fallen on the bed together and what she'd felt sticking into her belly. A twinge between her legs quickly followed. How could she be thinking about sex when her entire livelihood was in jeopardy? She no longer had a business or a home. Her sexual frustration should really be put aside for now.

"Then why are you calling from his house? Sweetie, you didn't sleep with him, did you? Please tell me you haven't entered into something casual, because you know that's not going to make you happy."

"No, Mom. I had to stay here because there was a fire at The Oar."

She heard Mom gasp and could almost see her pressing her hand against her chest. "A fire? Was anyone hurt?"

"No. Everyone got out safely, but we lost everything."

"Oh, Sophie, no. I'm so sorry. Where were you when the fire broke out?"

She realized now that she should have thought through exactly how much to tell her mother. Did she need to know how much danger Sophie had been in? Probably not. However, she would find out eventually, so it was probably best to tell her the entire story. "I was upstairs in the bathtub." She shared the rest of the details, including jumping out the window.

"That boy saved your life," Mom said. "You know what this means?"

"That he's a brave hero?"

"Yes, and now you're bound together forever."

"Did you just make that up?" Sophie asked.

"No, it's a Chinese proverb. I think."

"Mom." Sophie laughed.

"How did the fire start?" Mom asked.

"They think it was arson."

"But why? Who would do something like that?"

"I can't imagine. They wanted to know if I had any enemies, but I couldn't think of any."

"Are you sure? Maybe there's someone or something you haven't thought of," Mom said.

"It's probably unrelated to me all together. Arsonists don't necessarily target a place for a reason."

They spoke for a few more minutes, with her mother trying to convince her to come home and Sophie laying out all the reasons she couldn't. As much as she loved being with her parents, now was not the time. She needed to be here to help Zane.

After they hung up, she called her brother. She hoped he'd pick up since the number would be strange. He did, answering on the third ring.

"Zane, it's me."

"Sophie, hi. I'm so glad you called. I was about to drive up there to see how you're doing."

"I'm all right. You?"

She heard him sigh. "I'm thankful no one got hurt. I talked to the insurance people this morning. They'll process the claim for us to rebuild if we want."

If we want? Strange choice of words.

"When can we start?" she asked.

"I'm not sure."

"We have to get started as soon as we can," she said. "Nico said the guys will make us a priority. I say we shoot for a Christmas reopening."

"I talked with Brody this morning. He said you could move into their pool house until you decide where to go."

"You mean, until the apartment is finished?" She sipped her espresso and looked out at the pool. Jen had curled up in a patch of sun and appeared to have fallen asleep. She thought of her little apartment, and a wave of homesickness swept through her.

Zane cleared his throat, as if he were nervous. "Here's the thing. Are we sure we want to rebuild?"

His question was like a sudden splash of cold water on her face. She'd been afraid of this but hadn't expected it at the same time. "What? Why wouldn't we?"

"Maybe we should take it as a sign that it's time for a change. You need to do a little living instead of working all the time. Have some fun."

"I don't want to have fun," she said. "I want to work at The Oar." Not rebuild? How could he even suggest such a thing? "The place is an institution in this town."

There was a long pause from the other end before her brother spoke. "I went down there this morning. I wanted to see what was left, if anything. I had this weird hope that the surfboards Dad hung on the walls all those years ago might have made it." His voice cracked at the end of that sentence. "But as you know, there's nothing left."

"We'll put up new ones."

"What about the bar? He made that bar with his own hands, and now it's gone."

"We'll make it exactly the same," she said.

"It won't be the same because he didn't make it."

"But Zane, we're part of him. He's in us."

"The truth is, I'm not sure I can handle rebuilding without Dad." She heard tears in his voice, and the sound nearly broke her heart in two. "The Oar *was* Dad. His heart and soul were in that place. I hear him talking to me sometimes when I'm tending bar or back in his office. Even with the changes I made, it was still his place, his building. With it gone, I feel like I've lost him all over again."

"I understand," she said. "One of the reasons I love working there so much is because it makes me feel close to him."

"Right. And is that a good thing?"

"How could it be bad?" she asked.

"Because you should be out having adventures, not living like an old man. He'd want you to have fun, Sophie. I know he would. Instead, you're living the life he did. All you do is work and then drag yourself upstairs to sleep, then do it all over again. He never had the chance to travel or see anything. I don't want that for you."

"I went to Europe after Sebastian."

"For like three weeks. And that was over a year ago now. When was the last time you took a day off?"

She searched back through the summer, trying to recall. Was it possible she hadn't taken a night off since May? "Spring and summer are peak times. You know that."

"I'm too busy with the brewery and my family to help as much as I should," he said. "So it's been left to you."

"I don't mind. It's a privilege," Sophie said.

"Sophie, I need you to hear me on this. The Oar doesn't make enough profit for you to work as hard as you do."

"We're doing fine. Profits are way up the last few months."

"Because it's summer."

"I don't have many expenses. I don't need much," she said.

"The place barely makes enough to support you, let alone put anything away for savings."

"What are you saying?" A chill had settled somewhere deep inside her. He wanted out. She braced herself, knowing it was coming.

"I want to sell the lot," he said. "Let someone else have the headache if they want to open another bar or whatever else. You can take the insurance money and buy a house or take a long trip. Or something. Anything other than being trapped behind that bar every night for the rest of your life. You have a college degree in hospitality. You could be working for a big hotel, running events or catering at Kyle's lodge, not pouring beer." Kyle Hicks owned the new resort, which employed a lot of people. She knew he would find a place for her if she asked. But she liked running her own place. She liked being the boss.

"But Zane, I love it. Every minute of it. I love this town. I don't want to leave you and Honor and the kids, not to mention my friends. This is where I belong. Anything else feels wrong."

"You can work with me at the brewery full-time," Zane said. "We can do more with the wine bar. Maybe start hosting guest winemakers for dinners."

"I want to rebuild." She said it as firmly as she could. Technically, she owned half of The Oar. She should have equal say.

"Why could a young woman as talented as you want to spend her life mixing drinks for tourists?"

"Because I love it."

He made an exasperated noise, somewhere between a sigh and a sputter. "Well, I want more for you. A bigger life than behind that bar."

"I like my life just as it is. Half of the place is mine. What if I buy you out?"

"You want it that much?" Zane asked. "That you'd go into debt?"

"It's all I have of him," Sophie said.

There was another long pause on the other end of the line.

"Is that what this is about? Dad?" Zane asked.

"Partly, maybe."

"You know, all I ever wanted when I was a kid was to get out of here and make sure I didn't end up stuck here working my butt off every single day for no money. I never thought I'd end up running the damn thing. But then the dementia came and everything went to crap."

"But you love it here, don't you?" she asked.

"I do. Of course I do. Everything and everyone I love is here."

"Your worst fears are not mine, Zane. I crave a simple life.

This is my life, not yours. You're not responsible for me, you know."

"Seeing the ashes of Dad's life work made me realize..."

"Realize what?"

"As long as The Oar was there, I could almost pretend like he was too," Zane said. "And now it's gone. Just like him."

"Oh, Zane."

"I wasn't ready for him to go. I miss him so much. Every single day, I just want him to be here to see the kids and Honor doing so well. And to get to know you. I don't know if I can see his place resurrected without him there to tell us what to do."

She closed her eyes. His grief was palpable even over the phone. "I'll do it without you," she said gently. "You can be free."

He didn't answer.

"Zane, are you still there?"

"Yes, I'm here." Another pause. "Sophie, I'm afraid for you. I'm afraid you're going to end up all alone like Dad."

"He wasn't alone. This whole town was his family. If that's my life's legacy, then I'll be proud."

"If it's truly what you want, it should be yours. The whole thing. You don't have to buy me out. Honor and I are very set financially. I'll sign it all over to you. Your heart is there, obviously. But please, take some time to think it over."

She didn't need to think it over, but she would acquiesce for now. "Thank you, Zane."

She hung up, drained and relieved at the same time, and sat on one of the stools at the island, then buried her face in her arms and let the tears come.

"Everything all right, dear?"

She looked up to see Mrs. Coventry standing on the other side of the island. "Yes, I'm fine." She swiped at her cheeks, embarrassed to be found crying in a stranger's kitchen.

Mrs. Coventry had changed into a cotton sheath dress. Her

silver hair was dry now and fixed in a straight bob that fell at her chin. She had remarkably good posture, as if a stick ran from the top of her head to the base of her spine. Sophie imagined her sitting on the back seat of a convertible wearing a ball gown and a tiara, waving her small hand like a queen. Everyone was so casual now, especially in California. Mrs. Coventry, on the other hand, seemed to have come from a different time and place. One more formal and glamorous than the one where Sophie spent her days, that was for sure. Mrs. Coventry would never fill pints of beer, letting it slip over the side of the glass and splash her sleeve as Sophie did on a regular basis. Zane's words came back to her. *I want more for you.*

Why did all the men in her life seem to think they knew what she needed and wanted?

"Having yourself a little cry?" Mrs. Coventry asked, not unkindly but without a hint of sentimentality.

Sophie nodded. "I'm feeling a little sorry for myself."

Mrs. Coventry clucked her tongue. "Nothing to be ashamed of. You've been through a terrible ordeal. Even those of us made of steel have to cry it out every so often."

Made of steel? At the moment she felt more like a bowl of pudding. She stole a tissue from a box on the island and wiped under her eyes. "Since I've invaded your kitchen, may I make you a coffee?"

Mrs. Coventry brightened and clapped her hands together. "Lovely. Thank you. Double espresso with a splash of cream, please." She drifted over to a drawer and pulled out two precisely folded and pressed cloth napkins, then two spoons from another. As she spoke, she set two places at the table. "I imagine it seems impossible on a day like today that last night happened?"

An image of the orange and yellow flames shooting from the windows of her apartment flashed before her. "Yes. The whole thing seems like a bad dream."

"This too shall pass." Mrs. Coventry sat and spread a napkin over her lap. "Soon, it'll be only a memory. One you'll look back on and see it was the beginning of something new and delightful in your life."

"How do you know?"

"When you're my age, you look back and see how the pieces of your life fit into the overall puzzle. This happened because that happened and so forth. The particularly hard parts and terrible failures always seem to be the biggest turning points that lead to better than you could ever believe possible."

Sophie took in a deep breath as Mrs. Coventry's words filled her with hope. The sun had risen up over the eastern sky by now and shed bright sunlight over the pool. Beyond, the Pacific was covered by a layer of fog, typical of summer mornings here. Soon, it would roll out to sea and Sophie would wonder, as she always did, if it had been there at all. Fog was like the bad things in life. She must remember that over the next few days. *This too shall pass.*

"Thank you," Sophie said. "Your words help more than you know."

"Isn't it funny how sometimes the right person enters your life just when you need them? Even when you don't realize you need anyone at all?"

"It is." Sophie took down one of the small cups stored on the shelf above the espresso machine.

While the machine ground beans and dispensed espresso, Sophie rinsed out her cup and set it near the sink. When the perfect double was ready, Sophie added a spot of cream and presented it to Mrs. Coventry.

"This is divine. Thank you, dear." Mrs. Coventry brought the small cup close to her nose. "Smells glorious."

Sophie's stomach growled. "Now, about that granola. I'm starving."

Mrs. Coventry gestured toward one of the white bins on the

counter near the refrigerator. "He keeps it in there. The awful white yogurt is in the refrigerator." She paused, tilting her head to one side. "I wouldn't turn down a tablespoon or two of honey on mine."

"Sure thing." Sophie walked across the large kitchen and busied herself with putting together two bowls of granola with yogurt and a generous sprinkling of honey. When they were ready, she brought them to the table. They ate in silence for a few minutes.

"The granola is really hard to chew," Sophie said after the third bite. "My mom buys this same kind."

"I'm surprised I haven't lost a crown." Mrs. Coventry dotted her mouth with her napkin.

"And the yogurt's really sour."

"Awful. However, it's almost edible with the addition of honey. Nico doesn't believe in adding sweetener to this hamster feed."

Sophie laughed. "He has high cholesterol, so he's very deliberate in his food choices."

"Isn't it boring? For one so fit and young, high cholesterol seems impossible." Mrs. Coventry grinned, making her appear impish and mischievous. "I think he's making it up."

"Nico never lies." Sophie found herself grinning back at Mrs. Coventry. "He's incapable. Which is something we have in common.

"Does he ever talk about me?" The question kind of slipped out. Sophie regretted it instantly, but it was too late to pull the words back. That was the whole problem with spoken words. If only she could learn to keep things inside, she might do a lot less blushing.

Mrs. Coventry drank the rest of her espresso before answering. "Yes. He talks about you often."

"What does he say?"

Mrs. Coventry looked at her for a moment longer than was

comfortable. Sophie broke eye contact and moved a raisin around her bowl as if she were as interested in the dried fruit as Mrs. Coventry was in her. "I'm not sure I should betray his confidence, even if it's for his own good. He knows you're special, but he's been trying to distract himself with all the others."

"The others?"

Mrs. Coventry brought her hand to her neck and played with the silver chain around her neck. "The ones he brings home."

A dart of jealous heat rushed through her. *All the others.* She knew the others. Too many times, she'd had to endure him flirting with them at the bar, then taking them home. Each one had been a lesson in pain.

"They're not old souls like you," Mrs. Coventry said. "He knows that. Simply put, he's in love with you."

"I'm so in love with him." Sophie lifted her shoulders, intending to shrug, but instead let out a long, sad sigh. "I love him. Too much."

"There's no such thing as loving someone too much."

"Unless the other person can't receive it," Sophie said. "Or doesn't want to."

"Yes, as is the case with our Nico."

Sophie met her gaze, and by the sympathetic and knowing glint in her eyes, she knew the older, and probably much wiser, woman understood quite well the longings of her heart. "He's afraid I'll change my mind and he'll be hurt again. Isn't that stupid?"

"Sadly, our capacity for fear rises every time our hearts are broken." Mrs. Coventry pushed her bowl away. "And then there's his mother. It's her voice in his head that tells him he's not good enough. One only chooses a mate based on their own feelings of self-worth. Therefore, he cannot see himself with you."

She stared at Mrs. Coventry. "I've never heard it described that way, but you're right."

"When you're told your whole life you're worthless, only the miracle of love can make you see it's all been a giant lie."

"I wish I could be that miracle."

Mrs. Coventry spread her hands out in front of her. "Dear girl, you are his miracle. He ran into a burning building to save you without any thought of his own safety. He was willing to die for you."

A chill passed through her body. "Yes."

"Last night, it was you who needed rescuing. In the big picture, it's you who'll have to save *him*."

"But how? He keeps pushing me away."

"I admit, he's a hard case. However, this is not insurmountable. You need to love him unconditionally to counteract the conditional love his parents gave him. Secondly, you have to convince him that you're worth the risk and that unlike his fiancée, you'll never leave him for someone else."

"That seems impossible."

Mrs. Coventry tapped her temple. "Not with this old lady at the helm." She played with an earring, obviously thinking. "With a damaged heart, it's all about actions. We need a three-pronged approach. First, declaration of war. You tell him you're not giving up on him until he realizes you're here to stay. Second, seduction. You need to get him into bed. Once he feels what it's like to be with a woman who loves him, there will be no going back. Which means you're going to pull out all the stops. Go big or go home type of thing."

"I don't know how to seduce someone. I'm inexperienced in that area. Meaning, I have zero. I've been saving myself for the one."

Mrs. Coventry practically cackled. "This keeps getting better and better. After his run with the lesbian, the first time he makes you come, he's going to lose his mind."

"Mrs. Coventry!"

"What? Did he tell you the fiancée admitted to faking it during their intimate moments?"

Sophie shook her head. "No, he hasn't told me anything about that."

"He's going to know in his heart how much you love him when he has you in his bed. He'll feel your love then and start to trust it. And the way you'll love him will make him feel like king of the universe, which will give him the confidence he needs.

"My Paul used to say that all was fair in love and business. Soft-pitch was for amateurs. You, darling, must play hardball. Which is to say, you're going to have to go against your every instinct and be a bit of a seductress."

"How do I do that?"

Mrs. Coventry tapped her chest. "Darling, you're in luck. You're in the presence of a first-class femme fatale. I'll teach you my tricks. Now, don't look like that. This will never work unless you have a little fun connecting to your inner vamp."

"Vamp? No, that's not me."

Mrs. Coventry smoothed one slender hand over her silver hair. "Yes, obviously. You're almost completely hopeless. But I'm an excellent coach, so we'll soldier on. Seduction, my dear, is the name of this game. Looking the way you do, all luscious and curvy, with that tanned skin on display, there's no way he can resist you if you ramp it up a bit."

Sophie was now blushing from head to toe.

"You can't be afraid to touch him, flirt with him. Use your instincts."

"What's the third thing?" Sophie asked.

"If he still won't give in and beg you to marry him, you're going to have to leave. But that's only if he's not yet convinced that he deserves you. For the truly fearful, sometimes the only thing that works is their worst fear actually happening. You'll have to force him to chase after you." She paused to take a breath. "Don't worry, this is all going to work out in the end."

"How do you know?"

"Because you and Nico are just like my Paul and me. He was a hard case too, but I won him over eventually. We had forty-five terrific years together. And guess what? I was only twenty years old when I met him."

"How old was he?"

"Thirty-two."

"Just like us," Sophie said.

"That's right. So you leave it to me."

"I'm at your mercy." Impulsively she jumped up from her chair and gave Mrs. Coventry a hug.

"If we're already at the hugging stage, you'd best call me Judi."

Sophie smiled as she picked up both their bowls to take to the sink. "Judi, I feel like making some spaghetti sauce. If I'm going to seduce him, I need some carbs."

11

Nico

NICO JERKED AWAKE. Disoriented, he struggled to sit upright as the events from the night before drizzled into his mind. Sophie in tears. Fire. Sophie in his bed. He groaned as he set his feet on the floor and rubbed his eyes. Every muscle in his body ached. What time was it? How long had he slept?

Bright sunlight peeked through the gaps in the drawn shades. He looked at his watch. Just before noon. Jen was no longer at his feet. She wasn't in her doggy bed, either. He slowly rose to his feet and peeked through the open door of his bedroom. No Sophie. She must have taken Jen out and probably fed her. Where were they now? She couldn't have gone far without a car. Without the two of them, the apartment seemed abandoned and lonely.

Even one night with her here made him wish for more.

He was in so much trouble.

Nico used the bathroom, then brushed his teeth. He showered, hoping it would clear the fuzziness from his brain. The hot water did its job. As he dried off and dressed in shorts and a T-shirt, he felt somewhat restored.

Mrs. Coventry was probably worried about him. He never slept late. Would she have heard about the fire? He hadn't been up to make her breakfast. She might have forgotten to eat. Maybe Jen and Sophie had gone over for a visit? That would explain their absence. Jen often overstayed her welcome at the big house. Last week she'd decided it was a fine idea to take a swim in Mrs. Coventry's pristine pool.

He crossed the driveway to the big house. Jen's ball lay on the top step. Without knocking, he let himself inside, then paused in the foyer. The rich scent of coffee filled the space. Two soft, feminine voices were coming from the kitchen. The women were chatting away like old friends.

He walked down the hallway to the kitchen. Mrs. Coventry and Jen were seated side by side at the large kitchen island. Jen wore a red-and-white bandanna around her neck as if she were waiting for a steak dinner. Where had that come from?

Sophie was at the stove, stirring something that smelled of fresh tomatoes, basil, and garlic. She wore one of his sweatshirts and a pair of boxer shorts. He shuddered to think of her going through his drawers, then went hot remembering the large box of condoms he kept in the same drawer. Before he could look away, he noticed her nipples pressed against the fabric of the sweatshirt. Having Sophie around reminded him of being thirteen. An unwanted and spontaneous erection was a constant possibility.

He stopped in the doorway, surprised at the rapport between the two women. Mrs. Coventry kept most people at a distance. The woman who'd cleaned the house every other day for two decades was tolerated but kept at a distance. Mrs.

Coventry was a slow burner. Apparently, twenty years wasn't enough time in which to grow fond of a person.

Nico had no idea why she'd taken to him almost immediately. Like her, this was a mystery. When he'd answered the Craigslist ad for the bungalow in exchange for gardening, he'd expected to find a sweet, dithering old lady who smelled of lavender and cookies who dressed in polyester pants and bedazzled sweatshirts. The house, he assumed, would be outdated with cobwebs in the corners and maybe some hideous red carpet. However, the reality was quite different. Mrs. Coventry was more salty than sweet, and the closest she came to dithering was the rare occasion when she couldn't finish the *New York Times* crossword puzzle. She smelled of expensive French perfume and wore Chanel suits or expensive leisure outfits even though she rarely left the house. Her hair was cut into such a precise inverted bob that he suspected the ends could cut through skin if one came too close.

The house was a beauty. No cobwebs, only polish.

He stepped all the way into the kitchen.

"Oh, there you are," Sophie said. "We thought you might sleep all day."

Jen barked a hello and jumped off her stool to come greet him. He knelt to pet her and scratch under her chin. After a kiss on his hand, Jen ambled off to a spot of sun on the floor near the French doors and plopped over as if suddenly exhausted.

"We played a lot of ball," Sophie said. "She's tired."

"And chased a squirrel out by the pool," Mrs. Coventry said.

"A very naughty squirrel who ran up a tree and teased her incessantly," Sophie said. "We had to bring her inside and give her a treat to distract her from her new nemesis."

"Where'd the bandanna come from?" he asked.

"Judi found that in Paul's old things," Sophie said. "So after Jen's bath, I put it on her."

"She had a bath?" Had he slept a full two days?

"I worked at a grooming shop one summer," Sophie said. "Didn't I tell you that?"

"No, I don't recall that," he said. Was there anything this girl couldn't do?

Mrs. Coventry beamed at him. "Now she's making her homemade spaghetti sauce."

"It smells delicious," he said as he walked around the island to the cooktop where a red sauce simmered in a large pot. His stomach growled. "When's lunch?"

Sophie looked up at him. "This is for dinner, but I could make you something else."

Were they all having dinner together? "No, I'll just get some granola."

"Do you want me to make you a bowl of granola?" Sophie asked him from the refrigerator.

"Yes, please. But no honey. The granola's sweet enough."

Mrs. Coventry rolled her eyes.

"Do we have any berries?" Sophie asked.

"Nico says they're too expensive."

"You do?" Sophie asked with a note of horror in her voice. As if the lack of berries were a travesty of the deepest kind.

"Only because a certain someone won't eat them and they go bad," Nico said.

Mrs. Coventry shrugged both shoulders. "This happened one time, and he's punishing me forever."

"I'll get you some berries today." Sophie smiled, then scooped some granola from the tin on the counter into a bowl.

"Thank you, dear. That's so kind," Mrs. Coventry said.

"I'm starting to rethink inviting you here," he said to Sophie.

"Sophie's been telling me all about your heroic act last night." Mrs. Coventry's cheeks were pink, and her eyes sparkled. Sophie had her under the Sophie spell. No one was safe with the sunshine girl around.

"It was scary as hell," Nico said. Not wanting to talk or think about the fire, he changed the subject. Curious to know how long it had taken Sophie to charm Mrs. Coventry, he asked, "What time did you get up, Soph?"

"About nine. Jen woke me with a wet nose on my arm. She wanted to go out. I didn't want to wake you. You were sleeping so peacefully, and we'd had such a long night."

Hopefully he hadn't been snoring. Or worse, drooling.

Sophie turned to Mrs. Coventry. "I'm a light sleeper. Any little noise wakes me."

"I'm the same way," Mrs. Coventry said. "My late husband was the most exquisite sleeper. The man hardly moved and never made a sound. Often, I'd put my ear to his chest just to make sure his heart was still beating."

Sophie stirred the sauce and sighed. "That's kind of romantic."

"Sophie let me have honey on my rabbit food," Mrs. Coventry said as she folded her arms over her chest.

"Did she now?" He looked from one of them to the other, noting their shared smile. Why did he have this sense that the two of them were conspiring against him? "I'll have to get up earlier tomorrow."

"Honey never hurt anyone." Sophie shook the wooden spoon at him.

"She's delightful, Nico. Why haven't you brought her over more often?" Mrs. Coventry squinted at him with an accusatory glint in her eyes.

"I didn't think you liked visitors." Nico moved across the room to the espresso machine. He needed coffee desperately if he were to keep up with these two.

Mrs. Coventry clutched the gold chain around her neck and looked more affronted than even a moment ago. "Whatever would give you that idea? I love people."

"You do?" He raised one eyebrow as he pushed the button

for a double espresso. The loud grinding of the beans covered his laugh. Once the grounds were ready, he watched as the espresso dripped into the cup.

Mrs. Coventry lifted her chin. "Just because I don't have an endless number of people pretending to be my friends and taking advantage of my good nature like some older affluent women do does not mean I don't like people. I'm particular about who I allow into my home. Do you know how many of my friends have been bilked out of money by relatives and charlatans?"

"I don't think you're in danger of that," Nico said.

"Not with Nico here to protect you," Sophie said, flashing her guileless smile at him.

"Mrs. Coventry doesn't need protection," he said.

"Quite right," Mrs. Coventry said. "But I do like having you here. I've been lonely since I lost my husband. Sometimes a person doesn't seem to know they're lonely until just the right company comes along."

"Like a space you didn't know needed filling." Sophie's voice turned husky as she stirred her pot of sauce. "Until you meet the person who fills it just right."

Nico avoided looking at her, afraid of what he would see in her eyes. She believed they could fill each other's hollow spaces. For how long? That was always the question he returned to. How long until she left him with gaps so wide they destroyed him?

"That's how it was with my husband and me," Mrs. Coventry said. "We met and filled each other's emptiness."

Nico crossed over to the island and sat on one of the stools, unsure what to say to either of the women he'd come to love more than he should.

"I was like you, Nico," Mrs. Coventry said. "My family never provided the love and support I needed, so I found it with Paul instead."

"Do you have children?" Sophie asked Mrs. Coventry.

He sneaked a look at Mrs. Coventry, curious to see how she would answer. She'd told him once before that they'd tried to have a child but without success.

"No, we couldn't," Mrs. Coventry said. "And I didn't have a sister-in-law around to carry one for me."

Sophie's bottom lip started to quiver. "I wish I'd been there. I'd have had one for you."

To his surprise, Mrs. Coventry laughed. "Dear, you can't have a baby for everyone who wants one or there won't be anything left of you."

"Do you think that's true?" Sophie brows knit as if the idea deeply disturbed her. "Do we have a limited supply of generosity?"

"Some of us," Nico said under his breath. "Not you."

"Even people like Sophie have to look after themselves first in order to show up for other people," Mrs. Coventry said. "Women don't seem to know this innately. We only learn this truth after depleting ourselves until there's nothing left to give to anyone, including ourselves."

He studied Sophie from across the kitchen island, noting the twitch at the side of her mouth.

"You might be right," Sophie said. "But I can't help but think I'll probably never do something so meaningful ever again. Which is weird, right? I'm already done at twenty-two."

"Dear, don't be ridiculous," Mrs. Coventry said. "You have your whole life out there waiting for you. What you did for your brother was a wonderful gift, but it's not the first or the last. I've come to realize the biggest impact on the world comes from the sum of small acts of kindness or compassion made daily."

"I agree," Nico said.

"Well, for the record, I surely hope my life will mean something. Zane seems to think I should be flitting around getting drunk and laughing at memes on my phone."

"Oh, dear God, no," Mrs. Coventry said. "That's a deplorable way to live one's life. I don't care how young or old they are."

The women looked at each other and laughed.

The sound of Sophie's sweet giggle warmed him as if the sun had suddenly appeared from behind a dark cloud. Nothing, not even a fire in the dead of night, could keep the sun from rising.

12

S ophie

A FEW HOURS LATER, Sophie's legs trembled as she stood on the sidewalk in front of the smoldering mass that had been her home and business. She'd dressed in the clothes she'd borrowed from Autumn the night before. Later, she would stop by the clothing store and buy a few items, but first she wanted to see what remained. As Zane had said earlier, there wasn't much recognizable other than the metal parts of some of the kitchen. The singed leaves of the oak rustled above her heads, a reminder of how close she and Nico had come to death.

They'd blocked off the sidewalk in front of The Oar with crime tape. Clumps of people lingered just outside the boundaries, staring and talking. Sophie wanted to push them all away. This was not some spectacle to gawk at. This was her life.

Next to her, Nico touched the back of her hand with his. "I

know you wanted to see it, but let's go. I'll walk you to your car around back."

"Not yet." The hollow feeling in her stomach expanded. "I just realized something. What if the fire had spread? The whole town could've burned down." On the east side of her building was a surf shop, which had remained untouched, thanks to the precautions of the firefighters. A small park separated The Oar and the bookstore.

"But it didn't," Nico said.

"It didn't." She repeated the words, hoping they would sink into her consciousness. "This is the worst of it, right here."

"That's right."

"What are they all doing here?" she asked, gesturing toward the crowd.

"Curious, that's all." He looked down at her, concern in his eyes. "You want me to get rid of them?"

"I know you can't, but thanks for offering."

He put his hands on her shoulders. "Soph, what can I do to help you through this?"

"Nothing. I'm fine." She spoke stoutly as if she weren't about to cry. "I need some clothes and a phone. And a place to live for the next twelve months. That's all."

He took his hands from her shoulders. "Take this one day at a time. Today, buy the essentials and then come back up to the house. We'll have a nice Chianti with your red sauce."

She nodded, resisting the urge to throw her arms around his neck and cry into his shoulder. She would see him later. Anything seemed bearable with Nico there at the end of the day. "Chianti and red sauce never let you down."

"True." The corners of his eyes crinkled into fine lines as he smiled. She loved his face. God, she loved him.

"Zane wants to sell the lot," she said.

"You're kidding," Nico asked.

"He said he'll give me his half if I want but that he can't do it without his dad."

Nico turned slightly to face the wreckage, his features impassive.

"Maybe he's right," she said. "Seeing it like this makes me wonder if it's too much to do alone. Without him, I'll be tied to this place even more than I already am."

"You don't have to decide today," he said. "Give it some time. Any time I've rushed into a decision while in crisis, I've regretted it. Right now, you need to get a phone and some clothes."

She nodded. Later she would ask him what decisions he regretted. She hoped it wasn't coming to Cliffside Bay. "And a razor," she said lightly.

"Yes, that too."

She touched her fingertips against his bare forearm. "Will it bother you if I stay with Judi? I don't want to go out to the Mullens'."

He shook his head, chuckling. "How are you already on a first-name basis with her?"

"She likes me. What can I say?"

He turned toward her. "Of course I'm fine if you stay with her. I want you to do whatever makes this easier for you. I'm here for you too. Whatever you need."

Her eyes stung. "Don't say nice things or I'll cry."

"All right then. You and your hairy legs should get on your way."

She smiled as she took in a deep, ragged breath. "I can't look at this any longer. Not until it's cleared away."

"That's fair." He tweaked her chin. "Now go do your errands and meet me back at the house. I'll decant the wine."

She glanced back at the rubble. "The wine. All my wine. Just gone."

"We'll get more." Just as he turned to go, one of the firefighters approached, carrying a metal box. It took Sophie a second to realize it was her fireproof safe where she kept her passport and other important papers.

"Hey, Sophie," the fireman said. "We found this. Came through just fine. I cleaned it up for you." The fireman introduced himself as Jad Stokes as he handed it over to her. "We talked last night. But you were kind of out of it, so you may not remember."

"I'm sorry, I don't." She wrapped both arms around the safe. Although small, the metal box was heavy.

"Here, let me take it," Nico said.

She handed it over to him, then turned back to see Jad still standing there.

"You were in shock. It happens." Jad was the same height as Sophie, which made it easy to look directly into his eyes. They were a disquieting light color between blue and green. "But I certainly remember you. I'm sorry we had to meet under these conditions. I'd much rather be ordering a beer from you at the bar and slipping you my number on a napkin."

Was Hot Fireman flirting with her in front of the embers of her business and home? Wasn't there some kind of protocol against that? "It'll be a while before you can do that."

"Ordering a beer or slipping you my number?" Jad asked.

Sophie rocked on her heels and gave him a polite smile to hide her confusion. "We won't be open for a few months, and my phone burned up in the fire."

Jad gestured in the general direction of the phone store. "I hear you can just walk right in and get a new one."

"I'll look into that," she said.

"Don't you have fire stuff to take care of, Jad?" Nico's voice had lowered in pitch. He sounded a bit like a growling dog.

Jad either didn't notice or didn't care because he pulled a business card from the front pocket of his shirt. "I've had the same number for ten years, and my phone's working just fine. When you get a phone, give me a call."

"I'm unlikely to call," she said as she took the card.

"Why's that?" Jad tilted his head and grinned. "I promise to distract you from your troubles." He winked. She suspected Jad wasn't often turned down by women. Who wouldn't want to jump right into those muscular arms? She knew the answer. A woman in love with someone else.

"She's not interested, that's why." Nico's forceful tone caused her to jump. He stepped closer to her.

"Are you her spokesman?" Jad turned toward him, and the men stared at each other like two lions ready to fight for the last lioness on earth.

"She's just lost her business and home," Nico said. "Have a little sensitivity."

Jad put up his hands. "Whoa, man. You're taking this a bit far. I was just asking Sophie if she'd like to go out sometime. Unless you're with her, I'm not sure what business it is of yours."

Hot Fireman guy had made Nico jealous. She may not know much about men, but she knew a jealous one when she saw him. It was about time. Most women would flirt right back, but she wasn't that type of girl. Nothing good could come from playing with a man's heart. Jad was probably a nice man and didn't deserve to be used as a device in the seduction of Nico Bentley. Judi's words came back to her. She had to prove to Nico that her love was unconditional and that he could trust her never to hurt him. Actions, she'd said.

"Jad, it's sweet of you to ask me out," she said. "But I'm in love with someone else."

Jad turned his full attention back to her. "I didn't realize you were with someone. My bad."

"I'm not with him, but I hope to be soon," she said.

"Well, you have my card in case you change your mind," Jad said.

"Have it right here." She lifted her hand to show him.

"Awesome. Got to run now. Duty calls." He winked again as he walked away. "Talk to you soon, Sophie."

"We should go too," she said.

"Can you believe that guy?" Nico had crammed his hands into the pockets of his jeans.

"He's harmless," she said.

"He's too short for you."

"I think he's exactly my height."

"You'd never be able to wear heels," he said.

"Guys hit on me all the time. It's not a big deal."

"All the time? What does that mean?" Nico's voice seemed to have taken on a permanent growl.

She bit the inside of her lip to keep from smiling. "Happens a lot when you're a bartender."

"For God's sake. Men are pigs."

"Let's go to my car. I have a key hidden in one of those magnetic lock boxes."

"How come you have one of those?" Nico asked, sound surprised.

"My dad insisted."

"I wish I'd thought to get your keys and purse."

"Nico, you save my life and you went back for the journal. I don't think you need to feel bad about anything else."

"Fine then." Nico gently tugged her by the arm. "Come on. I'll walk you to your car before another fireman accosts you."

"He was just being friendly. Anyway, I told him I love you, so there's nothing for you to be jealous about." She kept her voice light as she followed him, enjoying the view of his trim backside in those jeans.

"I'm not jealous," he said.

They had to walk through the park to circle around to the

back lot of The Oar where her car and the others had managed to escape harm.

When they reached her car, he crossed his arms over his chest and glowered at her.

"What's the matter?" she asked as she knelt down to retrieve the lock box and used her secret code, Nico's birthday, to open it.

"You can't do that—tell people you love me."

"Why not? It's the truth."

"Because, Soph, people just don't do that when the other person doesn't..." He trailed off, then kicked a pebble with the tip of his shoe.

"When the other person doesn't love you. Is that what you were going to say?" she asked.

"Yes." He leaned against her car and looked up at the sky.

"If a man asks me out, it's not fair to accept when I know I'm only interested in one man. Really, your feelings for me don't factor into the equation."

"I'm such a jerk. I'm sorry I'm acting like a jealous boyfriend. I want you to be happy. I shouldn't hold you back."

She raised one eyebrow and poked him in the chest with her index finger. "Given your jealous behavior just now, it seems like you want me for yourself."

He caught her hand in his. "Dammit, this is not a joke."

"I know it's not. I'm about as vulnerable as a person can get. I've opened my heart and soul to you."

He let go of her hand slouched against her car. "You should go out with the obnoxious, overly confident fireman."

"He's too short for me."

"He's exactly your height," he said.

"No, I'll keep waiting for you to come to your senses, if it's all the same to you." Sophie patted the top of her sporty compact SUV. "In the meantime, I still have Mildred."

"And your surfboard," Nico said, pointing at the back.

"Wait, what? I forgot it was in there." She let out a happy yelp and threw her arms around his neck. "My board. I have my board." His arms seemed to instinctively wrap around her waist. He smelled woodsy and spicy. "You smell so good." She looked up to meet his eyes, but his gaze appeared fixed on her mouth. "What is it?" she whispered, knowing full well exactly what *it* was. He wanted to kiss her.

She resisted the urge to lick her upper lip like an ingenue in a bad movie. Her heart beat faster as he lowered his head. His mouth hovered just over hers. She held her breath as her heart raced. Would he kiss her? *Please, please kiss me*, she begged silently.

"Soph, you're killing me here." He still hovered over her mouth, close enough she could smell his minty breath. "How can you love me when I'm such an idiot?"

"I'll always love you," she whispered. "Nothing will ever change that. Even if you don't want me, I'll still love you."

"You're driving me crazy." He turned them so she was against the car and pressed against her. "Absolutely insane. Do you remember what you proposed last night while all loopy?"

"I remember."

"The sight of you in my bed is all I can think about. No man should be tested this way."

"I know the feeling." Boldly, remembering that seduction was key, she slipped her fingers under the waistline of his pants and pulled him closer. "The offer still holds. We can start tonight."

He groaned and spoke into her hair. "You were on drugs. You didn't mean it."

"Hell yes, I meant it." She moved her mouth closer to his ear. Seduction. What would tempt him to take this further? Judi had said to follow her instincts. Suddenly she knew. She nipped at his earlobe with just her lips and spoke softly. "What do you want to do to me?"

He made a sound between a groan and a growl. "Every damn thing. Again and again."

She pressed her mouth against the muscle of his neck and licked him. He tasted of salt. She wanted more. She wanted to taste every inch of him.

He lifted her chin with one finger and stared into her eyes. "What are you doing, Soph?"

"I'm taking what belongs to me."

He closed his eyes as if he were in pain and murmured, "I tried. I really tried to stay away from you." His hands moved from around her waist to her hair. "I want to feel this hair all over me when I'm inside you." Then he lowered his mouth and kissed her. She kissed him right back. They kissed hard, tongues clashing. Her entire body was on fire. She craved more and more of him. This was what it was like to be with a man she loved—this mixture of pleasure and need for release.

He moved from her mouth to drop his face into her shoulder. "Why do you have to feel so good? So right?"

"You know why."

Nico stumbled backward as if she'd kicked him in the shins and covered his face with his hands. "I'm in so much trouble here." He looked over at her, his eyes blazing. "What have you done to me?"

"You can run, but this thing between us isn't going away."

He simply nodded and turned and walked away. She leaned against the side of her car for support. With her arms folded around her waist, she watched him walk across the parking lot. Even his gait was etched into her consciousness. From behind, she would know it was him in a lineup of ten men of the exact same height and build by his long, loose-limbed stride. Yes, everything in her life was in turmoil, but she was alive. She'd survived. He'd survived. They could light up the night in a whole different way.

* * *

SOPHIE SPENT several hours running errands. She bought a new cell phone, stopped in one of two clothing stores to purchase a few pairs of shorts, tank tops, sandals, and a few other essentials. Before she left the store, she changed out of Autumn's clothes and into one of the new outfits. Wearing clothes that fit cheered her up considerably. The local drugstore had makeup and other toiletries. After she had all she needed for now, she drove up to Zane and Honor's.

As she exited her SUV, seven-year-old Jubie came running out of the front door and threw herself into her arms. "Aunt Sophie, is it true? Is The Oar all burned up?"

She lifted Jubie off the ground and held her tightly for a moment, breathing in the child's sweet-smelling hair and gathering strength from her warm body. "I'm afraid so." She set her niece back on her feet.

"Were you scared?" Jubie's forehead crinkled as she looked up at her.

"Very much."

"I'm scared just thinking about it," Jubie said. "But Dad said it won't happen here at our house because we don't have french-frying things."

"That's right. There's nothing to worry over," Sophie said as they started toward the door.

"We made cookies to cheer you up."

They held hands as they crossed the driveway and went into the house, which smelled of cinnamon and butter. "Snickerdoodles?"

"Your favorite, right?" Jubie asked.

"For sure."

The front room of the house perched on the side of the hill and looked out to the ocean. Honor had it decorated in the modern farmhouse style with cozy furniture and soft blues and creams.

They found both Zane and Honor in the kitchen. Zane was on his phone, pacing between the picture window and the table.

Honor was hunched over her phone typing furiously under a curtain of long blond hair. "Mama, Aunt Sophie's here," Jubie said.

Honor dropped her phone on the countertop and pulled Sophie into a quick embrace. "I'm so sorry." Their height difference always made hugs awkward as Honor inevitably landed right at Sophie's breasts. Her sister-in-law was just over five feet tall with a curvy hourglass figure, which she showed off today in a short cotton skirt and peasant blouse.

Honor's eyes were glassy. "When I think what could've happened..."

"I know. But it didn't."

From the corner of the kitchen, Sebastian bounced in his activity center where he was safely trapped with his fat legs dangling from the seat. He yelled out when he spotted Sophie. She went over to him and lifted him out of his bouncy seat and kissed him on his pink cheek. "How's my nephew today?"

He grinned and shouted, "Hi." His aquamarine eyes stared into hers.

"Hello, love." Sophie kissed the top of his head. His white-blond hair curled around his delicious ears. Honor hadn't yet given him a haircut, not wanting to cut off his curls.

"He's on with the insurance people." Honor gestured toward Zane, who had stopped pacing and was simply listening to whomever was on the other line. "Let's talk in the living room."

Still holding Sebastian, Sophie followed Jubie into the other room. Sebastian wriggled when he saw one of the three cats napping in a sunny spot. "Cat," he shouted, and pointed a chubby finger.

"Sebbie, remember, be gentle with the kitty," Honor said.

"Cat," he shouted again.

Sophie set him down and he toddled toward the cat, falling down twice before he reached his destination. The moment he got there, the orange-and-white cat woke and made a hasty retreat after protesting with a grouchy meow.

"Cat," Sebastian said, no longer shouting with glee. His bottom lip trembled. "Cat."

"Come on, Sebbie," Jubie said in an obvious ploy to keep him from crying. "Let's play with your trucks."

"Tuck." All memory of the cat appeared to vanish as he beamed up at his sister. Jubie shot Sophie a pious, long-suffering look as she led her baby brother over to the corner where Honor kept some of his toys in a basket.

The two women looked at each other and settled onto the couch. "How are you holding up?" Honor asked.

"I'm all right."

"Zane told me about your talk this morning," Honor said.

"Were you surprised he wanted to sell the lot?"

"I was. Shocked is more like it." Honor spoke softly, obviously aware her husband was in the other room. "He's not thinking straight."

"Right?"

"Losing it is like losing Hugh all over again," Honor said.

"We can rebuild." How many times would she say that in the months to come?

"Yes, we can. If that's what you want." Honor gazed at her with those big brown eyes that had transfixed her brother's heart. Given the kindness and intelligence that shone from them, no one would guess that Honor had been abandoned by her mother and in and out of foster homes most of her life. Yet here she was, a wonderful mother, a loving wife, and a friend to so many, not to mention an incredibly successful business-woman. She was the embodiment of second chances and rebuilding. If Honor could come through all that, surely they could restore The Oar.

"Zane just needs a little time. This was such a shock and blow to him." Honor lowered her voice. "It's bringing back so many feelings about his dad."

"I understand," Sophie said.

"I guarantee you by the time we're ready to rebuild, he will be too."

"I hope so. One of the reasons I've loved my job is working with Zane. It's a family business."

"He'll change his mind," Honor said.

"I'm just a little sick of men telling me what they think is best for me."

Honor shook her head and laughed. "Yeah, he's really all over this big brother thing, isn't he?"

"It's sweet. But annoying."

"Zane may see him in a whole new light now that he risked his life to save you from a burning building," Honor said.

"I'm not sure it matters. Nico's the only one who can decide if he wants to be with me."

Honor patted her knee. "Don't give up. You know I had a giant crush on Zane for years before he noticed me. Sometimes men just take a while to get a clue."

The doorbell rang. "Who could that be?" Honor asked as she rose up from the couch.

Sophie stood, watching as Honor opened the door to a man dressed in a blue suit. He flashed his badge. "I'm Detective Solomon. I'm working on the arson case. I'd like a word with your husband."

"Come in," Honor said, stepping back from the doorway. "My husband's on the phone with the insurance people, but I believe he's wrapping up. Can I get you a cup of coffee?"

"No, thank you. I won't be staying long," Solomon said.

Sophie introduced herself to the detective and led him over to one of the armchairs adjacent to the couch. "I'm Zane's sister and business partner."

"Excellent." Solomon was a slight man with small, keen eyes. His suit was wrinkled, and he looked like he could use a good shave and a long nap. "I was hoping to talk to you both at the same time."

"Zane wasn't there, and I was upstairs," she said. "I don't know how much help we can be."

"I understand. It's more that I've information to share with you. The questions I have for your brother won't be about the fire but about his connections with the..." Solomon took a small pad from the breast of his jacket and flipped through the pages. "What is it they call themselves? The Dogs?"

"His group of friends, yes."

Before she could ask a follow-up question, Zane and Honor came into the room. After introductions, Zane sat next to Sophie on the couch while Honor picked up a suddenly fussy Sebastian and settled into a chair.

Solomon glanced at Jubie, who'd come to stand by her mother. "Probably not a discussion for young ears," he said to Zane.

"Sweetie, can you go upstairs to your room for a minute?" Zane asked Jubie.

She looked as if she wanted to argue but knew better. Without a word, she trudged across the room to the stairway that led upstairs.

The sound of her footsteps up the stairs seemed to reassure the detective it was safe to begin. "I'll cut to the chase. The type of pipe bomb used in this fire was similar to the one that started a fire in an apartment complex in Stoweaway last month. We're not sure what the connection is or if the arson targeted these specifically. Most likely, they're random, but I'm looking for anything that could tie them together."

Zane leaned forward and covered both knees with his hands. "Did you say apartment complex?"

"I did. Why?" Solomon asked.

"We know someone who had an apartment in a complex that burned," Zane said. "In Stoweaway. Is it the same building?"

"There's only been one," Solomon said. "What's the name of the person you know?"

"Valerie Hickman," Zane said.

Solomon flipped through his notebook. "Yep, there she is. Apartment 2B. How do you know her?"

"Her son Kyle is one of my best friends," Zane said.

The detective's eyes narrowed to slits. "Tell me more."

"We've known each other since college," Zane said. "We're close with three other guys, too. We call ourselves the Dogs. Our lives are very intertwined."

Sophie's pulse sped as she pressed her damp palms together. Was this a repeat of the crazed man who'd tried to harm Autumn, Violet, and Pepper because of a vendetta toward Kyle? "Detective, is it possible the arsonist was targeting relatives of the Dogs? Kyle's mother? Me?"

"But why?" Solomon asked. "Is there a common enemy among you?"

"There was," Zane said. "But he was killed last month."

"This has happened to us before," Honor said casually, as if it were a completely normal explanation.

"And by 'us' you mean these Dogs?" Solomon drew out the sentence by putting space between each word. God only knew what he must think of them right now.

"And the Wolves," Sophie had to add, for accuracy. "The friend groups are kind of connected now. What with Trey decorating everyone's house and Rafael having protected the Mullens for so long and me having Zane and Honor's baby."

"Everything kind of merged," Honor said. "Like they do sometimes."

"Um, okay now." Solomon's eyebrows rose, bringing the skin of his forehead to the smooth pink of his balding scalp. "You two have lost me."

"Should I explain it to him or you?" Honor asked Zane.

Zane nodded. "I probably should. I've been here since the beginning of the Dogs."

"Agreed," Honor said.

"The whole thing started with a mentally disturbed nanny," Zane said. "And ended with her father's death after he kidnapped Violet, Autumn, and Pepper."

"Rafael's a sharpshooter," Sophie said. "Thank goodness."

"You better start at the beginning," Solomon said. "And I will take that cup of coffee."

* * *

AFTER HUGGING the kids and Honor one more time, she headed out to the car. The skinny road down the hill toward town was quiet on a Sunday. In just a few minutes she was in front of the fire site again. If she could drive with her eyes closed, she would. She gritted her teeth and headed out of town.

As she drove up the country road to Maggie's house, she thought about Honor's advice. Perhaps she was correct. There was nothing keeping her here. She could easily change her ticket for Paris. Staying here, hoping Nico would change his mind, was futile. The destruction would be hauled away by the time she got back. She would only see it in her dreams from then on.

When she pulled up to Maggie's house, her half sister came running out to hug her. Despite Maggie's baby bump coming

between them, her grip was so tight Sophie had trouble breathing. For such a slight person, her sister was strong from years of
dancing. When she withdrew, Maggie continued to stare at her
and shake her head back and forth as if she couldn't believe
Sophie was standing there. "Thank the good Lord for Nico
Bentley," Maggie said finally.

"True enough." Sophie smiled and tugged on a clump of
Maggie's copper-colored hair. "Now stop that. I'm fine. How are
you feeling?"

Maggie patted her slightly rounded stomach. "Much better.
Now that I'm in the second trimester the nausea is gone and I'm
not as tired."

"I can't wait to meet him or her," she said.

Maggie smiled. "The good doctor is hoping for a boy. Not
that he'd admit it."

"A boy would be nice," Sophie said.

"Do you want to stay with us?" Maggie asked as they
entered the house. "Until you figure out a new place to rent?"

It was a logical place to stay. They had room, but having
only recently gotten rid of houseguests, Sophie had a feeling
Maggie and Jackson were looking forward to being alone with
Lily and nesting before the new baby came.

"No, thanks, though," she said in response to Maggie's offer.
"Mrs. Coventry's offered up one of her guest rooms."

Maggie led her down the hallway to the kitchen. The
doors to the patio were open, bringing the scent of roses from
the garden. Lily was down for her nap, so they headed outside
to the pool to sit under the shade of an umbrella. Maggie
never sat directly in the sun. She was fair with about a million
freckles. The temperature hovered in the middle seventies
with a slight breeze that ruffled the fabric of the umbrella.
Maggie's guitar and sheet music were spread over her patio
table.

"Were you working?" Sophie asked.

"I had an idea for a new song and wanted to jot down a few things while Lily's napping."

Growing up, seeing a guitar had been a normal occurrence in Sophie's home. All through her childhood, musicians were in and out of the house. Often, in the middle of the night she'd wake to the sound of music from below.

When her father had heard Maggie sing at The Oar one night, he'd offered her a recording deal. The Oar. So many relationships in this town started with an encounter at The Oar. "Dad first heard you sing at The Oar. It's so hard to believe it's gone."

"It's true," Maggie said. "As long as I've been alive, The Oar has been the center of everything."

"I'm so proud and honored to run the place. Zane was so generous to offer it to me."

"How is he?" Maggie asked. "Jackson left him a message this morning, but we haven't heard from him."

"Not good. He suggested we sell the lot."

"What?" Maggie stared at her as if she hadn't heard her correctly. "Sell the lot? As in, not reopen?"

"That's right. He thinks it's sucking the life out of me and that I work too hard for a business that brings in too little cash. Like Hugh did all his life."

Maggie frowned. "That place meant everything to him and Hugh."

"Honor thinks he's in shock and that it's bringing his grief about Hugh back full force."

"Poor Zane. Losing Hugh was so hard for him." Maggie touched her hand. "What about you? Do you want the place to reopen? Or do you have another dream?"

"No, The Oar *is* my dream." She scrunched her shoulders together as a wave of sadness swept over her. Her eyes stung with the effort not to cry. No, she'd cried enough. "All I want is to have it back to the way it was at this time yesterday."

"Then we'll get it back for you." Her sister's sympathetic face was enough to bring the unwanted tears to her eyes.

"If we do, Zane wants out."

"I can't believe it," Maggie said. "He's spent his life in that place."

"Maybe that's the problem."

"If he wants out, then you'll just carry on without him," Maggie said. "Do you need money?"

"No, I'm fine. I have a lot in savings. My expenses are low."

"Because you do nothing but work all the time."

"I guess," she mumbled, thinking how often she'd heard that lately. Was it that obvious she had no life outside of The Oar? "But what about our employees? What are they supposed to do?"

"Maybe Zane can use them at the brewery? Or Kyle? You know he'd do anything for you guys. Give him a call. His manager at the lodge will find places for them for a few months."

"That's a good idea."

Maggie narrowed her eyes, as if studying Sophie for signs of stress. "Can I ask you something?"

Sophie nodded.

"Since you had Sebastian, you've been putting in really long hours at The Oar and down at the wine room."

"That's not a question," Sophie said, smiling.

"I'm wondering if it's been a way to distract yourself from your feelings about the baby. I know you had a rough time after he was born."

"It has nothing to do with that. I like working. The bar makes me feel part of something."

"You're sure Zane isn't right? Maybe the bar is too much responsibility for you?"

Sophie tilted her head. "No, absolutely not. I'm at my best

there. I don't get why everyone's stuck on the number. I'm a person, not an age."

"By everyone, do you mean Nico?"

"Yeah."

Anger sparked in Maggie's eyes. It was like watching a green lake with exploding fireworks above it, reflecting off the glassy surface. "If that man's too stupid to admit his feelings to the woman he risked his life for, then you need to walk away."

Sophie hesitated before asking the question. "Do you believe in soul mates?"

Maggie looked upward. "You know I do."

"Do you think they ever miss each other somehow?"

Maggie picked up her guitar and strummed a chord. "No. It may take a while for them to find their way to each other—or like Jackson and me, back to each other. But eventually they will."

Eventually. How long was eventually for her and Nico?

13

Nico

Two hours after he practically had sex with Sophie in a public parking lot, Nico sat in Autumn and Trey's living room. Their cottage was feet from the boardwalk and sandy beach. The door to the patio was open, letting in the comforting sound of waves crashing to shore and an occasional seagull's cry.

Trey handed him a glass of iced tea, then took the chair across from him. "So, let me get this straight. You acted like a jealous idiot and then you kissed her?"

"That's about right, yeah." He stared into his drink, watching the ice become porous. Like his heart. Full of holes.

"Is the age difference really that big a deal?"

He looked up to find Trey watching him intently, as if he were a wounded animal in need of help. "She was in high school like four years ago."

"Dude, she is twenty-two with a college degree, runs two

businesses, and was a surrogate. I think that qualifies as a fully mature adult. Plus, women are much more mature than we are."

"I was a complete dumb ass at that age. We both were."

Trey's mouth curved into a wry smile. "We really were. When I think of the stupid stuff we did, I'm surprised we're alive."

"By the grace of God," Nico said.

"Just because we were, doesn't mean Sophie is," Trey said. "She has it together."

"Maybe. But how can I be sure? What if there's something I'm not seeing?"

"Like with Addie?" Trey asked.

"Yes. I didn't see that coming." He hadn't seen a lot of things in his life.

"Regardless of your fears, you're in love with her, aren't you?"

Nico glanced up at his friend, then shook the ice around in his glass. Everything in him wanted to deny the truth. Even to Trey, who was like his brother. Most of all, he wanted to lie to himself. He loved Sophie Woods. His feelings were not just lust, although God help him, he wanted to drag her into his bed and touch every inch of her with every inch of him. Still, it was more than that. He loved being with her. She made him remember the possibilities of everything and notice all the simple, magnificent things the world had to offer. But what was she hiding? What was the thing he didn't yet know that would cause her to leave?

"You can talk to me," Trey said. "About anything."

This was Trey. He was the brother he'd wished his real brother had been.

"The truth is, I've never wanted a woman more in my life. Even Addie, who I loved so much, was nothing compared to this thing I have about Sophie. But what happens when Sophie grows up a little and realizes this is just a schoolgirl crush? If she left me, I don't know if I could handle it."

"If it wasn't for the age difference, would you be less afraid of Sophie changing her mind?"

He thought about that for a moment. His mind drifted to Addie. He'd been in such denial. "When she told me she was in love with her best girlfriend, I thought she was kidding around. That's how unbelievable it was to me. If I didn't see that, which in hindsight was about as obvious as my own hand in front of my face, how can I trust myself?" He put his wet glass on a coaster and ran his hands through his hair.

"Man, I get it about being blindsided," Trey said. "I was devastated when I learned about my wife's infidelity. However, Autumn is not like my ex-wife. Just because Addie had a secret doesn't mean Sophie will. From what I can see, she's about as authentic a woman as I've ever met. And dude, she adores you."

"Look at her, though. Do really think she's going to want me long term? She's going to see how all her friends are still out there partying and having fun, and I'm going to seem like a boring old fart."

Trey got up from the couch and wandered over to the window that faced the sea. Since he and Autumn had gotten engaged, Trey was like a new person. The cloud that had followed him around after his divorce seemed to have never been there at all. He looked ten years younger than he had a year ago.

"Do you know how Autumn thought she wasn't pretty enough for me?" Trey asked.

"Sure. Which was crazy. It's the other way around," Nico said.

Trey grinned. "Exactly. How she could think I'm even in *her* league is the true mystery. My point, however, is that she put those limitations up. She believed in this falsehood, which made her incapable of seeing how much I loved her and also doomed us before we even got started."

"Which is what you think I'm doing."

"I do." Trey wandered back to the couch. "You'll never know the depth of her love if you can't take the risk."

"I know that's true. I'm not sure I have it in me."

"Would you rather sit back and watch her fall in love with someone else? What if she comes back from the wedding in France with some guy on her arm?"

His stomach turned at the thought. "That would wreck me."

Trey squinted, watching him. "There's something else, isn't there? Something you haven't told me. Something that shook you beyond just Addie."

"There is." He placed his hands on his knees. "It's about my family. They're not who I thought they were. But I can't talk about it. Not yet. Not even with you."

"Whatever it is has shaken your faith, hasn't it?"

"To the core."

"When you're ready, I'm here."

14

S ophie

WHEN SHE RETURNED to Judi Coventry's house, Nico's car was parked in its usual spot. Sophie gathered her purchases and headed for the main house. Unsure as to whether to just walk in or not, she rang the doorbell. Seconds later, Judi appeared wearing a dark blue maxi dress and pearls.

"Thank goodness it's you, dear. I thought a salesperson had wandered up the hill trying to sell me a vacuum." Sophie sighed with pleasure at the sight of her. She was so glamorous with her slender frame and silver pageboy bob. Sophie could imagine her sitting with Jackie Kennedy having tea at the Biltmore or some such place.

Sophie glanced down at her shorts and tank top, feeling underdressed and sloppy all at once. Her hair was in a messy ponytail, and she hadn't had a chance to put on any of the makeup she'd bought earlier. Somehow, it hadn't even occurred to her.

"I don't think people sell vacuums door-to-door any longer," Sophie said.

"Do come in. There's no need to knock. Consider this your home for the time being." She held out her arms. "Give me a few of those bags. I'll show you to your room, and then we'll come back here and have manhattans before dinner."

She trailed Judi into the house and down a hallway to the guest room. Decorated in the same sparse, clean lines as the rest of the house, the room had its own bathroom and a king-size bed.

"Will this do?" Judi asked.

"Absolutely. I can't thank you enough."

"I'll let you get settled. Take a shower if you'd like before dinner. Nico said he'd be over in a few minutes."

Her stomach turned over, thinking of their interaction that afternoon.

Judi inspected her with those sharp eyes. "What is it?"

"We kissed this afternoon when he took me to my car. It was so hot. Then he tore himself away and said how wrong this was and all the usual stuff and walked away."

Judi played with her pearls around her neck. "He really is a dense one. But not to worry. You played it exactly right. I'm so proud of you."

"You were right about my instincts. It's like my body knew what to do."

"Yes, they always do." She walked over to the closet. "I had some things sent over from Le Chic in your size."

Sophie blinked. "Le Chic? The superexpensive shop up in Stoweaway?"

"That's right. We're taking it up a notch."

"What's wrong with what I'm wearing?" She looked down at her khaki shorts and tank top.

"Nothing, dear. You're adorable, but we need to shake him up a bit." Judi opened the closet. A half dozen dresses were neatly hung in a row. She chose a dark blue in a sparkly material with a scoop neck, and a classic black cocktail, then held them up for Sophie to see. "Which do you like better?"

Sophie stepped closer and fingered the material. The blue was a polyester blend that would cling to every curve. The other had an A-line skirt and fitted bodice with a boatneck collar. "I think the blue one would be best."

"Wonderful. I left you some perfume samples and jewelry in the bathroom. Choose whatever you like. And maybe put your hair up. Show off that young, elegant neck of yours."

"Um, okay."

"Don't hurry, but don't dawdle either. We've work to do."

Judi stopped at the door. "I also took the liberty of ordering you a bikini. Just in case you two want to enjoy the hot tub later."

Before she could answer, Judi was out the door, leaving Sophie standing there with her mouth hanging open. Judi Coventry had game.

* * *

"THIS IS A BEAUTIFUL MANHATTAN," Mrs. Coventry said as she held her tumbler up to the light. "My husband used to make them for us every evening before dinner. I haven't had a decent one since. Nico may make my flowers flourish, but he cannot make a cocktail to save his life. Or mine."

"Zane taught me how to make them, even though they're hardly ever ordered at the bar." She swallowed the lump in her throat. Her bar. Charcoal. Smoldering wood.

"You look stunning," Judi said. "He won't be able to take his eyes off you."

"Thank you." Sophie spun in a circle. "I feel like a movie star."

"Let's sit, shall we?" She arranged herself on one end of the couch. One slender leg crossed over the other, she sipped from her glass before setting it on one of the coasters from the coffee table.

Sophie plopped more than arranged her undainty self into the club chair adjacent to the couch. She caught a whiff of the tiger lily bouquet on the glass coffee table. Outside the picture windows, the sun hung low in the sky and colored the world in a gold slipcover. Cottonwood fluff danced in the rays like summer's snow. Nico had complained earlier about how the copious fuzz dirtied the pool and made him sneeze. Sophie thought it looked like fairies made of gossamer strands of silk.

"That's how we used to do it, Paul and me," Mrs. Coventry said. "Cocktails and expensive roasted almonds at five. He always sat in the big chair there by the fireplace and I'd take the couch here and he'd tell me about his day, and I'd tell him about mine. Very civilized, mind you." She looked toward the kitchen. "How I miss him."

"I'm sorry. How long has he been gone?"

She glanced at the gold watch on her wrist. "Four years, two hundred and seven days." Her gold bangles clattered as she lifted her hand to her face and touched a finger to the base of her throat. "He died in his sleep. Taking a nap, of all things. Doc Waller said his heart simply stopped. I don't have any idea how that could be when he loved me with that same heart for forty-five years. It was such a large one, figuratively speaking. As was he. A man larger than life seemed incapable of dying. I always thought it would be me who went first. Can you imagine my shock?" The edges of her mouth curved slightly as she picked up her drink. "The nerve of him. He knew I hated surprises."

Sophie imagined how it must have been to find him. Did she go to check on him, thinking his nap had gone on too long and found him dead? She shivered. "I'm so sorry," she said again.

"Thank you, darling. I'd like to be one of those people who says and thinks in platitudes." She raised the pitch of her voice and emphasized her Southern drawl. "I'm so grateful for our forty-five years together and that he went so easily and peacefully." She uncrossed her legs, then smoothed the fabric of her linen pants. Her voice returned to its natural buttery timbre. "Instead, I think only of the exact numbers of years and days and hours and wish for more. I've always been selfish and never guilty over having more than my share." She grinned as she fluffed her bangs. "Aren't I dreadful?"

Judi was the type of woman who could say ugly things but make them sound as pretty as a wind instrument's pure, low notes. Not that wishing for more time with the person you loved was wrong. "I think we all want more time. When we love someone as much as you loved your Paul."

"I never thought I'd have such an epic love. I was awfully flippant and thought of myself as a femme fatale with no need for the love of a man. They were for sex, like a toy one put away at the end of the day. I aimed to pursue more serious, important goals. Then I met Paul and it was all over. I realized one could love a man and still have goals and dreams of one's own. God's had a good laugh, hasn't he?"

Sophie had never thought of men as toys. She'd certainly never considered sex without emotion or attachment. She filled with wonder and admiration for this strong, independent woman.

"Poor Nico found me when I was still in the throes of my loss. Nasty thing, grief. All-consuming and black as the darkest night of the year."

"Does it get better?" Sophie asked.

"Yes, a little. Humans have a great capacity for acceptance of new circumstances. I still miss him, but it's a duller pain than a year ago. I've stopped calling out to him, as if he's in the other room, before remembering he's gone. I suppose that means I've accepted it finally. Sometimes I wonder if that's worse than grief. The moving on, I mean. As if it's a betrayal somehow."

Sophie's eyes filled with tears at the poignancy of Judi's words. How beautiful and tragic love was. "Not to sound like a banal platitude, but I think he'd want you to move on."

She raised one perfectly plucked eyebrow and nodded her head in mock disgust. "He would. He was always the most generous husband. I, on the other hand, would haunt him if he'd had the audacity to move on without me. I'd want him wallowing in grief, bringing flowers to my grave every day."

"You wouldn't," Sophie said, laughing.

"I absolutely would." Judi picked up her glass and gestured at Sophie in a toast. "Nice people like you always assume others are equally as good. We're not." The ice made a pleasant clinking sound as she made circular motion with her glass. "It's nice chatting like this."

"Agreed," Sophie said.

"I've noticed young people never sit unless they're watching television or on one of those tablets. You're all so very busy all the time. The art of conversation is going the way of the dinosaurs."

Sophie smiled. "Except in a bar. The people at my counter talk a lot. To me. To each other. You wouldn't believe the conversations I've overheard."

"Salacious?" Judi's eyes twinkled. "Do tell."

"Sometimes. Women mostly talk about things other women have done to them or said about them—basically wronged them somehow. Unless they're talking about the man in their life. If they're at my bar it's usually because a man has behaved badly and they want to talk to their friends about him. It always surprises me how many make excuses for them. Many don't seem to expect much from the one who's supposed to be their best friend."

"And men? What do they talk about?"

Sophie clicked them off on one hand. "To each other, it's sports or work, almost always. When they're talking to women, it's usually to pick them up unless they have them already. Those ones tend look at their phones or whatever game is on."

"More women should see themselves as the queen of the world and order heads to roll."

Sophie laughed, then quickly sobered. "A lot of women mold themselves into whatever it takes to keep their man. I don't think they even realize they're doing it."

They were interrupted by the sound of the front door opening.

"Go back to your room. I want you to make an entrance," Judi said.

"Really?"

"Yes, really. Now scoot."

15

Nico

NICO PULLED a cork from the bottle of Chianti and poured it through the infuser into a decanter. In one corner of the kitchen, Mrs. Coventry was teaching Jen how to roll over for a treat. So far, Jen had rolled over at least five times. "You're going to spoil her dinner," he said.

"Dogs always have room for dinner."

He tugged on the collar of his button-down shirt, still baffled as to the reason his landlady had asked that he dress nicely for dinner. But he knew better than to question her. Whatever eccentric reasoning she had was of no consequence. He was always happy to oblige if it made her happy. She'd been so good to him and now to Sophie.

After finishing with the wine, he made a salad. The pasta was happily cooking away on the cooktop. Sophie's pasta sauce simmered on the back burner. A fresh loaf of bread was already cut and on the table. Whenever Sophie appeared, they could eat.

Mrs. Coventry put the doggy treats in the cupboard and went to the sink to wash her hands. "Please find a white in the wine refrigerator. We'll have that before dinner."

"Sure thing." He leaned over to open the glass doors and pulled out the top drawer. Sophie didn't like oaky chardonnays, so he chose a French Chablis.

When he rose to his full height, his breath caught. Sophie stood in the doorway wearing a dark blue dress that accentuated her curves and high black sandals that helped to show off her long, toned legs. Her hair was piled on top of her head, and she'd done up her eyes with black liner. Her full lips were painted red, making her look utterly gorgeous and, as much as he hated to admit it, much less innocent than usual.

He pressed his fingers against his mouth to stop himself from looking like a hooked fish gasping for air. What had she done to herself? He flashed to earlier. She'd made him so hot he wanted to take her right there in the parking lot. And now this? It was as though she was trying to seduce him.

Jen, seeming equally surprised at Sophie's transformation, didn't run to her as she usually did. Instead, she came to stand next to him and simply stared at the vision in blue while wagging her tail in appreciation.

"Nice dress," he said.

"Thanks," Sophie said, as if dressing up like a supermodel going to a Hollywood party were perfectly normal.

"Dear, you look lovely," Mrs. Coventry said. "I knew the dress would be perfect for you."

"I might never take it off," Sophie said. "I'll sleep in it like my mother did when she was a kid and got new school shoes."

"You bought her that dress?" Nico asked. When and how and where? Why did he feel slightly betrayed by her doing so?

"I had my girl at Le Chic bring them down." Mrs. Coventry and Jen each took a stool at the counter.

"You have a girl?" he asked. "Never mind. I don't want to know."

"Sophie needed a few new things, so I called after you left this morning," Mrs. Coventry said. "Now, about that wine."

Slightly light-headed, he went to the cabinet where Mrs. Coventry kept the wineglasses. He had to pass by Sophie as he did so and caught a whiff of her perfume. This was not her usual fragrance, which smelled more like cookies. This scent was exotic and almost dangerous. Not almost. Totally dangerous. To him and his double-crossing body.

He took out three glasses and held his breath as he passed by the temptress. When he was safely back to the island, he poured them each a generous portion of Chablis. Meanwhile, Sophie settled on the seat next to Jen. Both women and the dog looked at him with an anticipatory countenance. He set a glass of wine in front of each of them. "I've nothing for you, Jen."

Jen angled her head to the right and whined softly.

"Do you see what you've done?" Nico asked Mrs. Coventry. "She thinks she's a person."

Sophie patted Jen's head. "She's better than a person, aren't you, girl?"

For the next few minutes, he bustled around the kitchen putting the rest of the dinner together as Sophie filled them in on the latest news. The insurance company was cooperating completely. They'd soon have a check for the assessed value. "All in all, it's probably a year before we can reopen."

"What an opportunity you've been given," Mrs. Coventry said.

"An opportunity?" Nico asked. All he saw was a year without a business. No income. Nothing but the hassle of a rebuild.

"She means, what can I do to take advantage of the fresh

start," Sophie said. "I can design a completely different place if I want to."

"It's exciting," Mrs. Coventry said.

"Maybe I'll find inspiration in France," Sophie said.

"A café," Mrs. Coventry said.

"I think people liked it the way it was," Nico said. "Local watering hole and all that."

"We'll see," Sophie said before taking a sip of her wine. "But that's not the most interesting thing that happened today. Wait until I tell you about our meeting with the fire detective. Do you remember when Stone and Autumn's mother had to move here because her apartment building up north burned down?"

"Sure," Nico said. The entire complex had collapsed. Fortunately, no residents perished, but they were forced to find other living arrangements. "That's when Valerie moved into the Victorian, right?"

"What's a Victorian?" Mrs. Coventry asked.

"The old house on Main Street that Rafael turned into apartments," Nico said. "Trey and Stone used to live there."

Mrs. Coventry waved her hand dismissively. "Oh, yes. Of course. I knew that house back when it was still a house. The saddest woman lived there with her seventeen cats."

"You'll have to tell us about that sometime," Sophie said. "I love old stories about the town. I wonder if Hugh knew her."

"Can we stay on topic, please?" Nico asked. "I want to know what the detective said."

As he took the pasta from the steaming water and mixed it into Sophie's delectable sauce, she told them about the possible connection between the two fires. "The minute he told us about the fire up north, we all thought of the same thing almost immediately. You should've seen the poor detective's face when we explained about the bad nanny and her father and everything else. He said Kyle attracted trouble like a bee to honey."

"I'd have to agree," Mrs. Coventry said.

"The detective is going to look into the whole thing and see if the nanny has any other disturbed family members. But Solomon—that's the detective—doesn't think it's related. He said if it were connected to Mel, then why would they have come after me? I had no involvement in any of that. And Zane didn't either, other than being a Dog."

"What else could it be?" Nico asked.

Sophie fluttered her fingers and lowered her voice dramatically. "He thinks the answer could be in the Dogs' past."

Mrs. Coventry pulled on one earring. "A deep dark secret."

The two of them were acting as if this were a murder mystery on television. "This isn't something to take lightly," Nico said. "We almost died in that fire."

Both immediately sobered. "You're right, dear," Mrs. Coventry said.

Sophie put one elbow on the counter and rested her cheek in her hand. He got a straight shot right down her cleavage. Her bra was black and lacy and pushed her breasts together. "He asked Zane to try to think about anyone who might have a vendetta against them. Zane said he couldn't imagine there was one. He said Kyle had a lot of old girlfriends who might hate him, but not the rest of the Dogs. Solomon said if they're targeting the Dogs' loved ones it has be for something they all did together."

"But wait a minute," Nico said as fear crawled up his spine. "If that's the case, then the rest of the Dogs' families might be in danger, too?"

"That's why they need to catch the guy soon," Sophie said.

"Or woman," Mrs. Coventry said.

"Until then, Sophie, you have to be on high alert." Nico sprinkled Parmesan cheese over the top of the pasta dishes.

"Maybe all the more reason to go on my trip early," Sophie said. "All signs point to Paris."

The thought of her leaving hollowed out his heart. He liked

it just like this. Sophie to come home to. He put those thoughts aside. "Are you two amateur detectives ready for dinner?"

"Bon appétit," Mrs. Coventry said as she raised her empty glass. "I think I'm a little drunk."

Jen barked in agreement.

When they were all seated at the table, the three of them dug into the pasta. They ate and chatted away about their experiences in Paris. After they finished, Sophie rose to clear the dishes, but Mrs. Coventry stopped her.

* * *

MRS. COVENTRY HAD TRICKED HIM. She was not coming out to the hot tub. Instead, he was going to be all alone with the hottest woman to ever wear a bikini. He should have known when she suggested they take a hot tub after dinner that she'd make some excuse not to join them. He'd been suspicious before, but now he knew for sure. Mrs. Coventry was trying to manipulate him. She wanted him with Sophie. The dress at dinner had been purposely purchased to show off Sophie's figure. Which it did. It definitely did. And now it would be a bikini.

When Mrs. Coventry had mentioned at dinner that she'd asked Le Chic to bring a few bathing suits for Sophie and why didn't they all enjoy a hot soak and another glass of wine, he should have known better than to agree.

None of Mrs. Coventry's interfering ways were going to work. He had a plan of his own. After almost doing her in a public parking lot that afternoon, he knew he had to do something drastic. Tonight, he would convince Sophie to leave the country. As much as he would miss her, she had to go. She would be safe from the lunatic arsonist. He would be safe from Sophie.

He stretched his legs out long and rested his neck on the

rim of the tub as the Jacuzzi jets swirled about his legs. The stars were vivid tonight in an almost-purple night sky. Out of the corner of his eye he saw Sophie come out of the house. He sat up straighter and watched as she padded across the patio wearing nothing but a red polka-dot bikini and carrying two plastic glasses filled with red wine. Mrs. Coventry was evil. How had he not seen that until now?

Sophie's hair was still up in the bun. He'd love to run his lips down the side of her neck. The bottom of the swimsuit was like two cocktail napkins connected by a shoestring over her hips. Sophie's generous breasts were barely covered by the equally small pieces of fabric. He couldn't tear his eyes from her as she climbed the steps up to the tub, still holding the glasses. She leaned over to set his glass in the holder closest to him. Great, a whole new angle from which to view her cleavage. Why did God and Mrs. Coventry hate him?

She grinned as she perched on the ledge with just her legs in the water and sipped from her wine. "This feels wonderful. Wasn't it thoughtful of Judi to think of a bathing suit for me?"

"Sure was," he said drily.

"What's the matter? Don't you feel well?" Her brow wrinkled.

"Perfect. Thanks."

"I've always loved polka dots." She drank more wine. "I used to have a suit just like this when I was a little girl."

"Given its size, it might be the same one."

She laughed and kicked his knee with her foot. "It's all that pasta I ate at dinner."

"It's not that you're too large. It's that the suit's too small."

She didn't say anything for a moment, then set her glass aside and slipped into the water up to her chest. "I've never heard a man complain about the smallness of a bikini before."

His stomach clenched as she moved over to sit adjacent to him. Under the water, her foot brushed against his. "I've been thinking. You really should leave for your trip sooner rather than later. I don't like the idea of this arsonist on the loose."

"Do you want to get rid of me?"

"Of course not."

"Liar. You're afraid you'll kiss me again."

"That should not have happened. I lost control."

She rose up slightly so that her cleavage was visible above the water. He tried to drag his gaze away. He truly did. But he was a weak, weak man. Sophie destroyed him, crushed every ounce of resolve to be an honorable man.

"Nico?"

Spell broken, he looked into her eyes. "I'm sorry. It's just that you're so damn beautiful. This isn't fair."

She grinned. "All's fair in love and war."

He wrapped one hand around her neck and pulled her toward him and kissed her. She returned the kiss, opening to him with complete trust. Before he could stop himself, he had dragged her onto his lap, and they attacked each other's mouths. Passion rose in him like a beast, all-consuming and unrelenting. He had to have her.

She moved to straddle him. He moaned as her strong legs wrapped around him. They kissed again. She ground her hips against him. His fingers brushed under the bikini top to stroke her nipples. She arched her back and let out a sound of such primal desire he thought he might lose it right then and there.

That's when it hit him what a total sleaze he was. Taking advantage of her like this when he had no intention of getting involved.

He removed his hands from her body before he explored another place. "Not like this," he said, panting. "This isn't how it should be."

She lifted her face away from him. "What do you mean?"

"Sophie, your first time should be special. Not in a freaking hot tub."

Her face fell. "But why?"

The hurt in her eyes made his fill with tears. "I'm sorry, Soph. This is all my fault." He had to physically lift her off his lap and set her aside. "You deserve so much better than this. Flowers and romance and a bed. I'm doing everything wrong here. This isn't how it's supposed to be."

"You mean, I'm not supposed to be with you. Isn't that what it always comes back to?"

"No, that's not what I meant," he said. But the words wouldn't come. They were stuck inside him.

16

S ophie

SOPHIE PULLED her legs up to her chest and wrapped her arms around her knees. Humiliated and still breathless, she stared at him, desperate for him to realize how simple it was. They were meant to be together. "Come to Paris with me. We can kiss on a bridge overlooking the Seine, and you'll see how we could go on and on together. Outside of the country, you'll understand age is just a number. Souls are ageless, and ours belong together."

"Paris?" He was looking at her as though she'd announced she was running for president.

"Yes, Paris. You'll understand then how these feelings we have belong to us and only us. No one gets to say whether this is right or not. Not Zane or society or even your paranoia that you're a dirty old man."

"No, I can't. I have work."

"You could. If you really, really wanted to, you would." Tears spilled down her face, mixing with the steam.

He reached for her and spoke into her damp hair. "Soph, please don't cry."

She twitched away from him and crossed her arms over her chest. "Nothing's going to put out the fire between us. Not even a real fire. It doesn't matter how far away I go or for how long. The moment we're back together, the flames start up again. You can keep running, but this thing between us isn't going anywhere." She was crying now, but she didn't care if he saw how sad and angry he'd made her.

"You're right," he said.

Everything seemed to rain down on her. All of it. The fire, and Hugh leaving before she could know him, and Zane's desire to sell the lot, and even the emptiness she'd felt after Sebastian was born. Most especially, Nico's rejection. All of these things made her heavy and weary down to her bone marrow.

Why was she fighting so hard for this man who was too much of a coward to seize this beautiful thing between them?

A quiet voice whispered to her. *You can't be with a coward.*

She had to walk away.

They could have died in that fire, and still he didn't see how precious and rare their love was. Here she was, throwing herself at him again.

"Why can't you admit you love me?" She dropped her head to hide the tears. "It's not hard, really. You just say the words, then take me inside and do what we both want so badly." She fought to catch her breath as the idea of life without him burrowed into her and filled her with a bleak, awful desolation like the coldest place on earth.

She watched him through her tears as he covered his face with his hands. He became distorted in her blurred vision, like an abstract painting. Yet she could see him clearly for the first time. He was a good man, but he'd chosen to live a diminished life because he was afraid to love again. This was not about her youth or her virginity. This was about him and his inability to see that she was his second chance, his prize at the end of all that pain.

Then she wanted to hurt him. "The fire reminded me how quickly life can change. In a second, we could be gone. You're right about yourself. You're a broken man. I thought loving you would put you back together, but I was wrong. I can't save you. You have to save yourself. You have to choose to move on, to be happy, to trust."

"I haven't known how," he whispered.

"I think it would be best for both of us if I left town." She couldn't stay in this town and run into him every other minute. "I'm not sure I belong here any longer."

She trudged across the hot tub, aware that he reached for her with both hands, but she shook him away. He might have even said her name, but she couldn't hear him. The roar between her ears was too loud.

She grabbed a towel and wrapped it around her as she sprinted across the cement patio. She managed to open the kitchen doors despite her wet, shaking hands. When she was inside, she ran across the cold floor and down the hall to her room. Forget it all. Let Zane sell the damn restaurant if he wanted to. Let Nico continue his solitary life with his flowers and taking home bimbos for meaningless sex. To hell with both of them. She was going to Paris. Maybe she'd stay forever.

In her room, she threw herself onto the bed, buried her face in the pillow, and sobbed.

A knock on the door startled her. She stopped crying. "Go away. I don't want to talk to you."

"It's Judi."

Her heart sank. Of course he didn't come after her. He never would. "Come on in." She sat up, wiping her eyes.

Judi approached the bed and perched on one end. "What's happened?"

"I need to get out of here." She waved toward Nico's bungalow.

"What did he do?"

"We kissed and kissed and then he pushed me away and I told him I'm leaving." She sobbed, knowing her face had folded into the ugliest cry ever. "And my heart's broken into a thousand pieces." She flung herself back.

"Oh, dear girl." Judi put her cool hands on Sophie's wet cheeks. "Men are such cowards sometimes. Especially after they've been hurt. They'll come up with every excuse in the world not to be with a woman, especially if their feelings are as strong as the ones this particular young man has for you.

"You're quite right. Leaving is the only thing to do. I didn't think it would come to this, but the third step is necessary," Mrs. Coventry said. "You need to disappear for a while. Let him miss you and see how empty his life is without you."

She nodded, miserable. "I'll go to Paris."

"I don't suppose you'd like company?"

"You'd want to come with me? I'd love that so much," Sophie said.

"We'll have to stay in only the finest inns," Mrs. Coventry said. "I'm snobby that way. I'll pay, of course."

"Whatever you want." She let out a long, sad sigh. "Nothing matters to me right now."

"Back to the plan," Mrs. Coventry said. "The last step, and it'll be the hardest. You must ignore his texts and calls."

"He might not call."

"He'll call. Trust me. You'll post on one of those social media sites all the pictures of places we're staying and how much fun you're having and all the people we're meeting, especially the handsome young men. It'll drive him crazy and right into your arms where he belongs."

"You're kind of evil."

"I know, darling. That's what I've been telling you." She stood. "Now, I'll need a few days to get some business sorted out. I have a meeting with my attorney in the city tomorrow. I'll call my travel agent in the morning. She can take care of everything."

Sophie sniffed. "I'll find someone to run the wine bar while I'm gone."

"That's easy enough, isn't it?"

She nodded, thinking of Bobby. He would probably welcome the work.

"Three days," Mrs. Coventry said. "And we'll make our escape."

Three days. Three long days.

17

N ico

THE NEXT MORNING Nico paced around the bungalow. Jen watched him from her bed. Her sympathetic eyes followed him back and forth across the living room. He hadn't slept much the night before, tossing and turning and thinking about Sophie. His eyes were dry and irritated, as if he'd been in salt water too long. A dull throb in his head reminded him of how wine and heartbreak didn't mix well.

He hadn't gone over to the big house for breakfast, not wanting to face Sophie or Mrs. Coventry. They were bonded against him at this point. His whole life was out of control.

He sank into the couch and rubbed his eyes. As if this were her cue, Jen crossed over to him and placed her head on his knee.

"What am I doing?" he asked his furry friend. "She says she's leaving. What should I do?"

Jen lifted her head and wagged her tail.

"Telling her that I love her might be the wrong thing for her. I mean, look at me. I'm a mess."

The fur above Jen's eyes twitched, as if she were frowning at him.

"I thought about it all night. If she leaves now, I've probably lost her forever. She'll probably fall in love with some French wine dude."

Jen barked.

"Of course I don't want that," he said in response. "But what if she's wrong about her feelings? What if she changes her mind and leaves me for someone else?"

The dog cocked her head to the right.

"I know, I sound like a dolt. You don't have to say it," Nico said. "I've been left many times. It's not like my fears haven't happened before."

Nico went to the window and looked out to the driveway. Sophie's car was already gone. She'd probably left early to avoid him. He wandered back to the couch and sat. This feeling of being left jarred him. There had been so many times in his life when he'd been left or abandoned. Not once had he seen it coming. There was Addie, of course, but before that there had been another girl. Someone in college who'd chased him for a year. When he finally gave in and let himself fall for her, she dumped him after only a few weeks. That had stung. In hindsight, that had been nothing.

Not like the devastating blow of Addie's decision.

Not like his parents.

He went to the desk and sat. The paperwork that had explained so much about his life lay on top. His parents weren't who he thought they were. They were not his parents.

That was it. The only knowledge he'd had of the girl who'd given birth to him and then committed suicide.

He'd come to Cliffside Bay to start fresh. In his new life, he could almost forget about his family and Addie—everything that came before. But not quite. This secret about who he really was, his parents' rejection, and Addie were intertwined. Nothing was as it seemed to him. His parents weren't his parents. His fiancée was a lesbian. He had obvious blind spots, especially when it came to people he loved. Which led him to the same conclusion about Sophie. She was not as she appeared. He assumed he was missing something. Whatever it was, there would eventually be the inevitable, heartbreaking revelation. Eventually, she would leave him.

The very thing he feared the most, he'd caused to happen. He'd forced Sophie to leave him.

What if he was wrong about Sophie? What if she was the thing not like the others?

A montage of images played through his mind: Sophie confessing her feelings; the first time Jen licked Sophie's face; her trusting eyes as he begged her to jump to the tree; the stubborn tilt to her head when she told him she would never stop loving him.

Despite all the ways he'd pushed her away and acted irrationally, she had been steady and resolute in her love. What if the problem was all his?

How was that even a question? The problem *was* all his. Sophie was the sunshine. She shone too brightly to hide anything. Like the sun, she rose every day without fail. He had to make this right.

He jumped at the sound of a knock on his front door.

"Mrs. Coventry," he said to Jen. "Here to give me a talking-to." Jen's claws clicked on the hardwood as they went to the door.

It wasn't his landlady. Zane Shaw stood there, looking big and angry.

Jen hid behind Nico's legs.

"Hey. What's up?" Nico put one hand in his pocket and crossed his fingers.

"I'm looking for Sophie."

"She lives in the main house. Not here." He knew that, didn't he?

Zane's eyes narrowed. He stepped forward a few inches, like a bull about to charge a matador. "She's not answering her phone."

"I'm not positive of her exact location at the moment." He forced himself to keep his feet planted on the ground. A guy like Shaw would take that as weakness and sink his teeth all the way into Nico's jugular.

"I need to talk to her." The muscle in Zane's left cheek pulsed.

Jen let out a soft whine and pressed against Nico's leg.

Nico put his hands in his pockets. "She might be asleep." *We had a rough night because I'm a bastard.* He left that part out. Taunting the bull with a red cape was not a good idea.

"Listen, Bentley, I know you did something to her. She sent me a text this morning to tell me she's going to Paris and that she wanted Bobby to manage the wine bar while she was away. She said she might be gone for two months, which led me here to your door. The only reason she would do that is if you hurt her."

Did he tell him the truth? "I did hurt her. Unintentionally."

Zane flinched. "What did you do?"

He wanted to deny his culpability. Even to himself, he'd love to paint his treatment of Sophie in a better light. However, the truth was the truth. "I told her what I've been telling her. We're not suited. She said she needed to get out of town for a while—to get away from me."

Zane cursed. He ran one hand from his forehead and over his nose, squishing his features into an almost comical expression. "Well, we agree about that much, anyway."

Nico shrugged, defeated and suddenly too tired to fight. "Whatever."

His nonchalance seemed to infuriate Shaw even more. "Why are you yanking her around, Bentley?"

A shot of anger woke him. "You know what, Shaw? It's way more complicated than you can understand. Anyway, it's really none of your business. You've been nothing but selfish since the fire. The bar is her life and all you can do is talk about how much you want to get rid of it."

His nostrils flared as he bit out each word. "She told you that?"

"Why wouldn't she? We talk about everything."

"Because this is a family matter. And you're not family."

"I care about her well-being more than anyone in her life," Nico said.

"That's such bullshit. You just want to get her into bed."

"You couldn't be more wrong."

Zane lunged at him, almost as if someone had pushed him from behind.

Nico stopped him by shoving him in the chest with both hands.

Zane stumbled backward. His face reddened as he lurched toward Nico again.

Nico put his hands up, less aggressively this time but still managing to stop him. "What the hell? We don't need to go here."

Zane shoved him by the shoulders. "You will stay away from my sister from now on."

"She's not giving me much choice, now is she? You can settle down. She's safe from the big bad wolf," Nico said, trying to stay calm. He wanted to punch him in his arrogant face. He had a lot of nerve coming to his house and threatening him after Nico had done nothing but thwart her advances. "For the record, I've never been anything but respectful to your sister."

"Respectful? You've done nothing but lead her on. How does she not see you're nothing but a predator?"

Nico let out a dry laugh. "Predator? Are you serious with this? I haven't touched her."

"That's a lie. I know you've kissed her, and God only knows what's been happening since she's been staying up here."

"Sophie has her own mind. She's an adult. If she wants to spend time with me, it's none of your concern."

"It's completely my concern. Our father would not want her hanging out with a guy like you."

Nico stared at him, truly astounded. "What's wrong with a guy like me?"

Zane gestured around Nico's front room. "Look at this place. You live like a college student."

That was it. He was taking this guy down. This time, he lunged toward Shaw and shoved him out of his living room and through the open door. Zane came back at him, grabbing hold of Nico's shirt collar as they danced like a drunken couple before falling into an arrangement of various-sized flowerpots. The clay pots crashed against the cement, spilling dirt and plants.

For the second time in a week, Nico was on top of a Shaw. This turquoise-eyed sibling, however, did not have the same influence on a certain body part. Quite the opposite, in fact. His base instinct was not to procreate but to kill. He raised his fist to smash it into Shaw's square chin. Before he could make contact, a cold stream of water hit his face. He yelped in shock and shook his head like Jen after a bath, then turned to find the source of the onslaught. Mrs. Coventry stood in the driveway with the garden hose between two hands. The jet stream aimed directly onto them.

"Get up. Both of you," Mrs. Coventry said. The force of her directive moved her arm, which made the water stream dance.

Nico rolled off Shaw into a pile of now totally wet dirt. A

sharp-edged piece of one of the broken pots pierced his back. Cursing and sputtering, the men struggled to their feet. Mrs. Coventry moved her wand of water on one, then the other. The fierce spray was like sharp needles against his skin. He put his arms over his face as another torrent of water pelted him. "Stop, please."

This seemed to do the trick. Mrs. Coventry lowered her wand of destruction. "What do you two think you're doing?" she asked calmly as she turned the nozzle off.

Neither of them answered. Shaw brushed dirt and several petunia heads from his shorts. Nico looked down at his beautiful pots broken on the cement. Blood grass lay flat, like dead soldiers. Creeping Jennies, with their low-reaching roots, had completely come out of the dirt. Worst of all, several stems of the pink peony bush had broken in half. A new surge of anger coursed through him. Peonies lived to be a hundred years old, and this lunatic had helped crush them.

Mrs. Coventry, perhaps sensing his anger, raised the hose. Very threatening for an old lady.

"Don't do it," Nico said. "Please."

"Mrs. Coventry, nice to see you," Shaw said. "Sorry about the pots."

She raised one eyebrow. "I'm sure you are."

"How have you been?" Shaw asked.

Mrs. Coventry nodded at him politely as if they'd just met on the sidewalk in town instead of after an onslaught of icy water. "I'm quite well, thank you."

Nico, unable to stop himself, stooped to try to salvage his flowers. The begonia seemed intact, although battered. Shaw knelt and started picking up broken pieces of the pots and putting them into a pile.

"You two acting like wild beasts is doing nothing to help Sophie," Mrs. Coventry said.

Both men straightened.

"Is she inside?" Shaw asked. "Because I need to talk to her."

"She's already gone this morning," Mrs. Coventry said. "She had some things to take care of before we leave on our trip."

"We?" Nico asked. "You're going with her?" How could she do this to him? No, he argued with himself. This was good. Mrs. Coventry would look after her, make sure she was safe.

"I am. She needs a break from both of you." Using the tip of the hose like a pointer, she directed it at Shaw, then Nico.

"This is not about her family," Shaw said. "It's about him. He's run her out of town." He tilted his head toward Nico.

Mrs. Coventry smiled. "Do you know what's delightful about being old?"

Neither of them answered. Nico knew she'd tell them without further prompting.

"My experience gives me certain insight into situations that might not occur to the younger, less experienced set. You two seem to be especially remedial when it comes to Sophie. I'm assuming, given the woman you're married to, Zane Shaw, that you must not be this slow when it comes to all females."

"No, ma'am," Shaw said. "But it took me a while to figure her out. My wife's a great teacher. I'm a perpetual student when it comes to her."

She nodded, looking him up and down as if he were a great disappointment to her. "It takes no imagination to see the truth of that statement."

Zane grimaced. "Yes, ma'am."

The sky was hidden in a layer of fog. Nico shivered in the morning air, cold in his wet clothes. Mrs. Coventry wasn't nearly done, however. He could tell she was gearing up for a stern lecture. They wouldn't be getting out of these wet clothes any time soon.

"Sophie is a smart young woman. She's an old soul, like Hugh. She doesn't need her older brother interfering in her life. Especially her love life. You don't get to decide who she dates. Furthermore, she loves that bar and grill. If she wants to rebuild, let her. What's it to you?"

Shaw hung his head.

"Seriously, what's it to you?" Mrs. Coventry asked.

"The Oar was my dad's place," Shaw said. "It was everything to him. I feel like I've let him down."

"Were you responsible for the arsonist?"

"No, but it feels like it's my fault," Shaw said. "I'm worried about Sophie spending the rest of her life behind that bar like my dad did."

"Again, not your decision," Mrs. Coventry said.

"Okay." Zane dropped his forehead into his hand and let out a long breath. "You're right. She's a grown-up and can make her own decisions."

"Except to date me?" Nico asked. Why had he just said that? Way to poke the bear.

Shaw's eyes narrowed as he turned to Nico. "She can do way better, and you know it."

"Zane Shaw, your father would be ashamed," Mrs. Coventry said.

"He's an outsider," Shaw said. "Not one of us."

"I'll ignore that for a moment," Mrs. Coventry said as she turned to Nico.

Nico's shoulders sagged. Here it came.

"She's desperately in love with you," Mrs. Coventry said. "Your rejection has cut her to the core. The only option she saw as viable was to leave town."

"She thinks she's in love," Shaw said. "But she's too young to know."

Mrs. Coventry played with the hose as if contemplating dousing them again. "Honor fell in love with you when she was only nineteen. How is this different?"

Shaw opened his mouth as if to answer. Mrs. Coventry's hand that held the hose twitched.

Shaw shut his big fat mouth and dipped his gaze to his shoes.

The lines in Mrs. Coventry's forehead grew deeper as she raised her eyebrows. "You might consider acting more like Hugh."

"What does that mean?" Shaw asked, a note of hurt his voice.

"Your father was very intuitive when it came to people, as well as generous. Nico's in love with your sister but thinks he's all wrong for her. Yet he can't stay away from her."

"I should've pummeled you when I had the chance," Shaw said to Nico, as if he hadn't heard Mrs. Coventry's explanation.

"When you had the chance? Good one." Nico made a scoffing noise deep in his throat.

"Boys. Enough." Mrs. Coventry raised the hose. "Don't make me do it again."

Nico raised his hands in surrender. "Okay, okay."

She fixed her stern eyes on Nico. "Tell Zane how you feel about his sister. Or you get the hose."

What did it matter if he told Shaw the truth? This was between him and Sophie, not her interfering brother. But then he remembered the sadness in Sophie's eyes when she walked away from him yesterday. He was the cause of her pain, all because he couldn't work through his own issues. Suddenly, it was important to him that Shaw know the purity of his feelings for Sophie. He cherished her, wanted only the best for her, and had thought with utter certainty that he wasn't it. "This isn't what you want to hear, but yes, I'm in love with her. I have been for months." That wasn't quite the truth. Really it had been since the first time she'd ever flashed that smile at him. He'd never recovered from that moment. "From the first time she smiled at me, I've been a goner."

"Then why have you pushed her away?" Shaw continued to scrutinize him as if Nico were not fit for the bottom of his shoe.

As quickly as it had come, the bluster and anger emptied out of him, replaced by a vast sadness. He looked Shaw square in the eye, imagining the entire scenario from his point of view. Who was Nico, after all? An older guy with nothing to show for himself except a bright green thumb and some friends who always had his back. He was estranged from his family, with no home to offer Shaw's sister or any kind of financial security. Nico couldn't blame him. Shaw was right to worry.

The outside lights turned on, brightening the yard. They were too vivid, too illuminating. Nico felt as vulnerable as a stage actor who had no idea of his next line. "I've been confused. And broken. And broke. And totally afraid."

Shaw brushed a few leaves from his right shoulder. His voice sounded softer when he spoke next. "What're you afraid of?"

"It's pretty simple, actually," Nico said. "You're right. I'm not good enough for Sophie. I've been afraid she'll figure that out sooner rather than later. I've already had my heart ripped out of my chest once, and I'm terrified it'll happen again when she wakes up and realizes how much better she can do than me."

"How ridiculous." Mrs. Coventry flung the garden hose onto the ground and stood there shaking her head.

Shaw tilted his head, studying Nico. "Someone ripped out your heart? Who?"

"My fiancée—Addie. She left me a few weeks before my wedding." He paused for dramatic effect. "For her maid of honor."

One eyebrow shot up as Shaw jerked his head back, like a crab retreating back into his shell. "Yeah? Wow." The lights that ran along the garden beds cast shadows on Shaw's face, but even so Nico saw his jaw unclench. "Same thing happened to me. Only it was a guy. Damn, it hurt like hell. Made me not want to give in to my feelings for Honor. It's hard to go there after you've been beat up that bad."

"Pretty much." Nico glanced at Mrs. Coventry. She'd wrapped her arms around her own waist and was staring up at the sky.

"What about all the women?" Shaw asked.

"What women?"

"The ones you take home from the bar. On occasion." The last was said in a tone exactly opposite of the words.

Nico let out a long breath. Shaw made it sound as though he was with a different woman every night, when the truth was quite different. When he'd first come to town, he'd tried to distract himself from his shock and grief with pretty tourists. "If you'd been left for a woman, you might need a little ego boost for a bit afterward."

"Fair enough," Shaw said.

"Men." Mrs. Coventry rolled her eyes. "Such destructive ways of dealing with grief."

"I can't lie," Nico said, ignoring Mrs. Coventry's commentary. "They've also been an attempt to get Sophie out of my system. It doesn't work."

"No, man. Not when you love just one," Shaw said.

"Nope." Nico flinched when he heard a bug hit the zapper that he'd hung near his front door. He shuddered, thinking of the fire. That thing might have to go. He'd have to find a more humane way to protect his plants from bugs.

Shaw ran his hands through his wet hair. "Let me give you a hint about Sophie. She's not going to change her mind about you. That's not how she works."

"Old soul," Mrs. Coventry said. "Like I said."

"Look, I'm not thrilled over the age difference," Zane said. "But my wife will kill me if she thinks I've interfered in true love. I know what it's like to feel like you're not enough for the woman you love. That said, my sister's a smart cookie. If she loves you and thinks you guys have something special, then she's probably right. I've been underestimating her and treating her like a kid when she clearly isn't. It's just that I only just found her, and I'm scared for anything to happen to her, including getting hurt by some jerk."

"I'm not a jerk," he said, even though he'd been acting like one. "But I'm afraid I've driven her away for good."

"If you love her, you're going to have to fight for her," Shaw said.

"Just stop all this nonsense," Mrs. Coventry said. "You're making all this much harder than it has to be. When you find the right person, thank the good Lord and then cling to each other for as long as you can."

"You make it sound so easy." Nico hung his head as shame and regret for how he'd made Sophie suffer enveloped him.

To his surprise, Shaw crossed over to him and put his hand on his shoulder. "I was just like you, man. After I got jilted, I was so afraid to let Honor in, so afraid to get hurt. I acted like a complete ass, if you want to know the truth. Sophie, like my wife, is a special woman. If she loves you, she's in for life. She's not going to run away. Honestly, she's solid as a rock. More solid than most."

"I'm sick over the whole thing," Nico said. "I drove her away."

"I'm guilty, too," Zane said.

"Both of you need to leave her a message," Mrs. Coventry said. "Let her know how you feel and that you're sorry."

"Yeah, okay," Nico said.

"Yes, ma'am," Shaw said.

Shaw held out his hand and Nico shook it.

"I'm sorry for acting like a lunatic," Shaw said.

"You're protective of her. I get it. I'm sorry for hurting her."

"Listen, Bentley, for what it's worth, tell her your feelings. Don't take the chance she might not come back." Shaw brushed the rest of the murdered plants off his shirt. "I've got to get out of here. Honor needs me at home this morning."

They said their goodbyes and watched his car pull out of the driveway. Nico wrapped his arms around himself and shivered. "Was the hose really necessary?"

"Boys who act like barbarians get the hose."

He turned to her. "Have I wrecked this? Is it too late? Yesterday she told me she was through with me and that she knew for the first time I was right. I wasn't the man for her."

"Honey, that girl will love you until the end of time. All you have to do is tell her what's in your heart." She patted him on the arm. "Now go inside and take a nice, hot shower, then send her a text that you want to see her."

Jen barked in obvious agreement.

"All right. I'll do it. I just hope it's not too late."

As she turned to cross the driveway, he detected a self-satisfied glint in her eyes. No ordinary man stood a chance against the wiles of Mrs. Judi Coventry.

18

S ophie

SOPHIE SPENT most of the day at the brewery training Bobby. The distraction of the work and his good humor kept her from dwelling too much on her troubles. Bobby was a quick learner. By dinnertime, she felt confident he would be fine without her.

She stood behind the counter with Bobby. "I'll order some dinner and hang around in case you have any questions."

"Good deal," Bobby said.

This room was usually quiet compared to the general chaos of the restaurant and brewery. A half-dozen book club members were sitting together on the couches in the lounge portion of the room. Several of the tables were occupied by couples who appeared to be on date nights. A few patrons occupied the counter, including Jamie eating dinner while reading a book. She wanted to ask Jamie about Darby the Dickens expert. She hadn't talked with her since the night of the fire. What had transpired between them as she and Nico were jumping out the window? Hopefully superhot sex while completely oblivious to the superhot fire down the street.

Sophie slipped onto the stool next to her. "Hey, mind if I join you?"

Jamie's face lit up. "I'd love it. I thought you were working tonight?"

"No, Bobby's fine without me." She told her about her plans for France. "I'll be gone for a few months."

"I'll miss you," Jamie said. "But I'm super jealous. Will it be a work trip?"

"Partly, plus Stone and Pepper's wedding."

"Hopefully by the time you get back, I'll have an inn."

"I'll cross my fingers," Sophie said.

She didn't say anything further. Not coming back to Cliffside Bay seemed impossible, but she would decide later. For now, she needed to put some space between her and Nico.

"I'm so sorry about the fire," Jamie said. "It's weird that I was there right before it started. I was completely oblivious about the whole thing. The next morning I woke up in Darby's room at the lodge and went down to the lobby doing the whole walk of shame thing, totally worried I was going to run into one of my brother's friends who would totally rat me out, only to find out that people had a much bigger thing to talk about than my one-night stand with some Dickens guru from LA."

Sophie laughed. "I'm glad the sounds of sirens didn't disturb your fun."

Jamie drew a little closer and spoke softly. "I don't think an earthquake would have distracted me from what that boy did to me. I've never in my life had sex like that."

She studied her friend, looking for clues. What exactly did she mean by "sex like that"? Her peers always assumed she knew what they were talking about when it came to this kind of thing, when in fact, she was clueless. "Like what? Kinky? He didn't do something weird, did he?" She'd read about some very strange activities certain people enjoyed. Like dressing up in furry costumes, for example.

"Oh my God, no. I mean, it was fantastic. He was just so... hot and skilled." Jamie fanned herself. "I don't know if it was just that we knew we'd never see each other again or if it was chemistry or his expertise, but the night was unbelievable." She paused, taking a breath. "But enough about my sexcapades. Let's talk about you. Is it true that Nico Bentley saved you? Were you really in the bathtub?"

"People know about that?"

"Girl, this is Cliffside Bay. Sophie Woods naked in the tub saved by gorgeous Nico Bentley was headline news."

She covered her face with her hands as heat flooded her entire body. "So embarrassing."

"No way. It's totally romantic." Jamie let out a long, dreamy sigh. "I'd love to have a man run into a house on fire to save me."

Sophie uncovered her face and looked at her friend. "It sounds a lot better than it really was."

"I'm just glad he was so brave. Trey said he didn't even hesitate."

"It was reckless, but he was the only one who knew I was up there. If it hadn't been for him, I wouldn't be here." Now if only he were brave when it came to his heart.

Bobby set her burger down on the counter.

"Bobby, did you know everyone knows about the details of my rescue?" Sophie asked.

"The naked-in-the-bathtub thing?" Bobby asked. "Um, yeah, everyone knows about that."

Sophie groaned. "Can I have wine, please?"

For a half hour, she and Jamie chatted as they ate burgers and drank wine. By the time she looked at her watch, she was surprised to see it was already after nine.

After Bobby cleared their plates, Jamie turned to her. "What do you think about taking an Uber home and having another drink?"

She thought about going home and possibly running into Nico. Best to stay out. "Since I'm basically unemployed, why not?" There really wasn't any reason she couldn't act like an irresponsible twentysomething for one night.

Jamie looked around at the patrons of the sedate wine bar. "Let's go out to the brewery and see if we can find some trouble."

Sophie signed for their check, treating Jamie to dinner. "You're saving your pennies for your inn."

"Thanks, Sophie. That's really sweet."

They waved at Bobby and headed out to the brewery. The bar area was busy considering it was a weeknight. Her chest tightened when she realized why. They had one fewer bar in town than last week. She wouldn't worry about it tonight. *Just have fun. Be in the moment with your friend. Do not think about Nico for at least a few hours.*

Jamie went up to the bar to order them drinks while Sophie secured a small bistro table in the far corner. From here they'd be able to people watch. There were a few locals she recognized but no one she knew well. Zane and his friends were all married with children and no longer came out much. When she'd first moved to Cliffside Bay, Kyle, Lance, and Zane used to spend a lot of nights carousing at the bar. One by one, they'd been tamed by the love of a good woman.

Jamie arrived with their cosmos and plopped into the chair across from her. "I ran into Sara Ness at the bar and invited her to join us. Is that all right?"

"Totally."

Sara showed up a few seconds later with a dirty martini in hand. Jamie stole an empty chair from another table and the three of them settled in with their drinks.

Other than that Sara was supposedly a billionaire heiress who had moved to Cliffside Bay with her baby daughter after her husband's death, Sophie knew little about her. She'd always seemed pleasant enough, albeit quiet and a little intimidating because she was so well-spoken and stunning with her thick auburn hair and creamy white skin. Sophie could imagine her as a commentator on the news or a criminal defense attorney.

"Thanks for letting me join you," Sara said. "Autumn was supposed to meet me, but she has a cold. I'd already asked my nanny to stay late, so I decided to come out anyway. It's been a long time since I was out or even had a drink."

"We're out spontaneously," Sophie said. "The more the merrier."

"I don't know if I've ever seen you anywhere but behind the bar at The Oar," Sara said. "By the way, I'm so sorry about the fire."

Sophie mumbled a thank-you and took a sip of her drink.

They talked for a few minutes about the fire, but Sophie steered the conversation away from the topic as soon as she could. She wanted a night where she didn't have to think about reality.

The cocktail was starting to give her a nice buzz by the time they'd covered the niceties. When asked, Sara said she was adjusting to small-town life just fine and yes, her full-time nanny was a godsend. The chatter moved to her experience with Wolf Enterprises, who'd built her mansion just up the road from the Mullens' palatial estate. Sophie hadn't been there, but Nico had told her it was first-class everything.

"Trey had a lot of fun working on your house," Jamie said when her brother's name came up.

"He's a wonderful designer. So talented." Sara was talking faster than her usual measured cadence. She'd downed her martini fast and had already ordered another round for all of them. "You'll have to come out to the house sometime. He found the most exquisite pieces. The entire team was a dream. Contractors can be total nightmares, but these guys were incredible. Other than David Perry, I consider them all friends."

"You weren't happy with his work?" Sophie asked.

"His work is marvelous," Sara said. "But I don't care for the man himself."

"How come?" Jamie asked. "He's so good-looking. I mean, not that looks are the most important thing."

Sara chuckled as she plopped an olive into her mouth. "He's fine to look at, but his personality is so condescending and disapproving. Like the grumpy old man who doesn't want children on his lawn."

"He's grieving," Sophie said. David had always been extremely sweet to her. She sensed he was sad and still reeling from what happened to him. "He lost his wife before he moved here."

"I'm sure he's a fine person," Sara said. "But the two of us were like oil and water. I'll tell you, though, your Nico is such a doll." She gestured toward Sophie.

Your Nico.

"He isn't mine," Sophie said. "I wish he were." She and Nico were not like oil and water. They were like the perfect blend of cabernet and merlot. Someday they could have little cab franc babies to add even more joy to their blend. *Do not go there. Stay present. Nico does not want you.*

They paused their conversation as the server brought the second round of drinks. Sophie thanked him and took a good look at the new cosmo. Was this a good idea? Probably not. But hadn't she vowed to have fun? As she'd said earlier—she had no place to be tomorrow.

Sara picked up her drink. "I just assumed you were together. He talked about you a noticeable amount when he was designing my yard." She elongated the word *noticeable.*

"Is that right?" Jamie raised one eyebrow. "Tell us more."

"You know how guys do when they're in love? 'Sophie this' and 'Sophie that,'" Sara said. "It was charming and endearing, just like him."

"Then what's his problem?" Jamie asked. "I just don't get it."

"He thinks I'm too young," Sophie said. "And he's scared."

"Because his ex-wife ran off with a girl?" Jamie asked. "What does that have to do with you?"

Sara's eyes glittered. "Being betrayed changes a person. I can understand why he's cautious. He doesn't want to get hurt." She brought her glass to her mouth and sipped a good portion off the top.

Sophie wondered if Sara had been betrayed by her husband before he died but was too polite to ask. Jamie, however, was not deterred by this social hindrance. As usual, she dived right in without any sense of boundaries. "What's your story, Sara? How did your husband die?"

"You haven't heard?" Sara smiled, a little drunkenly in Sophie's opinion. Not that she should judge, as the alcohol was definitely going to her head as well. "It was all over the papers in Denver."

"No, we have no idea," Jamie said.

"But you don't have to talk about it if you don't want to," Sophie said, with a pointed look in Jamie's direction.

"I don't mind," Sara said. "All you'd have to do is google my name to learn it all anyway." She splayed her hands on the table. "My family is kind of well-known in Denver for our business enterprises."

"Wait, are you the Ness like the beer?" Jamie asked.

"Yes, we are," Sara said. "I mean, not anymore, of course. But my great-great-grandfather founded the company."

"That's like the first beer I ever had," Jamie said.

"You and every other person in the country," Sophie said.

Sara nodded. "Right. At one time we owned a basketball team and a few other things, including a partial stake in some high-tech stuff. I don't even know the half of it, truthfully. When my father died, I inherited everything because I have no siblings and my mother died when I was young."

"You're like a real-life heiress," Jamie said.

"I suppose I am," Sara said. "I was still in college when Dad died, and I was completely unprepared for any of this. But he'd left me in the care of his best friend—whom he trusted with his life—and it's all been fine."

"It must be great to have your own money and not have to answer to anyone," Jamie said. "I can't lie. I'm not sure I can like you now."

"Financial freedom is great," Sara said. "However, when you're a billionaire, you can never be sure if people like you for you or for your money. I was a fat kid. I was still fat when I was at college, where I met Matt. That's my husband. My dead husband."

"But he loved you for you, didn't he?" Jamie asked. "Please say he did."

"I thought so. I mean, that's the thing. Don't we always think so? As a matter of fact, I believed so strongly he loved me that I lost fifty pounds. It was like he loved the weight all off me. Then we got married and I was happy even though I was still grieving my dad. We were living in Colorado. Skiing and hanging out with all the 'it' people. He thrived in that scene even though he'd been raised very middle-class. I couldn't have cared less about who was who, but he jumped all in and was completely ensconced in that world." She took another drink of her martini and kept her eyes lowered when she picked up her story. "Then I got pregnant. It was a complete surprise. I was thrilled, but he wasn't. He liked things the way they were and all that. Long story short, he started having an affair with one of the women in our social circles. A married woman." She paused as she looked up at them. "A woman married to an erratic man with drug and mental health issues. He killed them both at my home. My daughter was weeks old."

For once, Jamie seemed stunned into silence.

"I'm so sorry," Sophie said.

"I had no idea he was having an affair until they were killed. Can you believe that?" Sara widened her eyes and made a face. "Like could I have been a bigger idiot?"

"It's not your fault he was a cheater," Jamie said. "I hate cheaters. My dad's currently living with the woman my age that he cheated on my mother with. Disgusting."

Neither of them had a chance to respond to that because just then a man appeared at their table. He looked familiar. It took Sophie a moment to realize he was the firefighter from the other day. The flirty one who'd given her his number. She couldn't remember his name. Jake? No, James? That wasn't it, either.

"Hey, Sophie."

"Hi," she said.

"Jad Stokes," he said. "We met the other day."

"Right. Hi, Jad. These are my friends." She introduced him to Sara and Jamie.

"Out for a ladies' night?" he asked.

"Sure. Something like that," Sara said.

"Can I buy you ladies another round?" Jad asked.

Sophie was about to say no when Sara blurted out, "Heck yeah."

"Nothing for me," Sophie said, indicating her almost-full glass. "I'm good for now."

"A light beer for me," Jamie said. "A Ness Light."

Jamie and Sara laughed and high-fived like a couple of middle school boys.

Jad ambled off to the bar after winking at Sophie. He was really into winking.

"He's a yummy drink of whiskey," Sara said. "He likes you."

She told them about their conversation from the other day. "He gave me his card, but I couldn't remember his name just now."

"He's cute," Jamie said. "Maybe some no-strings-attached sex is just what you need to get Nico out of your system."

"Could be." Sophie played along. Jamie didn't know she was a virgin. She suspected Jamie wouldn't understand why she was saving herself for her one true love. Jad Stokes was not that. Not even close. Nico was the one for her. *No, don't do it. No more thoughts of Nico.*

"Maybe that's what I need. Some meaningless sex," Sara said. "With a stranger who I can kick out before breakfast."

"I don't think that's what you need," Sophie said.

"What do you think I need?" Sara asked, grinning. "Because right now it's all chocolate and online shopping. Do you know how many pairs of shoes I've bought in the last six months?"

Jad returned with the drinks for the ladies plus a beer for himself. "Do you mind if I join you?"

"You bought a round, so that means you get to stay." Sara made a motion as if she had a magic wand in her hand.

Jad grabbed a chair and set it next to Sophie. After he sat, he pointed at her handbag. Leaning close, he spoke into her ear. "So, is there a cell phone in there?"

She smiled. "Yes, there is."

"And yet my phone has not rung."

"You didn't really expect me to call, did you?" she asked.

"Ladies always call if I invite them."

"Surely not all."

"Ninety-eight percent," he said.

"I like being in the two percent," Sophie said. "Being different is my one of my best qualities."

He winked. "And here I thought it was those gorgeous legs of yours."

Out of the corner of her eye, Sophie saw Nico and David

Perry walking through the main doors of the brewery. Her breath caught, and her stomach churned. Why, why, why did he have to come here tonight? Didn't he have the decency to stay away from her place of business?

She caught Jamie's eye and tried not to cry. "Nico's here."

"Is that bad?" Jamie asked.

"Very bad," Sophie said.

"The insufferable bore is out at night," Sara said. "Amazing."

"That guy again," Jad said. "Is he like your overprotective uncle or something?"

Sophie shot him her best scathing look. "No, he's my good friend who I happen to be madly in love with."

Jad shrank back slightly, then grinned. "He's the one you're in love with? That's why you're able to resist me. I get it now."

Nico and David hadn't yet seen them, she felt certain. They were in the bar area now, winding their way through the crowd toward the counter.

"Jad, you're really kind of awful." Jamie giggled cheerfully as she tapped the tabletop with her short nails. "We're not the type of women taken in by your type."

"At least not again," Sara said. "Been there, done that."

Jad appeared baffled, then affronted before his usual smugness settled over his features. "What does that mean exactly? What kind of type do you think I am?"

Sara gave him a long, appraising examination before she answered. "You think a lot of yourself, which makes others do the same even though behind all the muscles and handsome features there's just a vacuous hole."

"Wow, Sara, that's rough," Jamie said. "You're kind of my hero right now."

"That's what happens when you're a bitter old lady like me," Sara said. "You just don't care any longer."

Jad grinned and raised his hands in a gesture of defeat.

"Fine, we've established I'm not taking any of you home tonight. How about we lighten up on the ol' Jadster. We can be friends. I promise, I'm not as bad as I seem. Harmless, really."

"A good-looking man is never harmless," Sara said. "The minute you think they are is the minute you screw yourself."

"Same could be said of women. But we'll put a pin in that one." He turned to Sophie. "What's the deal with your uncle? Why doesn't he want you? I mean, how could he not? Plus, he seems like the type who wants to settle down and have babies. What gives?"

"Please stop calling him my uncle." Sophie sighed and looked over at Jamie for help.

"He thinks she's too young for him," Jamie said.

"Even though he's totally into her," Sara said.

"And a year ago his fiancée fell in love with a girl and called off the wedding," Jamie said. "He's all messed up in the head because of it."

"Harsh blow," Jad said. "But still, he must be out of his mind to walk away from you."

"Thank you." It surprised her that his words bolstered her damaged ego. Jad might be full of himself, but there was a sweetness under all that bravado. Someday he would grow up to be a man ready for a relationship.

"Tell you what." Jad ran his hands down his torso. "How about we use all of my parts to make him a little jealous."

"Great idea." Jamie clapped her hands together. "Get his competitive juices flowing."

"No, I don't think so," Sophie said. "I don't like to play games."

"No offense, but that's probably half the problem," Jad said. "Men love the chase."

Sophie smiled despite the embarrassment that made her cheeks flame. "Honestly, just leave this alone. He won't respond well to me trying to make him jealous."

"They're coming this way," Jamie said under her breath. "Look natural."

"I am natural," Sophie said.

Nico and David came to their table, each holding a beer. They were both dressed in khakis and button-down shirts. The client dinner must have gone long. As much as she'd love to ignore him completely, she couldn't stop herself from staring at him. "Hey, ladies." Nico's gaze flickered around the table and stopped on Jad.

Jad stood and held out his hand to Nico. "Hey, man. Jad Stokes. We met the other day."

"Sure, how's it going?" Nico asked as they shook hands. "This is my friend David."

David nodded a greeting. "Hey."

"Good to meet you." Jad moved a few inches closer to Sophie, then draped his arm around the back of her chair. "You guys want to join us?"

Nico's eyes shuttered to slits. Sophie couldn't decide if the nerve of Jad Stokes was funny or frightening. Maybe it took someone with this kind of rashness to be a firefighter?

"Pull up a seat," Jamie said. There were several unoccupied chairs at other tables.

"We can stand." Nico positioned himself between Sara's and Jad's chairs.

David came around to stand between Jamie and Sophie.

"Hello, David," Sara said in a bored tone, as if his mere presence was tedious.

His jaw seemed to tense at the sound of her voice. "Hi, Sara." David set his beer on the table, then directed his gaze toward her. "How are things?"

"Just peachy," Sara said. "You?"

"Same." He suddenly seemed interested in the contents of his beer glass.

"Let's have another round." Sara raised her hand and

lurched precariously close to one side of her chair. The legs of the left side raised off the floor a few inches. Jamie's hand darted out to steady her.

"You guys been here awhile?" Nico asked with a pointed look in Sara's direction. "And how are you getting home?"

"I'll make sure they get home safe," Jad said. "Rescuing cats from trees and beautiful women from too many martinis are kind of my things."

A nervous giggle escaped before Sophie could stifle it.

Nico's expression darkened. "David and I will take them home. We don't actually know you."

"Not a problem. Take Sara and Jamie home. I'll be sure to get Sophie to a safe place."

Nico gripped the edge of the table. The veins on his forearms bulged as though he'd just lifted a heavy weight. For a moment, she thought he was going to flip the table. Instead, he turned to Jamie, then Sara, and gave them a tight smile. "What brings you two out tonight?"

19

N ico

NICO HAD NEVER KILLED A SPIDER. Not once in his thirty-four years. He scooped them into a cup and took them outside where they could live out the rest of their lives in peace. Martin Luther King and Gandhi were his heroes. However, at this precise moment and for the second time in twenty-four hours, he wanted nothing more than to punch another man in his arrogant face. Was Sophie here with him? Had she agreed to a date, or had they just run into each other?

She'd laughed at his joke about rescuing cats and women. What the actual hell was going on here? Did she like this obvious player? She might not know he was a player. She didn't know about these kinds of men. What if she offered herself to him?

His stomach turned at the thought of this idiot touching her. His Sophie. A voice in his head berated him.

She's not yours. You've done nothing but force her into this very situation.

From the platform at the other end of the bar, the singer from the live band announced the beginning of the first set. No sooner had the first guitar chord played than Jad had whisked Sophie off her feet and practically dragged her to the dance floor. He tried not to watch them, but it was impossible. Did the bastard have to hold her that close? She didn't even know him. He could be a predator.

He felt David watching him from the other side of the table. When he looked over, his friend gave him a sympathetic smile. Was it that obvious that he was about to lose his mind?

Sara put her hand on his arm, drawing his attention to her. She was more than a little loose. He suspected that wasn't her first dirty martini. "It's just a dance, you know."

"What? Sure. I mean, it's none of my business who she dances with," Nico said.

Jamie threw her head back in laughter. "Dude, you're absolutely pathetic."

David ducked his chin and massaged his temple as if he wanted to disappear. Nico had talked him into coming out for a drink, hoping they'd find Sophie. He was sure to be regretting it by now.

"What Jamie's trying to say," Sara said, slurring her words slightly, "is that everyone in this town knows you're in love with Sophie, and we're all wondering why you're so determined to be miserable."

Jamie leaned back in her chair and tilted her head as if she were studying an alien creature. "We do wonder that, yes."

"Were you a fat kid?" Sara asked Nico.

"No. Kind of skinny," Nico said. "Why do you ask me that?"

Sara's shoulders sagged as she peered at him with glazed eyes. "Because I was, and even though I'm not fat now, I still feel like that little girl. I thought that might be part of your self-esteem problem."

He stared at her for a moment. She was right. "There are other ways to feel like crap about yourself. Many, many ways."

"Totally," David said.

Sophie and Jad arrived back at the table. She was all flushed and obviously a little drunk. That was it. He had to get her out of here. Take her home and get her to bed. His bed.

Sara made a sad little squeak. "Wow, I've had way too much to drink. I think I should go home now. Are we sharing an Uber? Or do you want to stay longer, Jamie?"

"I'm good to go now," Jamie said.

"Let me drive you home," David said. "Nico and I came in separate cars."

"Does your car have a heater?" Sara asked. "I imagine it's like a refrigerator in there." She hiccuped.

"What?" David asked.

"She's just kidding," Jamie said. "We'd love a ride home."

"We accept."

David offered his arm to Sara. "Let me help you."

Sara tilted her head and looked across the restaurant to the front. "It's so far to the door."

"Don't worry, I've got you," David said.

Sara took his arm, and the two of them headed toward the entrance.

Jamie patted Nico's shoulder on the way out and whispered in his ear. "Don't let her leave with him tonight."

He waited until they were out of earshot before he turned to Sophie. "It's time for us to go, too."

"You go ahead," Jad said. "Sophie and I are staying."

"Like I said, we don't know you. I don't feel comfortable leaving my friend to ride home with a stranger." He tried to keep the threatening tone from his voice but was failing miserably.

"It's okay, Jad," Sophie said. "I should probably go."

The conspiratorial look they shared made his temperature rise at least another ten degrees.

"Whatever you want," Jad said.

He reached the boiling point when Sophie leaned over and gave him a kiss on the cheek. "Thanks for the dance and for understanding."

"My pleasure." Jad pretended to tip his hat.

This guy practically begged to be punched.

"Come on, Soph." Nico held out his hand. "We're going home."

She sucked in her bottom lip and stared at him with those giant eyes as though she wasn't sure what he'd just said.

"Take my hand." He reached out to her. "You're a little drunk, and I don't want you falling."

"I am a tiny bit tipsy, so that's the only reason I'll accept your offer." She placed her hand in his, and he led her through the crowd and through the front doors.

He almost wept with relief when they stepped into the cool night air. If he'd stayed indoors for another second, he might have unleashed on the man.

Sophie jerked away from him, then leaned over at the waist as if she might be sick.

"You okay?" Was she drunker than he thought? Then he realized she was silently laughing so hard that her whole body shook. "What in the hell is so funny?"

She straightened. Her eye makeup was smudged from hysterically laughing. "You, Nico. You're funny. Funny and aggravating and so stupid sometimes I just don't even know what to say anymore." Clutching her bag to her chest, she lifted her face to the sky. "If you're going to drive me home, let's just get it over with. The sooner I can get away from you the better." She started walking toward the parking lot, and he had no choice but to follow her.

S ophie

SOPHIE STARED out Nico's car window all the way back to Judi's. Her thoughts looped round and round. Jad's plan had worked. Maybe too well. Nico was jealous and he was mad. She didn't care. She was mad right back. The trick was to *stay* mad. There was no way she was backing down from this fight. He was acting like a big fat jerk. The vehicle lurched to a stop in front of his bungalow. With his hands still on the steering wheel, he stared out the front window.

"What were you doing there with that jackass?" Nico asked through clenched teeth. "Please tell me you didn't meet him there on purpose."

She crossed her arms over her chest and concentrated on shooting a hole through his brain. "Do you really think you get to be jealous?"

"I'm not jealous. I'm concerned over your judgment. He could be a serial killer for all we know."

She barked out a laugh. "That's the most absurd thing I've ever heard. He's a firefighter."

"That means nothing. You have no idea what he's like other than he seems like a stalker."

"You're so full of it, and you're so jealous."

"I swear to God, Sophie, every time I turn around some jerk's all over you."

"Then why don't you do something about it instead of just getting mad and acting like an ass?"

His head snapped backward as if she'd smacked him in the nose. When his gaze returned to her, his eyes glittered with an intensity that almost scared her. "I've been trying to be a good guy. How can you not see that?"

"I don't even know what that means." She stared at her lap. She would not cry. Not here in front of him.

His voice was husky. "Soph, I'm sorry. You've made me into a crazy person."

"I've not done one thing to you except love you with all my heart. Your crazy came along way before me."

He hung his head. "It's true."

"Maybe everyone's right. If you don't want me, maybe I should be with one of the guys who does." She fluttered her hand in the direction of the brewery. "Jad's nice. He's a hero who saves cats from trees."

He jerked upright to glare at her. "Dammit, Sophie, don't mess with me."

"I'm not messing with you." She swiped at the one stupid, betraying tear that leaked out of her eye. "You're the one messing with me. Just leave me alone." She yanked open the door and practically hurled herself out of the car, then headed across the driveway toward the front door. By the time she reached the steps, she heard the driver's-side door open and slam shut.

"Sophie, do not walk away from me."

She really wanted to give him the finger but having never actually flipped someone off, she thought better of it and continued up the stairs.

A second later, he was on her. "Listen to me." His eyes filled as he looked down at her. "I'm the one who ran into a burning building for you while the firemen took their sweet time to get there. I'm the one who would have died for you. I'd do it again. A thousand fires. A thousand nights. Over and over to make sure you're safe. Don't ever forget that." Then, without warning, he lifted her off her feet and into his arms.

"What the hell do you think you're doing?" She tried to wriggle free, but his grip was like that of a drowning man.

He stormed across the driveway. "I'm taking you inside and doing what I should have done months ago."

What was that? What did he mean?

He opened the door to his bungalow with one hand and charged inside. Breathing hard, he crossed through the living room and into the bedroom. Jen, clearly startled out of her slumber, looked up at them from her bed.

"Stay put," Nico said to Jen.

Jen wagged her tail and did as he asked.

He tossed Sophie on the bed. She bounced slightly. "What's happening?" she whispered.

He shut the bedroom door, then sat next to her, gently pinning her arms to her sides. "Soph, I need to say this to you even though I'm terrified of every single thing about you. I love you so much it hurts. It's bigger than anything I've ever felt before. I've acted like an idiot, and I'm so sorry."

"You. Love. Me?" A boundless surge of joy flooded her. Was this happening? Was her dream unfolding before her eyes?

"Yes, I love you. I've been an idiot, and it's all because I'm so afraid to let you in and give you the power to crush me. Being away from you makes me ill. My life without you is like living without sunshine. You make me want to be brave. I've decided it's worth the risk. I want you by my side for the rest of my life."

"Nico, really?"

"Yes, really." He lay beside her and looked into her eyes. "I've loved you since the first time you smiled at me. The thought of you going to France and not coming back was awful. I don't want to live without you."

"I don't want to live without you," she said.

"I'm sorry I've acted so ridiculous. At first, I was simply trying to do the right thing. I thought you were too young for me. But as time went on, I realized there was more to it. More to me that I haven't told you."

"I know you were, but you were totally wrong about what that should be. The right thing is for us to be together."

"I know that now," he said. "I'm sorry I hurt you. I was trying to tell you all this last night, but you left before I could get the words out. When I saw you with Jad, I lost all reason."

"All is forgiven." She stroked his cheekbone and let herself fall into the pools of his eyes. He loved her. She'd begun to doubt that he was the one, but being here with him like this, she knew. She knew with utter certainty. This was him. The one she'd known from the time she was a little girl was out here waiting for her. "You can spend the rest of your life making it up to me."

"Do you mean that?" he asked. "Do you really want me for the rest of your life?"

"It's what I've wanted from the first." She held his face in her hands. "I told you the truth. When I was eight years old I had a terrible fever, and the vision of you and Jen came to me. Only you guys were standing in a field of sunflowers. Which is sort of weird, but I think that was just a symbol for your profession."

"The whole thing's weird," he said.

"I'm weird."

"The world according to Sophie is weird but wonderful."

"I'm glad you're finally understanding that," she said.

"Soph, I want to go to France with you. I want to kiss you on a bridge overlooking the Seine. Will you let me?"

The vulnerability in his voice and eyes touched her heart in a whole new way. "I would love nothing more. What about work?"

"I talked to the guys about it at dinner, and they said they could spare me for a few weeks. All in the name of love."

"That's really sweet," Sophie said.

"They're your fan club. They've thought all along I was being stupid."

"The path to love isn't always a straight line. It hasn't been for any of the Wolves."

Her breath caught as he kissed her with new tenderness.

"When I thought you might be trapped upstairs when that fire broke out was the single most terrifying moment of my life," he said. "The thought of losing you made me brave. I realized that if I could run into a burning building to save you, surely I could risk you leaving me someday."

"I'm not going to leave. You can always count on me. Today and every single tomorrow."

Tears swam in his eyes. "Besides Trey, I've never had someone in my life who truly supported me or understood me. Growing up, my parents' love was conditional. Or at least it seemed that way to me. With Addie, I thought I'd found the woman who would love me for me, but she loved someone else. It's been unfathomable to me that you would feel this way about me forever. I didn't trust it. But no matter how I tried to convince you that we were all wrong, you never gave up on me. You never wavered. I saw that finally." His cheeks were wet now. Sophie dried them as best she could with her hand. "No one has ever loved me the way you do. I don't really get it, but I finally decided to stop questioning it and be thankful."

"Judi told me that the way to make you see that we're meant to be was to offer unconditional love to counteract your parents' conditional love. She was right."

"She figured that out pretty quickly, didn't she?" His lips twitched into a half smile.

"When I think about the little boy who simply wanted to be loved...I don't know how to say it...how sorry I am."

He scrunched his eyes closed as his chest rose and fell.

"You don't have to pretend it doesn't still hurt," she said. "Not with me."

When he opened his eyes, the pain that reflected from them pierced through her. "Soph, there's something I haven't told you about my parents. I tried so hard to get them to like me. But they couldn't. It never made sense to me. Maybe if my brother hadn't been born or if they'd gotten me as a newborn, things would've been different."

The truth to what he was saying felt like a boulder had dropped onto her chest. "Nico, were you adopted?"

"They don't know I know. All my life, I couldn't figure out why they loved my brother and not me. I was the easier kid, always compliant, whereas my brother was a hellion. Ironically, Addie was the one who convinced me that I might be adopted. She didn't think any natural parents could act the way they did. We sent in for a DNA test. My father was a zero match. My mother was at twenty-five percent. Which means she's my aunt. I haven't asked my parents for the truth yet, but I have every reason to believe that my mother's younger sister is my real mother. She committed suicide at age fourteen."

"Oh, Nico. I can't believe it. I'm so sorry. How come you haven't told me about this until now? Or Mrs. Coventry? Of all people, we would understand."

"Only Addie knows. I haven't told anyone else. Not even

Trey. I haven't known how to talk about it. The whole thing seems so unreal. Until I get the courage to confront them, I'll never know how everything went down. I don't know if I want to. When I think about a fourteen-year-old girl giving birth and then ending her life, my heart breaks. How bad must her home life have been? Maybe they forced her to give me to her sister and her husband. Maybe that's what caused her to kill herself. My grandparents were wealthy. Maybe they forced them to take me in exchange for money. Who knows where my real father is? Was she raped? Was it a boyfriend? Did he ever know about me?"

"We can find try to find him."

He moved his arm over his eyes, as if he wanted to hide. "What if he's a monster? What if that's what I come from?"

"Wouldn't it be better to know? Whatever we find, you're not a monster." She peeled his arm away from his face. "You're a kind, good man. The very best person. I wouldn't love you so much if that weren't true."

"What if what we find makes you not want to be with me?"

"Nothing will ever cause that to happen," Sophie said. "Not anything. But you have to face this. Confront your parents. Find out the truth. I'll go with you. I'll be there every step of the way."

"You'd do that for me?" His eyes searched hers.

"I'd walk to the ends of the earth for you. I'd run into a burning building for you. Again and again to make sure you were safe. I'm your family now. It's you and me forever. No matter what we find, we'll have a home in each other."

"They never loved me, Soph. I always knew it, but I never knew why. I was a burden to them."

He buried his face in her hair and sobbed. She wrapped her arms around him and held him close. His heart pounded against her chest as the little boy in him wept. The rejection and criticism—the coldness where there should have been warmth—had forced the hurt child to hide deep inside him. On the outside he'd appeared whole, but he wasn't. He was broken. Like so many others, he was broken. She was not. She was whole. She was made to love him, to reach the places he'd never been touched. He was a virgin of a kind, too. He'd never been loved properly.

He hadn't believed she could love him because he didn't know what it felt like to be sheltered by the people who love you. Protected and nurtured as she'd been. Even Hugh, from afar, had loved her so much that he left behind his words for her. Her real mother in heaven had been her guardian angel, always by her side, steering her in the right directions. Micky and Rhona had loved her every day of her life as though she was their miracle. They were the reason she was whole. But this beautiful man had been denied the only thing that will keep a person truly alive. Love.

"You'll never have to feel this way again," she whispered. "I'm going to love you so hard you'll understand what it's like to have a family. I'll never let you go one day without feeling my love."

"I don't think a man ever loved a woman as much as I love you."

"All men in love think that," she said. "I'm glad it's me you feel that way about."

He raised his head from her hair and kissed her. For the next few minutes, she forgot everything but the feel of his hands and mouth and body.

"Is this how it is?" she asked, panting, desperate to have her clothes off. "Does it always feel like this?

"You mean sex?"

She nodded, feeling shy suddenly. "You know I don't know anything."

He brushed her hair away from her neck and nibbled on

the skin above her collarbone. "We can wait to go the next level if you're not ready."

She tugged at his button of his jeans. "Undress me. I've waited long enough." She gasped as his hands unclasped her bra in one quick flip of his thumb and finger.

"I'll be gentle, but it might be unpleasant. I promise the second time will be better."

"As long as there's a next time, I'm good," she said.

21

N ico

IN HIS BED, Nico held Sophie in his arms and stroked her hair. They were both damp from the physical exertion of their second encounter. The first time had been a bit rushed, albeit satisfying. They'd waited so long to be together that it was a heated, intense exchange that had left them breathless. They'd fallen asleep curled together like two cats, with him promising it would be better next time. When they woke in the early morning, he took his time, savoring her. While the birds chirped outside the window and Jen slept in her bed, his world expanded. This was what it felt like to make love to his soulmate.

Now, she brought his free hand to her mouth and kissed his fingers one by one. "Do you think I scared Jen with all that noise I made?"

He laughed, ridiculously pleased with himself for the sounds he evoked from her. "You *were* kind of loud."

She smacked him playfully on the chest, then hid her face in his neck. "Don't talk about it."

"There's plenty more where that came from," he said.

She sighed and burrowed more deeply into him. "Was the first time with other girls like the one we had?"

"I've never been anyone's first time," he said.

"In that way, we were both virgins," she said, sounding happy.

"Are you sure you're not going to want to try some other guys?" The thought of it turned his stomach, but he had to ask.

She lifted her head. All that hair splayed over his chest as she looked into his eyes. "Don't ever ask me that again."

"Got it. Never again." He let out a long, relieved breath and vowed to himself that he would do everything in his power to make sure she always had whatever she needed and wanted from him.

She settled back against him, resting one arm over his stomach. If she weren't careful, he'd be ready for round three.

"Soph?"

"Yeah?"

"If I asked you to marry me, would you say yes?"

"You know the answer to that question," she said, her voice wobbly. "Are you going to ask me soon?"

He chuckled and kissed the top of her head, which smelled unbelievably good. "The proposal has to be perfect, so it might take a bit to come up with just the right thing."

"The proposal doesn't have to be perfect. You're perfect for me. That's all I care about."

"What about a wedding?" he asked. "Do you want one?"

"As long as I get to marry you, then I don't really care how we do it."

"But what about your mom? Will she care?"

"She will care," Sophie said slowly, as if imagining how it would play out if he were to whisk her off to Vegas. "She will care a lot."

"Then we'll have a wedding. Whatever you want."

"My dad will insist on paying for the whole thing. Maybe we can get away with something small, though."

"Not a château in France?" he asked.

"I'd like that just fine, but it would mean more to do it here where we live. Where we found each other."

His chest ached with love for this woman. His Sophie. She would be his wife. How was he this lucky?

"Small sounds good," he said. "I'd vote for our church in town for the ceremony."

He smoothed hair from her eyes. "I can't lie. I feel bad that I don't have a house for us," he said.

"Since I have no stuff, moving in here with you won't be a problem."

"That does work out nicely," he said. "But someday we'll need something bigger."

"Don't worry about it. Everything will fall into place when it's supposed to."

"I've been thinking," he said. "Would you be willing to fly to San Diego with me before we head to Paris?"

"Absolutely. We'll have to let Judi know why."

"I'm ready to talk about it," he said as he reached for his phone. "Okay, I'm doing it. I'll text that we'll be there tonight for dinner."

"Do it."

He sent a group text to both his parents.

I've met someone I want you to meet. We're coming to town tonight. I'd like to bring her by for dinner.

He deleted the last sentence. No asking. He would tell them.

I'm bringing her by for dinner.

Surprisingly, his mother texted back right away.

We eat at 7. I'll expect you to be on time.

He showed the exchange to Sophie. "Oh, we'll be on time," she said.

A bark came from outside the room. "Poor Jen," Sophie said. "We have to let her in. She's probably sad out there all alone."

"Spoiled pooch." Nico got out of bed to open the door. Jen wasted no time. She leaped onto the bed and hurled herself into Sophie's lap.

"Hey girl, that's my spot," Nico said as he pulled on a pair of sweatpants.

Jen answered by burrowing deeper into her new mistress's lap and grinning.

Nico joined them on the bed and for the next few minutes there were many kisses of the canine variety.

* * *

Nico's hands were shaking when he rang the doorbell of his parents' house at five minutes after seven. "We're late."

"Just five minutes." Sophie's voice sounded a little shaky, too. "We shouldn't have stopped for the flowers."

"Maybe we shouldn't have come." He was seriously doubting the wisdom of this idea.

"This is the right thing." Sophie squeezed his hand.

He gave her a quick kiss on the cheek. "You look beautiful, by the way. If I haven't mentioned it." Mrs. Coventry had picked out her outfit: a flowy dress in light blue that tied in the middle with sleeves that fluttered when she walked. He couldn't stop fantasizing about untying the package. And her legs in strappy sandals were enough to cause a riot.

"You told me earlier." Her eyes shone up at him. "But I love hearing it again."

"You've got something on you." Pollen from one of the

flowers had left a yellow residue on the shoulder of Sophie's dress. He brushed it with his fingers but only managed to embed it further.

"Don't worry about it," Sophie said. "I'll wash it off later."

A housekeeper dressed in black opened the door. Short and plump, she was around fifty with white hair and a sweet face. He didn't recognize her. Not that he'd expected to. His mother went through housekeepers like some women changed outfits.

"Hi. I'm Sophie." She vigorously shook the housekeeper's hand and flashed that Sophie smile.

"I'm Merry." She lifted her startled brown eyes to Nico, clearly unsure if she were to shake his hand too.

"I'm Nico," he said, offering his hand in a quick shake. "Nice to meet you."

"Please come in," Merry said. "Mr. and Mrs. Bentley are waiting for you in the living room."

The house was all white marble floors and pale walls. Large and cold with cathedral ceilings, he always imagined there would be an echo when he talked. A spiral staircase led up to the second floor. A giant chandelier glittered over the entryway.

Sophie's heels click-clacked on the hard floors as they followed Merry through the house to the sitting room.

His father sat near the grand piano reading the *Wall Street Journal*. He set aside the paper and stood, smoothing the front of his linen shirt. Casual attire for his dad was Nico's best dress clothes—the difference between a landscape architect and a lawyer. One of many, for which Nico was glad.

"You're late," Mom said from the wet bar where she was pouring martinis into glasses. She wore a pair of black slacks and a red silk blouse that tied at the neck. Most likely what she'd worn to the office. Both his parents were tall and slim. In their midfifties, they were fit and youthful.

"Sorry. We had to wait for a cab," Nico said as he shook his dad's hand. "This is Sophie Woods."

"Nice to meet you, Sophie," Dad said.

His mother stepped forward. "Welcome, Sophie." Her light brown hair was cut in flattering layers.

"These are for you," Sophie said. The bouquet they'd chosen looked paltry in the large, formal room.

"Thank you. So thoughtful." Mom took them, and without doing the obligatory sniff, placed them on the wet bar. "I'll have Merry take care of them later."

Mom's long red nails hovered over Sophie's shoulder. "You've got something on your dress."

Sophie looked at her shoulder and laughed. "A little pollen from the flowers. No big deal."

Mom's eyes expanded slightly. "Would you like to use the restroom to wash it off?"

"Nope. I'm good."

Dad gestured toward the couch. "Have a seat. We like to have a drink before dinner, Sophie. Would either of you care for one?"

They both declined as they sat together on the stiff couch. He never worried about slouching on his mother's furniture. They all seem to have stiff backs.

Mom set two martinis on the coffee table and sat in the armchair next to his father.

"This is quite a surprise," Mom said. "Sophie, we had no idea you existed until this morning. We hardly hear from Nico since he moved north."

"I exist," Sophie said, smiling. "And I'm here to stay."

His mother's gaze flickered to Sophie's hand.

"We're getting engaged," Nico blurted out. "Soon."

"Nico, really?" Mom said. "I'm glad you brought her to visit before you proposed at least." She said this stiffly, as if he'd committed a mortal sin.

"We're happy for you," Dad said. "What happened with Addie was rough."

"It was the talk of the club, that's for sure." Mom smoothed the front of her blouse. "For months."

"Until old Larry ran off with his son's fiancée," Dad said. "Then they moved to that subject for several months."

"That's some family drama," Nico said. At least they weren't that bad.

"And what do you do for a living, Sophie?" Dad asked. "Are you in the landscape business?"

"I own a bar with my brother."

As though they were lifted by strings implanted into her forehead, his mother's plucked eyebrows rose in tandem.

Dad crossed his legs. "What kind of bar?"

"Old-school bar and grill. It's been in my family for three generations," Sophie said. "We're very proud of it."

"The Oar is a part of Cliffside Bay's history," Nico said.

"We had a fire," Sophie said. "Nico saved my life by rescuing me from the bathtub."

"The bathtub?" Dad asked.

Sophie nodded. "Yes. It's now the talk of town, to my mortification." She explained that her apartment was above the bar. Then she gushed about how he had saved her.

Embarrassed, he wished he'd asked for that martini. He said as much to his mother, then rose from the couch to pour one from the pitcher.

"Do you need money?" Dad asked. "How's business?"

Derek Bentley was always one to get right to the point. "No, I'm good. Thanks for asking." Nico sat beside Sophie and took a swig of his martini and coughed. "That's strong."

"Yes, Merry does a wonderful job with the drinks," Mom said. "Which almost makes up for her lack of dusting ability."

"They've had a few high-profile clients," Sophie said, circling back to bragging about him. His heart ached with love for her. "Sara Ness just had them build her a mansion."

"Of Ness beer?" Dad asked, brightening.

"That's right," Sophie said. "She can't stop raving about Nico's design. Her gardens are spectacular. He even put in a creek."

"A creek? She must have a large piece of property," Dad said.

Nico realized he needed to get on with things. They were here for reason. "I came down to talk to you about something specific."

"We figured," Mom said.

He took in a deep breath, then let it out slowly. It was best to say it straight. "I had a DNA test done. I know you're not my biological parents."

No one moved for at least thirty seconds. He'd never seen his mother at a loss for words.

"Why would you do that?" Mom's face had lost all color.

"Addie suggested it, back when we were together. Then everything blew up and I left town before she got the results back. They were mailed to our old apartment. She wasn't sure whether to contact me or not. The way we left things wasn't good." *Stop babbling. Get yourself together.* "I'm down here to learn what happened. And why it was a secret."

His mother finished her martini and got up to pour another.

He would stay quiet. Wait for her to speak.

Nico sneaked a glance at his dad. He looked like he wanted to run out of the room.

Mom sat back in her chair, appearing calm and unflappable. She was accustomed to the courtroom. "Why would you think to do this?"

"Because I wondered why you've never loved me." Damn, his voice cracked there at the end. *Keep it together.* Sophie squeezed his knee.

Mom's voice was sterile and without emotion as she launched into her explanation. "I'll tell you everything I know.

And then we'll never speak of it again. My little sister became pregnant when she was thirteen years old. Derek and I were newlyweds. Father was preparing to run for a conservative seat in the House of Representatives. They asked us to take you and pretend you were ours. We didn't have a choice."

"Which made you resent me." Of course they had. They'd been forced to do something they didn't want to do. He understood, actually. All his life, they'd tried to make him into something he was not. Knowing the truth explained everything. Every moment of his childhood suddenly made sense.

"I was in law school," Mom said. "Which I had to put on hold to *pretend* I was pregnant. That was my father's plan. We had to go along with it for the sake of the family. I lost an internship in the law firm of my choice, which took me years to recover from professionally. The minute you're seen as a mother, the old boys' club marks you as damaged goods and dismisses you from the partner track. So yes, I was resentful."

"You had Zander five years later," Nico said. "How come he didn't make you resentful?"

"Because he was mine." The words seemed to spill out of his mother's mouth before she could stop them. The moment they were out, she snapped her jaw closed with the force of an angry alligator.

Next to him, Sophie stiffened. "How could you not love him? He was yours. He needed you. I'm adopted, and my parents think of me as a miracle."

"I won't apologize for my feelings," Mom said. "My stupid little sister couldn't keep her legs closed. Then she decided to hang herself in the bathroom to break our mother's heart for the second time. She was never the same, you know. Tina's selfishness ruined our family."

Sophie's earrings were jangling. He turned to look at her and realized it was because she was shaking her head with great force, as if she couldn't believe what she was hearing. "She made a mistake. She was thirteen years old."

"My life shouldn't have been defined by her actions," Mom said. "From the time she was born, everything in my family was about her, not me. And then, in the end, I was stuck with her mistake. Her child."

Her child. Him. The baby no one wanted.

"Why did she commit suicide?" All the moisture in Nico's mouth had disappeared. The feeling of cotton balls stuffed at the back of his throat made it hard to speak or breathe. Regardless, he had to ask. He had to know. "Was it because of me?"

His mother hesitated. She took another sip of her martini before she answered. "Does anyone ever really know the reasons for such a thing? I imagine she was ashamed."

"There was more," Dad said. "They wouldn't let her see you. Or the boy. They locked her away in that house."

"The boy? The father?" Sophie asked, her vocal pitch elevated. "Did the family know who he was?"

Nico inhaled a sharp breath that hurt his chest. His heart beat hard and loud between his ears. Time slowed. The wall behind his mother's head wavered, like pavement on a hot day.

"He was the gardener's son," Dad said. "After everything I did for you. Priming you for a spot in my firm, treating you like my own—you end up a goddamn gardener like your father."

Nico was surprised to hear the anger in the response. "I'm not a gardener." He mumbled this under his breath as he processed what this meant. His choice of profession had seemed like rejection to his father. Was this the reason he cut him off financially? Had it come from a place of pain rather than a desire for control? *How have you never seen this?*

His gaze flickered to his father for a moment. He felt the urge to apologize, but he wasn't sure for what. Being born? Being himself? For his DNA that was not his father's?

"He worked for the family?" Sophie asked. "Was he young too?"

"He was eighteen the year he worked for us," Mom said. "One measly year. That's all it took to ruin everything."

They sat in silence for at least a minute. Nico's entire body hurt. Secrets destroyed families. This one had almost destroyed him.

"Dad, is this why you didn't want me to go to landscape design school?" Nico asked. "Because I was like him?"

"I wanted you to be at the firm with me. Like so many things through the years, you wanted nothing to do with anything I did or liked. In fact, you chose to do the opposite. It was like you knew you were someone else's son. As much as I wanted to influence you, your heart belonged to someone else. When you suddenly announced you wanted to be a gardener—I'm sorry, a landscape architect—it was another blow."

"You never acted like us," Mom said. "Whatever we did, you did the opposite."

"It wasn't rebellion." Nico put his hands in his pockets and crossed his fingers. Then, thinking better of it, he took out his left hand and placed it in Sophie's. She was his shield now. Finally, he had someone on his side. He paused, taking in a deep breath to keep from crying as waves of pain washed over him. "It wasn't about you. It was about me being myself. I tried my best to please you but at a detriment to myself. Had I taken the path you wanted, I would be completely dead inside. I couldn't be a lawyer. It's the antithesis of how my brain works. Let's be honest, I'm not sure I could've gotten into law school even if I'd tried. People are good at what they love. I love plants, Dad. That's simply who I am. I'm sorry if that felt like rebellion."

"I suppose it was in your blood," Dad said softly. "We were stupid to think otherwise."

"Do you know what happened to him?" Nico asked. "Did he know about me?"

"Do you know his name?" Sophie asked.

His mother's gaze dropped to her lap. "Why do you want to open this up?"

"Because I want to know who my family is," Nico said. "It's my right to know. I might have other family out there."

"He knew about you," Dad said.

"But he didn't want me?" Nico asked.

"Father paid him to stay away," Mom said. "Five thousand dollars was all it took to get rid of him."

Five thousand dollars to wash his hands of a baby no one wanted.

Sophie leaned forward. He could feel the heat radiating from her skin. "Tell us his name."

His father reached for his martini. "His name was James Baylor. He went by Jimmy."

"Do you have any idea where we might get information about him?" Sophie asked.

"It's been thirty-four years," Mom said, as if it were a stupid question.

"Did you ever plan on telling me?" asked Nico. "Why did you keep it from me?"

"We thought it would be better to leave it alone," said his mother.

"Jimmy left for money," Dad said. "We thought it would hurt you to know that."

"You're making us out to be the bad guy," Mom said. "We were the ones who did the right thing. We never asked for this. But we did it without complaint."

"Did it without complaint," Nico said. "How good of you." He'd been nothing but a burden to them. A responsibility they took on to save the family from scandal.

So many things made sense now. All the times he felt

rejected. His mother's coldness toward him but not Zander. Feeling as if he didn't belong. The shame of being unwanted had clung to him like a second skin. He'd carried that shame into every moment of his life. Understanding, however, did nothing to ease his pain. Would the ache ever leave? Or did this kind of wound fester for the rest of his life?

"That's not how I meant it," Mom said, sounding impatient. "It wasn't easy to change my life for a baby I didn't ask for. I wasn't ready."

"Your mother's family was always about their secrets. No matter the cost." His father uncrossed his legs and looked to the ceiling before turning his gaze to Nico. "I know where your father is. He died twenty years ago. I'm sorry."

His mother flinched, obviously surprised. "Derek, are you sure?"

"Over the years, I kept track of him." Dad closed his eyes for a moment as a wave of pain crossed over his face. "I'm not proud of what we did. I was never sure it was the right thing to keep it from you. I worried that you'd discover the truth. If you did, I wanted you to know where he was."

"Do you know how he died?" Nico asked.

"Car accident," Dad said.

"Did he have a wife? Other children?" Sophie asked.

"The paper didn't list any," Dad said.

"I suppose that's a disappointment to you," Mom said.

Taken aback, Nico looked to his mother. "Why would you say that?"

"It's obvious you would love to replace us," Mom said.

"You just told me I was a burden to you," Nico said. "Isn't that what Zander's always been? Your real family?"

They sat in uncomfortable silence for a moment or two. An urge to flee almost overwhelmed him, but he stayed put. This was the conversation they must have in order for him to understand who he really was. "Why didn't they just offer me up for adoption?"

"That was my mother," Mom said. "She couldn't stand the thought that her grandchild would be raised outside of the family."

Nico's stomach turned as he imagined his fourteen-year-old mother. How scared she must've been. How ashamed. How misunderstood. Then he thought about the woman who raised him, the one who had given up so much of her life to take him in. He filled with a deep sadness, for all of them. He fought tears. "I'm sorry, Mom. I can see how unfair this was to you. But did you ever love me just little?" His voice broke. Despite his best intentions, the tears came.

"It was you who didn't love us," Mom said.

"That's not true," Nico said. "I loved you. I tried so hard to be good. It hurt to never be quite right. Nothing I did ever seemed to please you."

"That's ridiculous." His mother's grip on her martini glass seemed as if she might break it in half. "I didn't understand you. It's not the same thing."

"It felt that way to me," Nico said.

"We were kids ourselves when they asked us to take you," Dad said. "We didn't handle things as well as we should have. I see that now. We did the best we could with the resources we had. I'm sorry we didn't do better. If I had it to do over again, I would make different choices. If I could go back...if I could see it then as I do now, through the lens of maturity, I would have acted like an adult, instead of a spoiled child. Sophie, your parents are right. You were a gift to them, just as you are to us, Nico. I thought about it a lot over the years—how different things might've been had I been supportive of your decision to study what you love. I'll regret that for the rest of my life. My only excuse is that it seemed to be the final proof that I would never really be your father."

"You are my father," Nico said. "Forging my way alone made me the man I am today. You don't need to carry that burden. I love my life. I'm proud of the life I've made."

"You *should* be proud," Dad said. "You've made it on your own without the help of anyone." He paused, looking at the floor. "I wish you'd needed me just a little."

"I have needed you, Dad. Just not in the ways you thought I did. I've wanted your approval all my life."

"I'm saying it now. I'm proud of you. I love you. I'd love nothing more than to be part of your life again."

"I'd like that too." Nico swallowed a lump in his throat.

His mother shifted, looking uncomfortable. "I know I've been overcritical. I pushed too hard. I want too much from the people I love. I wanted you to be successful, so that my sacrifices were worth it. I'm sorry if my parenting hurt you."

He supposed that was the closest he would ever get to hearing his mother's confession that she loved him, despite all he had cost her.

"I'd like it if you'd stay for dinner," Mom said. "We could answer more questions for you, if you wanted."

He glanced at Sophie. She met his gaze and gave him a nod of approval.

* * *

AFTER DINNER, his father asked him to join him in the study. He left Sophie with his mother, who was telling her the details of the fire. Mom was asking questions like the criminal defense lawyer she was. Maybe they should put his mother on the case.

"Cigar?" Dad asked as he lifted the humidor.

"No, thanks. I don't smoke."

"I noticed you skipped the roast beef tonight as well."

"I have high cholesterol," Nico said.

"Well, you didn't get that from me."

They looked at each other and laughed.

"Too soon?" Dad asked as he closed the humidor without taking a cigar.

"Probably. Although, the only way to get through life is to laugh at the absurdity of most things."

Burgundy-colored paint on the walls and mahogany furniture gave the room a serious, lawyerly vibe. His father's diplomas, awards, and photographs with various important people hung on the walls. The slight smell of cigars lingered in the cushions of the leather chairs. When he was a child, Nico had been forbidden to come into this room. Now, standing here with his father, he felt as if he'd entered another life. An existence that had no connection to his current one but not to the past, either. A new chapter. One based on the truth, not lies.

"I have something for you," Dad said. He walked over to a cabinet in the corner and pulled open a drawer. He rummaged around for a moment, then turned to face Nico. In his hand was a small box. "I never thought Addison was the right woman for you. I didn't see the eventual outcome." He chuckled. "No one saw that coming."

"I certainly didn't."

"Now that I see you with Sophie, I can see it was for the best. Although it must've hurt like a son of a bitch."

"No question. However, if I'd known Sophie was waiting for me, I would have seen it as a blessing."

"That's the thing about life. You can't see the reason why until it's over. Looking back, you understand how it all fits together. How one thing leads to another. Or at least, that's what they say." He handed Nico the box. "This has been in my family for several generations. After meeting Sophie, it seems perfect for her. Open it. You'll see what I mean."

He lifted the lid. An antique wedding ring made of silver and three rather large diamonds glittered back at him. "You're right. She'll love this. She's an old soul. So perfectly herself. I've never met someone as comfortable in their own skin. She lives her life exactly how she wants to with no apologies."

"I can see that. Which makes her a good match for you."

"Thank you, Dad. I can't afford to get her a ring like this. Even though I wish I could."

"Well, you don't have to. You've done everything on your own. Let me do this for you. It'll make me happy to give it to you."

"What about Zander? Wouldn't he want it for his bride?"

"I want you to have it."

And in those words, that simple sentence, forgiveness and acceptance and everything he wanted from his father rained down on him. He wanted to give the ring to him.

"I accept. Thank you. Thank you for everything."

"New chapter, though? One where I see you more?" Dad asked.

"Absolutely. You could come visit me sometime."

"I'd like that."

"We're going to Paris in a few days. Sophie asked me if I'd kiss her on a bridge overlooking the Seine. With this ring, I'll be able to ask her to marry me."

"Sounds like a good plan." His dad slapped him on the back. "You found a good one. She's even charming your mother, which is no easy task."

"That's just the world according to Sophie. You'll get used to it."

22

Sophie

IT WAS early morning when Sophie, Nico, and Judi landed at the Charles de Gaulle airport. Judi paid for first-class upgrades from both San Francisco to New York and New York to Paris. The seats were so comfortable that after a glass of wine, they'd all slept for a good portion of the seven-hour flight from New York to Paris.

Now, in the backseat of a taxi, sitting between Nico and Judi, Sophie clung to her purse as they made their way in stops and starts down the Paris streets toward central Paris where Judi had booked them two rooms at Hotel Villa D'Estrées. The cab driver rolled down his window to yell an obscenity at the car in front of them, then laid his hand on the horn for a few seconds. She assumed they were obscenities as the intent couldn't be mistaken, given the hand gestures. Although she couldn't imagine what the other car's offense might have been. There seemed to be no rules on the Paris streets other than to be as aggressive as possible.

"Paris is crazy," Nico whispered in her ear. "There's no way I'm driving here."

"Agreed," she whispered back.

"I can't believe I'm here with you," he said. "This feels like a dream."

On her other side, Judi sighed. "Paul and I had so many wonderful times here. You two have to promise me you'll come again and again."

"That's a promise I'm willing to make," Sophie said.

They crossed over the mighty Seine to the Right Bank, where they would stay in the sixth neighborhood, or arrondissement, as the French called them. The river was a dark green today. A whisper of clouds streaked the autumnal blue sky, shedding an ethereal light over Paris. As they passed over the bridge, Sophie pointed to Notre-Dame, which was under construction and surrounded by cranes and scaffolding. The first time she'd come had been before the fire. Fortunately, the cathedral didn't go the way of The Oar.

The sidewalks were quiet this time of day. Parisians weren't early risers. A woman on a bicycle wearing a cotton skirt and sandals pedaled past them. Baguettes stuck out of the bike's basket. "I should get a bike to pedal around Cliffside Bay," Sophie said. "I want one with a basket."

"You really should," Nico said.

"I can see it starting a trend," Judi said, sounding happy. "I'll buy you one for Christmas."

They passed attractive cafés, not yet open. A woman in heels and a tight red dress ran in front of the car and into a bakery. Several workers swept the sidewalks in front of businesses. Another watered a flower basket that hung from the front of a bistro.

They lurched rather than turned down the skinny cobblestoned Rue Gît-le-Coeur and came to a halt in front of Hotel Villa D'Estrées. Sophie, slightly nauseous from the ride, stumbled out of the cab. Nico steadied her and gave her a quick kiss. "Welcome to Paris."

Judi spun in a circle, giggling like a girl. "Isn't this the best, y'all?"

"I adore this street," Sophie said, as she breathed in the cool, crisp air.

The front of the hotel was painted black with large paneled windows. Sophie pulled her jacket closed as she peered down the quiet street. An apartment building was directly across from them with a very French-looking Café Latin next door. How she would have loved to peer inside the rooms of the apartments, but the shades were all drawn. Directly next door to the hotel was an Irish pub, of all things. She couldn't seem to get away from bars.

The driver took their suitcases out of the trunk and grunted to them in French before heading toward the lobby doors. Nico grabbed the third bag. "After you, ladies."

They walked through heavy doors into the colorful lobby. Unlike the sparseness of an American lobby, this space was filled to the brim in a complex combination of bright colors and ornate furniture. Tables with delicate carvings were paired with red, green, and yellow striped chairs. Heavy burgundy drapes hung in the windows. Every table had a fresh bouquet of lilies and roses. She sighed with pleasure as their scent mingled with that of coffee. At artfully arranged tables, guests dined on pastries, yogurt, and fruit. In the middle of the room, several men read newspapers while their younger cohorts looked at tablets or phones.

As tempting as the buttery croissants were, Sophie trudged up to the desk in the far corner where a young woman with a sleek brown hair and dark eyes worked on a laptop computer. Her name tag read "Collette."

"Bonjour," Collette said.

"Bonjour," said Judi in perfect French. "We're the Coventry party."

Collette responded back in English with a hint of a French accent. "Welcome to Paris."

After getting the rundown about breakfast and other housekeeping items, they were told to take the elevator up to the third floor. "We'll send your luggage up straightaway," Collette said.

Sophie wondered why they wouldn't just take their own luggage up with them but didn't want to ask. She understood when the elevator doors opened. There was barely room for the three of them. Nico had to bend his head slightly in order to fit. Luggage must come up a different elevator.

"The small elevators and bathrooms in Paris are compensated for the charm of everything else," Judi said.

"When I was here last time, I walked into a bathroom and a man was in one of the stalls doing his business," Sophie said. "A stall with no door."

"The French are not nearly as uptight as we are," Judi said. "And they're much better dressers. Speaking of which, I'd like you two dressed for dinner. Not your usual shorts, Nico."

Nico nodded good-naturedly. "Sophie made sure I brought clothes that look like my dad should be wearing them."

They agreed to meet in the lobby at noon to find a café for lunch. Sophie let out a squeal of delight when she walked into their room. Decorated in black and white with yellow accents, the room had a king-size bed and two darling chairs arranged in front of a window. A small black desk had a writing pad and an orchid in a vase. She peeked her head into the bathroom to discover a deep bathtub with a handheld shower.

Nico grabbed her from behind and kissed her neck. "We can have some fun in there."

"This sex thing is turning out to be just as fantastic as everyone said it would be."

His hands lifted her skirt as he nibbled her ear. "We have time before lunch."

She pressed her backside into him, feeling his arousal. She could recognize it now. What surprised her was how often it rose to attention. "Let's take a shower first, and you've got a deal."

His hands moved farther up her thighs. "How about we take one together, and I'll show you a few of my shower moves."

She shivered. Each time was a new lesson in ways Nico could make her scream. "Good idea."

SHE WOKE a few hours later to the buzzing on her arm from the alarm. For a moment, she couldn't remember where she was until it all came back to her. She was in Paris. With Nico. She rolled over to see that he was still asleep. With one arm flung over his eyes, he didn't stir. She would let him sleep a few more minutes.

Her phone beeped to tell her she had a message. Yawning, she grabbed it from the bedside table. There were two voice mail messages. One from her mother and the other from Zane.

She listened to her mother's message first.

"Just making sure you got to Paris okay, honey. Send me a text if you get this message."

Before she listened to Zane's message, she texted her mother that she was doing fine and would send pictures in an email later.

With that sent, she listened to Zane's message.

"Hey. I hope you arrived safely in Paris. I just wanted to say I'm sorry for acting so stupid lately. The fire really threw me. I want you to do whatever you want with the place. If you want to rebuild, do it. Or if you want to make it into another type of place, do that. Dad would be happy to see you there, carrying on where he left off. I'll help you however you want, but the place should be yours now. I've got the brewery and the kids and Honor. When you get back, we can talk more about everything. Also, I'm sorry I was such a douche about Nico. He's a good guy, and I'm just ridiculously overprotective. You should feel bad for Jubie. Okay, have fun in France. I love you."

She teared up at the end of the message and had to wipe her eyes before she could get Hugh's journal from her bag. There was a passage she wanted to read. Something Zane had reminded her of. She flipped through until she found the one she was looking for.

Dear Sophie,

I was at your school play today. You were a wonderful dancing banana. The plot was a little thin. It's hard to make a story about the food groups riveting. However, I was riveted by you. You're eight years old now. You're tall for your age and have shiny long blond hair. You look like Zane and me, but you're graceful like your mother. I can't believe how fast the years roll along, even though there isn't a day goes by I don't think about you and wish I could know you. Right now is not the right time to disrupt your life by introducing myself. Someday, though, you'll be an adult and I'll contact you and we can become friends. I've observed your parents a lot over the years, and they're such good people and so good to you. I feel in my heart that they'll give their blessing for me to meet you once you turn eighteen and can decide for yourself if you want to.

This spring, Zane and Maggie will graduate from high school. Zane and Maggie have a best friend named Jackson Waller. The three of them are thick as thieves. Have been since they were little. After Mae died, Jackson's family took Maggie in. Dr. Waller and his wife, Lily, have been like parents to her. A year or so back Maggie and Jackson fell in love. Maggie and Jackson are soul mates. There's no doubt in my mind about that. Mae was mine. Even though we had so few years together, they were the best of my life. I never regretted loving her even though it hurt to lose her. The memories we made together give me so much comfort, even after all this time. And we made you, of course.

It's been a sad time for all of us because Lily passed away from cancer last week. We're all devastated. She was the heart of this community, always doing things for others in need. The cancer took her quickly. I'm trying to see that as a blessing because she didn't suffer too long, but it's hard to comprehend it as anything but a terrible tragedy. Doc's taking it really hard. So have the kids. Now all three of them are motherless and left with just Doc and me, which doesn't feel like nearly enough.

All this to say that my deepest wish is that someday you and Zane and Maggie will have a relationship. They don't have much family. I know sure as I know anything how happy they'll be to find you. Zane has a hot temper but underneath all that bluster is a kind, good heart. No matter what, he'll look after you. Maggie's an angel like her mama. Just like you.

I can imagine the three of you around my dinner table someday and it makes me about as happy as any image could. I wonder what you'll be interested in when you grow up? What your job will be? I'm thankful you'll have all the opportunities I didn't have.

Well, I best go now. This place isn't going to close itself, and I have a suspicion one of the bartenders is skimming off the till. Love, Hugh

She closed the book and held it against her chest. Silently, she talked to Hugh. "Some of your dreams came true. Maggie and Zane and I are close. I wish you were here to have dinner with us. I found my soul mate. He's right here with me and loves me so much he risked his life for mine. It's just like you said it would be. And guess what? What I wanted to be when I grew up was to run a bar in Cliffside Bay. Isn't that funny? I wish you were here to help me build it back up. We'd have so much fun together, wouldn't we?"

A voice came to her. "We sure would, angel. But I'm watching you from up here and I'm so proud."

Silently, she promised, "I won't let you down."

* * *

THE THREE OF them spent several hours walking around the neighborhood looking at shops and stopping in a café for a light lunch. By the time the cafés closed at three, they opted for another nap. After another love session, Sophie fell fast asleep for a good two hours and woke feeling refreshed. Per Judi's instruction, she chose a black taffeta dress with a flared skirt and fitted bodice. Black pumps completed the outfit. Feeling sophisticated and very Parisian, she opted to put her hair up and made up her face with special care.

When she came out of the bathroom, Nico was sitting in the chair by the window. His phone was in his hand, but he stared out the glass. Her heart fluttered as she watched him, knowing he hadn't heard her come out of the bathroom. He wore a dark gray blazer over a blue button-down shirt and black slacks. The table lamp shed a pale light on his profile.

"I'm ready," she said.

He turned and put his hand on his heart. "Soph. God."

She blushed. "You look good too."

"Come here. I want to see you in the light," he said.

She crossed to him. He stood, taking her hands. "I'm not sure I should let you out of this room."

"A girl needs to eat. Plus, you'll need your strength for later." She tweaked the collar of his shirt and lifted her face for a kiss.

They stopped at Judi's room to escort her to dinner. She came to the door wearing a red sheath dress and tall boots. "You look wonderful," Sophie said.

"Paris is made for me, dear. You two should be on top of a wedding cake. You clean up well."

They took the skinny elevator to the lobby and stopped at the desk to ask Collette for a recommendation for dinner. She suggested Café Latin on the corner.

Sophie wobbled slightly on the cobblestoned street as they walked to the restaurant. She clung to Nico's arm. "How do Parisians always wear high heels?"

"They're used to it," Judi said.

At Café Latin, they dined on *moules marinières* and *frites maison*, which in English translated to mussels in white wine sauce and homemade fries, as well as crusty, warm pieces of bread.

"Have you ever tasted better bread?" Sophie asked.

"I can't say I have." Judi smacked her lips as she pried a mussel from its black shell.

After the dinner plates were cleared, Judi picked up her glass of wine. "I have a proposal. This is going to sound a little crazy. Or at the very least like something Sophie would come up with."

"I can't wait to hear this," Sophie said.

"As you know, I wasn't blessed with a child of my own, so I would love to extend the offer of adoption."

Sophie laughed. "Perfect. Everyone needs another parent. This will bring my count to five."

"I understand I can't *actually* adopt you," Judi said, completely serious. "However, I can give you something that would tie us together as a family."

"You don't have to give us anything," Sophie said. "We're already family."

"Yes, that's all well and good," Judi said. "However, being Southern, I feel a great need to give you an object instead of just my love and gratitude."

"Gratitude?" Nico asked. "We're the ones grateful to you. You're one of the reasons I stopped being such a dummy when it came to Sophie."

"That's true," Sophie said. "And you taught me how to be a seductress."

Nico shot her a sidelong glance. "Seductress? I thought I was the one seducing you."

"Let's not get off topic here," Judi said. "You two can go back to the room when we're done. I have an agenda, and I need you to stop making eyes at each other long enough to hear my proposal."

Sophie put a finger to her mouth. "Sorry, I'll be quiet."

Judi continued. "I think of you two as my family—as the children I wished I'd had. Which is why I'm giving you my house."

Sophie's mouth dropped open. Was she joking? She must be. People didn't give away houses. "You're joking, right?"

"I would never joke about anything to do with money," Judi said. "It's too big a house for just me. Soon you'll be having children, and you'll need the space."

Nico raised his hand in an obvious protest. Judi glared at him. "Hear me out now. I have the best idea. I'll move out of the master bedroom and into one of the other bedrooms. That way you two can have the master suite."

"No way," Nico said.

Judi shut him down with another stern look. "You stay quiet or I won't be able to get through this little speech. Before you came, Nico, I was lonely and depressed. I wanted to give up and join my husband in heaven. You brought life back to my house. You brought life back to me. When Sophie came, it was like we were family. I found myself looking forward to life again. The thought of you two moving away is heartbreaking."

Sophie couldn't believe what she was hearing. "Judi, we're not going anywhere. We plan on living in the bungalow."

"We're very happy there," Nico said.

"Don't be so bossy," Judi said to Nico. "You remind me of

myself sometimes, and that's not necessarily a good thing. I need y'all. This is a selfish offer, actually."

Nico tapped his fingers against the tabletop. "This is a generous offer, obviously. That said, we cannot accept it. I'm a man, after all. I have to make my own way."

Judi, looking disgruntled, shook her head. "Listen up now. I've had the most wonderful life. I've traveled all over the world. I spent forty-five years with the love of my life. Everything I ever wanted was mine, except for children. You two can fill that emptiness for me. I'm an old lady now. I'm in my last act. Giving something of value to people I love is the best way to spend the rest of my life. I've thought a lot about this. I've imagined the little children you will have. How much joy they will bring me. My wealth is what I have to offer you. I mean, really, who wants a fussy old lady in their house? The gift of your companionship is worth much, much more than a house, even one that looks at the ocean. I've already set the paperwork in motion. In exchange for the house, you'll allow me to live there for the rest of my life."

"This is too much," Nico said.

"Listen up, young man. You didn't have to be kind to me. All that I asked was for you to keep up the yard. I can't think of another human being, except maybe Sophie, who would have done what you did for me. You brought me back to life. Don't take it away from me now."

Nico and Judi stared each other down like roosters in the henhouse.

"This is absurd," Nico said. "You do know that, don't you?"

"Not in the least," Judi said in a haughty tone.

Sophie smiled at Nico and then Judi. "I think it's a wonderful idea."

"See there, Nico? Sophie always understands me."

Nico planted his forehead in his hands, then mumbled something under his breath about how much easier plants and dogs were than women. "I give up. If it makes you two happy, then it makes me happy."

Judi looked so triumphant that Sophie laughed.

"When will y'all be having that first baby?" Judi asked.

"We have to be married first," Sophie said. "Or my father will want Nico's head on a platter."

"Don't worry," Nico said. "I've already asked and received his permission."

Sophie's hands flew to her mouth. "You called him?"

"I had to. A man worthy of you calls your father. I called him earlier today. He was happy to give his permission, by the way. In case you were worried."

"I wasn't," Judi said. "Were you, Sophie?"

"Not in the least. He knows my feelings for Nico."

"He did ask for one thing," Nico said. "He wants to walk you down the aisle. I had to promise him we wouldn't elope in Paris."

"My mother would kill me," Sophie said. "She's been dreaming about my wedding since I was four years old."

"Well, that settles it." Judi said. "Now someone just has to buy a ring."

"I don't need a ring," Sophie said. "But I do need a proposal. One we can tell our children about."

"Don't you worry," Nico said. "You'll get that and every single thing you ever want. I'll find ways to give you everything you want."

"I already have it," Sophie said. "All I ever wanted was you."

23

N ico

NICO AND SOPHIE stood together on the Pont des Arts, the scenic bridge over the river Seine. A full moon hung high in the sky and reflected on the water. A boat loaded with passengers made its way slowly up the river. The ripples in the water looked like ribbons. Paris was beautiful, but even she couldn't match Sophie.

Sophie's skin was luminescent in the moonlight.

"Isn't it magical here?" Sophie asked.

"Even more so than I thought it would be."

She lifted her face to him. "Isn't this where you're supposed to kiss me?"

"Not yet. I have something I have to do first." He reached into his pocket and pulled out the box with the ring inside it. He knelt on one knee and presented the box to her.

Sophie's eyes went wide. "Is this it? Is this the moment?" She flapped her hands in front of her chest. "I'm not ready."

"What?" His chest tightened.

"I mean, yes, I'm ready. But I didn't think it would be tonight."

"What better place?"

"You have a ring? Where did you get a ring? Okay, okay. I can't stop talking. I'm wrecking the moment, aren't I? It's just that I've imagined this so many times. And it wasn't here. I don't know why but this never entered my mind. I thought it might be at home on the beach. Or at the bar. Maybe in front of our friends. No, no. That's not right. It's supposed to be here. I should shut up now, right? My God, I'm so sorry. I'll stop talking right this instant."

He simply watched her, vowing to always remember what she looked like in this exact moment. He would tell their children someday how she got so excited that she couldn't stop talking.

As for talking, he'd had a speech planned but now he couldn't think of one word. The rough surface of the bridge was starting to hurt his knee. "I need to get this out. I'm nervous. I wanted it to be perfect, and now I can't think of what to say."

She tented her hands under her chin and bounced on her toes. "Just ask me. Nothing fancy. Simply the words. You already know my answer." She held out her arms for him to see. "Oh my gosh, I have goose bumps."

"Which is why it has to be perfect for you. You should have the most romantic proposal that's ever been given. I'm not sure how to say it—how to capture exactly what's in my heart. All I know is that you light up the world. You're the sun to me, Sophie Grace Woods. Will you be my wife?" He opened the box to show her the ring.

"Oh my God, Nico, did you rob a jewelry store?"

"Be still, I'm trying to put this on your finger."

Despite her erratic movements, he managed to get it on her. She held her hand out in front her. "Where did you get this? It's so pretty—like the prettiest ring I've ever seen."

"My dad gave it to me the other night when we were there. He said he couldn't imagine it on anyone else's hand but yours. I agree. Now, about that answer."

"Didn't I answer?"

"Not yet, no."

"Yes, yes. I'll be your wife."

And on the Pont des Arts overlooking the Seine, they kissed. He hoped Sophie would remember every detail of this moment, but if she didn't, he certainly would. When a man convinces the sun to always shine for him, it is not a moment he will ever forget.

THE END.

ABOUT THE AUTHOR

Tess Thompson Romance...hometowns and heartstrings.

USA Today Bestselling author Tess Thompson writes small-town romances and historical fiction. She started her writing career in fourth grade when she wrote a story about an orphan who opened a pizza restaurant. Oddly enough, her first novel, "Riversong" is about an adult orphan who opens a restaurant. Clearly, she's been obsessed with food and words for a long time now.

With a degree from the University of Southern California in theatre, she's spent her adult life studying story, word craft, and character. Since 2011, she's published 20 novels and 3 novellas. Most days she spends at her desk chasing her daily word count or rewriting a terrible first draft.

She currently lives in a suburb of Seattle, Washington with her husband, the hero of her own love story, and their Brady Bunch clan of two sons, two daughters and five cats. Yes, that's four kids and five cats.

Tess loves to hear from you. Drop her a line at tess@tthompsonwrites.com or visit her website at https://tesswrites.com/

ALSO BY TESS THOMPSON

Cliffside Bay Series

Traded: Brody and Kara

Deleted: Jackson and Maggie

Jaded: Zane and Honor

Marred: Kyle and Violet

Tainted: Lance and Mary

The Season of Cats and Babies, A Cliffside Bay Novella

Missed: Rafael and Lisa

A Christmas Wedding, A Cliffside Bay Novella

Healed: Stone and Pepper

Scarred: Trey and Autumn

Jilted: Nico and Sophie

Departed: David and Sara (coming early 2020)

Blue Mountain Series

Blue Midnight

Blue Moon

Blue Ink

Blue String (Coming early 2020)

River Valley Series

Riversong

Riverbend

Riverstar

Riversnow

Riverstorm

Historical Fiction

Duet for Three Hands

Miller's Secret

Legley Bay Series

Caramel and Magnolias

Tea and Primroses

Novellas

The Santa Trial

Made in the USA
Monee, IL
21 April 2020